MISTER YAM

YENG K TAN

This book is dedicated to James J. Paderna.

1

It was hard to tell how long I slept, but a pulsating noise was vibrating through my room. Above and below me were two layers of blankets, of which I was snuggled optimally in between. The bed I was on was firm, but not too firm. "Luxury firm" was the description used by the mattress company. Supposedly, it contours comfortably to the body whilst supporting the back.

> "REMINDER! Thirty minutes until the event: Meet Lorenzo at the career event."

Though they might sound like marketing terms (which they were), I wasn't about to argue semantics with the company; my lumbar spine did actually feel great. Not only were the inner coil springs of high quality, but the memory foam in the middle meant that the pressure points were just right, as if cycling between the palms of a massage therapist. Push and pull. Push and pull...

> "REMINDER! Ten minutes until the event: Meet Lorenzo at the career event."

A series of words entered my consciousness. Thoughts about pizza manifested in my mind. Was it Neapolitan pizza? Mmm...I'd really enjoy some thin crust...

"REMINDER! Two minutes until the event: Meet Lorenzo at the career event."

I woke up. An intensely persistent alarm was coming from my phone. The sun had just barely risen outside. What could possibly be so urgent?

"REMINDER! One minute until the event: Meet Lorenzo at the career event."

Oh.

~

I laced on my Allbirds sneakers. The recruiting fair was just a short walk from my house. Fifteen minutes on a regular day, except that I was running considerably late. I had only myself to blame for this, but I wasn't too earnest with being on time; punctuality for *Corporate America* left a sour aftertaste on my moral conscience. Picture this—fifty or so companies, fighting to get your attention, only for you to serve as nothing more than an extra cog in the wheel. I had little affinity for such events. But personal opinions aside, I promised my friend Lorenzo that I would support him on his big day.

Glancing at the street signs, I arrived at the supposed area. I strained to see anyone though. Squinting, all I could see were bland buildings after bland buildings. The architecture looked as though it served as the backdrop of a generic stock photo, like I was in the mezzo of the Wall Street Journal's most uninspiring catalogue.

I adjusted my glasses and squinted harder. Sure enough, I spotted a swarm of people at the tail-end of a corner. The majority of the group were dressed in business casual—an aesthetic I couldn't help but recognize as I approached the line. The impression I received from their professional attire was that they were in queue for the career event. Yet, scanning around, I couldn't spot my friend anywhere. Perhaps he was already inside the building?

"Mister Yam! Mister Yam!" echoed a voice. It was Lorenzo, waving at me by the registration desk before the stairs. "You're here, finally!" he shouted. Colorful and full of expression, he stood in great contrast to the soggy stale people in line.

As I waved back at him, I noticed the company banners spread across the entrance. Wells Fargo, Walmart, McKinsey—all the big conglomerate names were here, advertising themselves in the form of the plastered sponsorships on the walls. "I thought you were going to bail on me again," said Lorenzo. He reached for a hug as soon as I made my way to him. A nervous hug. "I was worried you weren't going to show up."

"Of course I came! I promised you, didn't I?" It was surreal seeing my friend in a suit. I had known of him since our first year, living in the dorms together in college, on the same floor just three doors apart. More specifically, I knew him as the crunked guy who set fire to our kitchen, for the painfully stupid reason of overcooking popcorn in the microwave. He was a goofy person; a clumsy, frustrating fellow with a knack for never being on time. But he was also honest, genuine, and kind.

"I'm so nervous, oh my God!" he exclaimed. "I shouldn't have drunk coffee this morning. My anxiety is through the roof!"

"Relax. You'll be fine," I said. "Remember what I told you earlier? Keep your introduction simple and concise. Don't overstate yourself, but not undersell yourself either. Make sure you use a bunch of eye contact, and—"

"I know, I know," he interrupted. Lorenzo had heard this spiel multiple times by now. "I jotted down notes on the bullet points you gave me. But..."

"But?"

"What if they don't like my resume? Or my face? Should I lie about my experience then?"

I shook my head. "No, no. That's a terrible idea." How was he so nervous? "Besides, it's totally unethical. You should just be forward with what you don't know. Curiosity compensates for a lot more than you'd think."

"Ahhhh! Why is this so difficult?! I just want to land a job somewhere!" he screamed, catching weird looks from bystanders.

I shook my head again. This was the most stressed I had ever seen my friend. "I understand your frustration, but you have to stay calm. If anything, they'll use your anxiety against you. Confidence is key, especially once—"

Boom, he was gone. Just like the wind. I'm betting he didn't realize I was still talking to him. I was confused though; wasn't he the one that wanted my advice on something? I guess such things didn't really register with my friend. After all, he was new to this game—the rat race. The endless pursuit of bi-weekly paychecks. The meaningless facade of black suits and ties.

I guess I'm free? - I dialogue with myself; as I reflected about my time in his shoes. I recalled moments where I'd stay up all night, trying to optimize my chances for a promotion. There was a time in my life when such goals were equally as important to me. I had seen them as noble aspirations. But they were not aspirations. They were a type of egotism that had disguised itself in the form of an aspiration. Soy milk pretending to be real milk.

But what was real milk then? That was a question only the dairy connoisseurs knew—a simple question; yet one with reaching depth when considered carefully. I thought about what Dutch milkers might have thought. It had to be easy on the body, and also something rich and smooth. Was it pasteurized or unpasteurized?

I had no idea, but a desire for a cold beverage struck me. How about a cocktail, then? That sounded pretty good. Eleven o'clock before noon might be a touch early for a drink, but I also figured I needed to pass the time.

Navigating through the various company booths, I made my way to the makeshift bar by the corner of the auditorium. Once seated, I ordered myself a Moscow mule.

"Can I see some identification, sir?" asked the bartender.

I took out my driving license and placed it on the countertop to his peripheral view.

"Thank you...Mister Yam," he remarked. Strange name, his eyes said. He wasn't the first person to think oddly of my name, and I didn't blame him for it; there weren't many people named after a starch found in a grocery aisle. But it could have been a lot worse. My parents could have named me Mister Potato—imagine the international lawsuits that would follow from that.

The bartender arrived with my ginger drink; I took a sip and looked around the bar. The only other people mingling around here were executives dressed in pencil skirts, nursing expensive wine. They were most likely corporate higher-ups from the various companies in attendance. Compare this scene to that of their lowest associates, who were drudging diligently. They weren't even trying to hide the inequality.

I took another, bigger sip of my drink, and felt the headrush pulsating from my brain. For not having slept much at all last night, I was surprisingly awake. My body was tired, of course, but my mind kept swimming around in circles. Some greater quantity of brain synapse was firing more restlessly than usual. A specialist in behavioral psychology might have more insights to offer on this, but usually I'd just eat some cheese to calm myself. I couldn't think of anything in the world better than smoked Gouda with strings of *prosciutto di parma*. Life seemed more robust when it was there, in the background.

Why not Parmesan then? Or Mozzarella?

"*Parmigiano-Reggiano*," said a voice.

Who was that?

"Me," said Lorenzo. He was sitting on the stool next to me.

"When did you get here?" I asked.

"Two hours ago."

I shook my head clear. I pondered about cheese for two hours? "That's ridiculous."

"Not as ridiculous as what I'm about to tell you!" he exclaimed in an exceedingly happy tone. He clearly had no interest in my recent epiphanies of cheese.

"Well, I'm listening..."

"I landed an interview! With...uh...some company. Woohoo!"

Clearing the remainder of my drink, I gave my heartfelt congratulations. "Hell yeah!"

"Sheesh, Mister Yam, have you just been drinking alone this whole time?" he asked.

"And thinking about cheese," I corrected.

"Well, I feel bad. I didn't mean to ditch you like this, or for you to wait around drinking," continued Lorenzo. He took out his phone and glanced at the time. "Do you have any plans after this?"

"I can't say I do."

"Alright then, let me buy you lunch somewhere."

Lorenzo's words caught me off guard. Suddenly, my thoughts of *prosciutto di parma* rushed back to me. "Buy me lunch? Did I hear that right?" I asked.

"Yup. I know a place we could check out," he said.

Cold weather made for busy restaurants, so it was no surprise that the noodle houses here were especially packed, catering to the seasonal craving that only a hearty soup can satisfy. The front-of-house staff kindly informed us that it would be at least an hour wait before a table would open up.

"Do you mind waiting?" I asked.

"No, not at all," Lorenzo replied. They gave us our number in line and told us to wait by the side.

I had read online reviews of this place just moments ago; to my surprise, they were pretty mediocre, neither positive nor reflective of the true enthusiasm I was seeing around me. Families laughing, friends drinking...it was only upon closer reading that I discovered that the negative reviews written were almost unanimously about the service and nothing at all to do with the food.

Most Asian restaurants were victims of this, it seemed. Typically, someone would come to your table and take your order. Sometimes, they would flip a notepad and write, or miraculously, they would memorize the entirety of the order in their head. Either way, they would come back with food, you would enjoy it; when you were done, you would head to the counter and pay the bill. Some Americans may consider it poor service, if even any service at all; and they're right. Service in an Asian restaurant is a job you get done quick, almost matter-of-fact. Small talk is non-existent, and any attempts at doing so will get shot down by the servers' death glares. Was it a bad thing?

It depends on who's asking, but you get great food at a reasonable price.

～

After about an hour, the maître d'hôtel informed us of our now ready table. Sitting in the corner of the restaurant, we waited for no longer than a minute before our server arrived, already prepared to take our order.

"Can I get the pho combo special, please?" Lorenzo pointed.

"I'll get whatever he's having, plus some extra beef balls," I followed.

The server smiled and left. Despite the chaos of the place, she arrived with our food shortly after. "Here you are, sir," she handed me a rich selection of condiments—bean sprouts, lime slices, yellow onions—as she generously plated the side dishes for us to choose from.

Already, I could imagine the warmth that would fill me as I drank two spoons, three spoons of the rich, delicious broth. Beef bones, ginger, scallions, star anise, fennel seeds, and cinnamon as a base, topped with basil, tendon, brisket, and some rice noodles. I plucked every single basil, squeezed every lime, and dumped all of the beansprouts into the soup. Like entering a cozy cabin in the middle of a winter storm, the broth was warm and delicious; the noodles were just the perfect texture—thin yet firm, smooth yet subtle.

"Pretty good, huh?" Lorenzo remarked. "I figured you'd enjoy this place."

"Very tasty," I said. "Very tasty indeed."

With wooden chopsticks of the proper kind, I attacked the noodles. The more strands I slurped, the more enthusiastic I became, until my excitement almost caused me to choke. "Take it easy, Mister Yam! Your face is all sorts of red right now."

I didn't respond. All I could observe were the chewing motions in my mouth—how did texture influence taste? The teeth and the tongue had their respective tabs to keep track of, of which the brain then attempted to make sense. But what about scent? How did that contribute to the equation? I started going down this rabbit hole of thought until Lorenzo kindly reminded me that I was still dining with him. "You know, It's been a while since we hung out like this," he said. "When was the last time we ate together?"

"I don't know," I said. "Time flies when you're an adult."

"By the way, check these out." From his wallet, Lorenzo pulled out a small business card and placed it on the table. "I ordered these online before today. Not too shabby, eh?"

I brought myself forward and squinted my eyes. It looked like the average run of the mill business card you'd see across the business world. Inscribed on the front was Lorenzo's full name, alongside his contact information, like emails and phone numbers. "These look pretty good," I said. Flipping the card over, the back revealed a minimalist, blank canvas of white. In its center was a logo of sorts. It looked like... a sheep? How random.

"Anyways, enough about me!" said Lorenzo. "How are you doing? Are you still dating Michelle?"

"No. We broke up a while ago."

"I'm sorry to hear, I had no idea. Was it the distance?"

"It was definitely part of it, but there were some other reasons too," I said. "I'm still trying to process the whole thing."

About five months ago, I broke up with my girlfriend. We were in a long-distance relationship, which in this day and age is not too difficult, but there was only so much a phone and a text can do to compensate for the loss of touch and presence. I loved her, and I still do love her, but love is such a tricky subject for me, and the relationship didn't make sense at the time.

When we broke up, as I lay awake in my bed, I suddenly spoke in verses so strange and abstract and hopeless that I did not bother to capture them. In the morning, it was all gone—still, to this time, they lay stowed away in me. Which is to say, I think about her a lot.

~

The server made her way to our table, checking up on us as we ate our noodles. She had fair, silky skin and an enchanting smile; though she was soft-spoken, her voice had a soothing, comforting tone. "Is there anything else I can help you with today?" she asked.

"Yes, actually! Could we order some spring rolls?" Lorenzo suggested.

"Of course. Just give me a few minutes."

There was something familiar about her; not just that I had known of her, but that we had interacted, or even been close at some point. It was a bizarre sensation, especially when you had only just met a person.

"I worry about you sometimes," Lorenzo said, looking directly at me. "No, that's not true. I worry about you all the time. Believe it or not, I think it's healthy for you to socialize once in a while."

I nodded. "You might be right, but you know how I am," I said, my mouth still busy chewing. "I don't do well with large groups of people."

"My roommate's hosting a party this weekend," he continued. "I'd love to see you there! Maybe you'll meet someone there and forget about your breakup."

"Hmmmmm."

"All I'm suggesting is that you drop by; say hi, and stay as long as you'd like."

"OK," I told him. "I'll think about it."

~

The sun was beginning to set as we left the restaurant. Though there was barely any light outside, little specters of lights broke through the foggy clouds like flower crabs in a beach full of sand.

I got into the passenger seat of Lorenzo's car and swept aside the

Bose headphones presiding there. A messy car, I thought. But I didn't comment on it.

Once seated, he revved the engine and began to drive. The hills in San Francisco made for an anxious drive uphill, but Lorenzo distracted me from this by spending the next fifteen minutes rambling about all sorts of things—relationships that didn't work out; his ever-changing expectations about life; this one big fight he got into with his sister. Through all of this, I was reminded of the memories we shared, in the same car four years apart. Back then, the distressing reality of adulthood had yet to reveal itself. The world was more idealistic, life was more romantic. People were more interesting to me. I was much happier.

"Do you mind If I asked you something, Mister Yam?"

"Go ahead," I said, hands clutched on the overhead handle.

"How do you know if something is real?" he asked.

"Real? Like, are you asking me how I would define *reality*?"

"Yeah"

I coughed. It sounded bizarre, almost as bizarre as the question. "Well, if you're talking about your senses—what you see, what you smell, what you taste—then reality is just a matter of what's in your head, no?"

Lorenzo nodded his head. "I see."

"What about you? What do you think?" I asked.

Silence. He seemed uncomfortable pondering the question. "I'm not sure," he answered, after some time. "Honestly, I don't even know why I asked the question. I guess I've just been pretty confused with some things recently."

"What are you confused about?"

"I...can't really say. I think it's just clutter in my brain, but I get these weird visions. And...I get these thoughts in my head that I can't seem to push out."

"Are you talking about hallucinations?"

"Not exactly," he answered. "It's not a vision thing per se, but I experience certain parts of my day differently; and they lead me to places. Unpleasant places. Have you experienced anything like that before?"

"No, never," I said.

The car came to a complete stop. "Let's talk about it at another time then. We're outside your house."

"Oh, right."

With the beep of his keys, he popped open the door for me. "Thanks for joining me today. It was really great seeing you."

"Likewise," I said. "Thanks for the ride."

"Good night, Mister Yam."

Unlocking the apartment gate, I paced myself to the front door of my place. Once inside, I leaned back against the kitchen tabletop and stared straight at the sink. I reflected on my day. It got me drunk by noon, but at least I had noodles to wash it off. What was up with my friend's behavior though?

Usually, I wouldn't care about these sorts of things—but I couldn't stop overthinking it. There was just something different about his tone today; something off about his body language. It was digging at me in a strange way, like a kind of aggravating migraine that wouldn't leave me.

Was he hiding something from me?

This was what I thought about as I went to sleep, and what I went on to think about frequently after. It would only be much later that I'd recognized the importance of it all.

PART I

2

I took the local BART train to Berkeley every Sunday for no other reason than to wander around the famous university. The University of California is a hub for a lot of things - the radiation lab for the Manhattan Project research; the 1960s counterculture protests; the rigorous and prestigious engineering and science programs. Perhaps most wonderful about wandering around the campus was the feeling of being a part of something much bigger than yourself.

And so I would walk for hours, typically with a latte in hand, and do nothing but think. I would allow myself to be free—I would see the magnificent blue sky and shelter in its shine. I would see the birds fly by, eating the bread so generously offered by the elderly couple on their stroll, and be reminded of small, simple joys. I would catch students conversing in the parks—some with stressed faces as they dealt with classes and examinations. It seemed that everybody here was engaged in some capacity of learning, either forced by homework or from genuine excitement. Being in a space where everybody was engaged, exchanging ideas about the absurd world, the delicate balance of discovering the new and challenging the old, was the most crucial part, and perchance the whole point.

I was in the middle of eating when my phone rang. Inspired by a deli advert I saw a few days ago, I had made myself a pastrami sandwich—filled with cheese, tomatoes, pickles, and Dijon mustard—and was just about to sink my teeth into the sourdough's crust when the phone rang again. There were only a handful of people who had my contact, and I rarely received any calls beyond the occasional birthday wishes. I let the phone ring a few more times before I picked it up.

"Hello," said an unfamiliar woman's voice.

"Hello," I replied.

"Are you the one they call the purple starch?" she asked.

"...yes?"

"How are you doing today?" she said. "I am doing well. Are you doing well? I hope you are doing well."

"I'm doing fine. Thank you," I said. "Can I help you with something?"

"No," she zapped.

I stood waiting for more, but nothing else came. "...uhh, okay. I guess I'm going to hang up now—"

"Mister Yam, wasn't it?" she interjected. "The name's kinda funky. It has a catchy ring to it."

Her tone of voice was rather unusual. It was aggressive—aggressive in the way you'd expect from a close relative, not an unfamiliar stranger. "Can I help you with something?"

"Yes," she zapped again.

"Well?" I asked, rather warily. "I'm here, aren't I?"

"Why are you so impatient?" the woman pushed back. "Just wait for a few minutes. All your questions will be answered then."

Just great, I thought. Was this a phone call for some kind of food survey? This better resolve with one of those two-in-one Pizza Hut combo coupons.

After a few minutes, the woman asked: "How are you enjoying your sandwich?"

"I like it," I said. "It's one of those things that I make often enough."

"I see," she responded, her voice sounding a little piped in. "I'd imagine you'd include a slice of cheese somewhere in there too?"

"Yeah. Usually, I'd do pepperjack," I answered. "Why do you ask?"

"Because I know that you typically enjoy eggs on your sandwich," she said, and then continued, "hard-boiled or soft-boiled—I might even guess the spread of Dijon mustard you'd have tucked under-neath the generous shreds of spicy Italian salami you top over—"

(What the hell? I looked up her phone number from the registry list, but she was calling from an anonymous line.)

"—fresh slices of mozzarella, drizzled in fresh olive oil and balsamic vinegar. But ignoring the flavor profile for just one moment, it's even more of a shame that you don't use eggs anymore. Because, honestly, I love the way you crack them open; the gentle, circular motion that you'd carry as you whisk in your copper bowl. When did you stop?"

I didn't reply. I kept my sandwich techniques very secretive—so much so that I had the notes stapled beneath my desk. "Who are you?" I asked. "How much is Pizza Hut paying you?"

"Nothing. No amount of money could convince me to work for them," she said. "Have you seen the inside of one of their kitchen?"

I didn't believe her for a second. "Don't lie to me—I've seen all the ads. I've blown through more than enough money on your soggy uncrusted pizzas."

"I see. Well, that's a shame. Except that I don't work for Pizza Hut."

"What are you calling about then?"

"That's not for me to say," she said. "Don't you know how this works?"

"I can't say that I do."

"What does my voice sound like to you?"

"I have no idea," I said.

"You must know. We've spoken a few times before."

I had no recollection of ever hearing her voice.

"No, I don't think so," I said, shaking my head. "You must be calling the wrong number."

"Perhaps, except I know everything there is to know about you. Like, the kind of outfit you are currently wearing—black denim, blue flannel, black joggers, chukka boots. And the kind of sandwich you're eating. Not a bad choice, I'll admit. But a tragedy for your sodium intake!"

That made me silent, if only for a bit. "What the hell do you want from me?"

There was no response. The line had been cut.

I stared at my phone, partially stunned, mainly confused. I had never imagined Pizza Hut to be so intrusive with their marketing campaigns.

The phone rang again, and I left it in my pocket as it rang and rang until, about five minutes later, it stopped. My sandwich had gotten stale by now. *Undesirably mushed,* to be specific. But I had lost my appetite anyhow.

Who on earth was that woman? I didn't appreciate her vagueness one bit, and thinking about her motives just flustered me further. Was she really not from Pizza Hut? Perhaps she was a food scientist doing a study. That'd make some sense; I belonged in the perfect demographic for that—single adult male with no appreciation for spices and little aptitude in cooking. I was concerned about the degree to which she knew of my sandwich recipe though. That required an impressive due diligence far beyond the norm.

How did she know?

I needed to calm down. I needed something warm, and easy on the body.

Tea. I needed some tea.

Leaving the university, I walked to a nearby cafe and ordered a cup of black tea. A recent backpacking trip I did in Japan had left me obsessed with the herbal drink. I discovered the drinking process itself to be quite cathartic; a kind of fallback activity I do when I'm feeling off.

Tilting the tea kettle, I observed the kocha leaves flow down to the china porcelain. The woman, whoever she was, had intel on me; awfully specific intel on me. I've never been one to care much about privacy, but the majority of my restaurant reviews on social media were done anonymously. I did, however, put my name on a specific review regarding the Cheesecake Factory a couple of months ago. Namely, I docked a few points of four stars for a bone-ribeye steak slightly overdone. Was she seeking revenge on their behalf?

Speculations aside, the phone call probably had nothing to do with me.

I finished the remainder of my tea and made my way to the train station. I had about a month's worth of laundry that needed to be done. And all the paperwork I had to get done for a kitten I had wanted to adopt. Ideally, I'd raise it to have a personality like Garfield. Just like in the comics, maybe we'd even share a lasagna together.

Feeling chilly, I flapped my arms en-route to the station. It was an attempt at heating my body, but I felt exponentially worse after. Why was the weather so cold though? Usually, my leather jacket was enough to keep me warm. But since a minute ago, the cold had developed into something unbearably worse.

With the breeze facing me, my walk became a jog, and then a sprint, as I ran to the train station. Once at the front gate, I swiped myself in and sat on the first bench in view. I sat silently as the cold dissipated, my body slowly adjusting to the warmth inside. Soothing and sensual, it was the poor man's equivalent of entering a cozy cabin. There was some tranquil mix of sweat and relief.

Once I was ready, I walked towards the platforms and caught the train as it was arriving. Scouting for an empty seat inside proved remarkably easy; there was not another soul in sight.

I sat on one of the cushioned seats and glanced at my watch—the time read 5:42 pm. I felt the sinus accumulating around my cheeks. In approximately twenty minutes, I would have a stuffy nose. What a useless intuition to have. Perhaps the world's most useless superpower. One can only imagine the glory and fame that would come from being saved by a man with a chronic nose condition.

Then, an air whistle—the train had come to a stop at West Oakland. I was now exactly halfway between the East Bay and San Francisco. I stood from my seat and did a little stretch, starting with the arms, and then with the shoulders. I twisted my waist and did a little scan around the car. But there was nobody else in sight—not in the station, not on the platform. Even the vending machines by the booths were void of their drinks.

I was left contemplating the various possibilities that would cause this. For such a popular route, the train was notably empty. There could have been a major concert going on, or a special episode airing for a popular TV show. Or maybe a worldwide pandemic that caused people to stay at home? As the train departed with no new passengers, all that was left with me were empty speculations.

I took out my phone and attempted to occupy myself with social media. My sister had recently shared a video of a British Shorthair drawing on an iPad. The cat was fat. Really fat. It reminded me of a few street cats I once saw near a deli. They were so fat I thought they were raccoons at first. I wouldn't be surprised if they would waddle and roll down hills in their free time.

I glanced at my watch again, mainly out of boredom, but the hands remained unchanged—5:42 pm.

Was I hallucinating?

I waited in place for some time, counting the seconds as they went. But the time remained unchanged—5:42 pm.

My brain began fogging over. Perceptiveness was not an adjective I'd ever use to describe myself, but it was clear that something was off. Like cucumber on a steak, the mismatch was obvious. But if strangeness was the cucumber, then the silence was its sauce, which descended upon me as I sat in the deserted space. I had some difficulty explaining why, but it'd been a while since I felt this lonely. I noticed how momentarily depressing some experiences can be—unaccompanied on this train, void of any aspirations. Was seclusion always this heavy?

It wasn't long before I heard a thud, and then later, some faint footsteps. The sounds were coming from the neighboring cart on the right.

Peering out the window, I watched a man walk through the transit door. My initial assumption was that the man was homeless, given that he was dressed in his pajamas; and not that it mattered, but he was also spectacularly bald, to the extent where the reflected light from his scalp was causing different diffractions in the space.

The absence of hair is not usually given a positive connotation, but how shiny and lustrous his scalp was! I found myself completely in shock! He took a seat a few inches in front of me, but it was impossible for me not to stare at him. How in the world was he so perfectly bald?

"Stop staring at my head," he said, sounding miffed.

Crap. Did he catch me looking?

"Do you think it's okay? Staring at a stranger's head like that?" he continued.

"Sorry, I'll mind my own business."

The bald man went silent. He was kind of weird-looking. I couldn't help but notice the birthmarks around his forehead. From a distance, it looked like a smudge, but I could point out some very specific details on it. There was a shape to it that looked rather circular, but had pointy edges. And his face—button nose, craggy jaw, high cheekbones—looked vaguely familiar. He wasn't very tall, but he wasn't short either; his shoulders were within some happy medium of slightly above average.

"Chin up, kid. I was just messing with you," he laughed. "I'm used to people staring at my head."

I shook my head. "No. No, no. That was really rude of me. I shouldn't have done that."

The bald man frowned, and gave me a hard look. "You're being too hard on yourself, but I bet it's because you've never seen such a bald head before, eh?"

"It really is quite magnificent," I remarked. "How'd you do it?"

The old man paused. It seemed as though he was digesting my question fully. "I'm not sure. Once I stopped eating royal jelly, all my hair went away. *Poof*—just like that, it disappeared," he said. "Take it with a pinch of salt though. I'm no scientist."

"I had no idea that honey was that potent."

"Yeah, most people don't. It's one of the world's best kept secrets," he stated, his voice slightly hushed. "Consider it a tip from a bald stranger."

"Duly noted," I said.

"Either way, It'll be a while before you start worrying about this. How old are you?" he asked.

"Twenty-five."

"Twenty-five…" he mulled. "Barely an adult. Eh?"

"*Semi-functional* adult," I corrected. "Great on paper, terrible on ink."

"Ha! we've all been there," he blurted out in amusement. "Forty-seven years ago, I was just like you. Working and living in the city. Mind you, the concept of working was very different back then. It's nothing like it is now."

I nod. And nod. "What did you do in the city?"

"Well, I worked in agriculture with my buddy. We focused on

organic produce, and farming methodologies," he said. "It might not sound exciting to you, but it was a really big deal then. I grew some pretty big tomatoes!"

I closed my eyes and imagined steamed broccoli. Oof. An undesirable lack of umami...

"Anyway," he went on," what I'm trying to say is that I was vegan before it was cool. These modern salad shops have no idea what a *paneer tikka* is."

"I see." I had no idea what a *paneer tikka* was either, but I rubbed my belly anyhow.

"You're not very talkative, are you?" the bald man asked. "Maybe you don't think I'm worth your time."

"No, not at all," I responded. "I just don't really know what to talk about."

I see, his face said. "Would you like to see something interesting then?"

"Sure..?"

The bald man stood up and made his way towards me. Only a couple of inches separated us when he was seated. He reached under his jacket and pulled out a tiny rectangular box. He took out a handkerchief from his pocket and gave it a quick wipe. "Pretty cool, eh?"

I pulled myself forward to examine it. Perfect in symmetry and unison in length, it looked like the standard wooden box you'd see at a jewelry store. Yet, it had no visible opening; no visible lock. Flipping the box over, he revealed an intricately engraved emblem on its bottom—a carving of a sheep. Was it symbolic of something? I recognized it from somewhere, but I couldn't remember exactly. It had wings. A winged sheep; how strange.

"Where did you get this from?" I asked.

"A friend of mine gave it to me. It was his farewell gift," he said. "What do you think? I think it looks really pretty."

"Er, I guess so."

"C'mon, no need to be shy!" he said. "It's a beautiful little box. If I listed it for auction, I bet I'd be able to get quite a sum. Maybe I'd be able to seduce an old lady in the process, hah! But, unfortunately, it's completely useless."

"Useless? What do you mean it's useless?"

The bald man stretched his finger and placed his thumbs on its center. Then, he made exaggerated movements to illustrate his failed attempts at opening it. "See, it won't open!," he said. "No matter what I try, it won't budge. And I've tried everything—jigsaw, nail gun, chainsaw, impact driver, you name it."

"I see." I glanced at my watch. I should be back at the station any second now.

"Mhmm, which is why I'd like you to have it," he said, out of the blue.

"I beg your pardon?"

"Consider this a gift, from one man to another."

"You want me to take the box from you? I asked.

"I do, indeed," said the bald man. He let out a gentle smile; an infinitesimal movement from his jaw shaped his face. "Though I'm not sure if *take* is the word I'd use."

Screech. The train made its arrival in San Francisco. A sizable influx of people joined the train as hustle and bustle now occupied the space.

"Ciao," said the bald man, waving his hands. "And whatever you do, don't get lost."

By this point, congestion overwhelmed the train. Like crammed sardines, numerous passengers had already set their eyes on the impending scramble for my seat. I was flustered, but as soon as I stood up to leave, a realization hit me—the bald man was gone! There was no trace of him anywhere in the crowd. He had vanished as miraculously as he had appeared, from the outskirts of nothingness onto the teeming crowd.

Great. How wonderful. As entertaining as that whole skit was, did he really think I'd be happy to receive this? What if this box was drug-related? For all I knew, the old man could have been using me as some sort of cocaine mule. Smugglers come in all shapes and forms; I'd seen those El Chapo videos.

I turned my attention to the object. Outside of its bizarre symbol, it looked like just about any other wooden box. Tapping it made it give off a kind of bouncy sound; there was quite evidently something inside. It didn't feel like drugs though, which relieved me. But, still, I found the whole situation bizarre. Did the Pizza Hut woman on the phone have anything to do with this?

Hmm…

I placed the box in my bag. What was the worst that could happen? If anything, I'd bring it down to a pawn shop and get some quick cash. Perhaps I'd even strike gold and find a thick bar of it inside.

3

I woke up the next morning and headed to work. Today was the end of the financial quarter, and so a lot of different groups within the company took this time to share their financial earnings. The team that I was a part of achieved some pretty substantial wins this time around, so it was particularly important for us to highlight our successes.

I was tasked with delivering the presentation for my team . Though I had already prepared for it, I arrived earlier than usual at my desk and did some last-minute touch-ups.

My manager, Max, was already seated at his desk and waved at me as I walked in.

"Ready for your big day?" he asked.

I nodded. Max was an interesting guy. For one, he was incredibly smart and focused, but perhaps more noteworthy, he held within himself a plethora of political attributes, of the kind that allowed him to climb the precarious corporate ladder. He was organized and ambitious; it took him just ten months to land back-to-back promotions.

The presentation went well. Max was visibly delighted. As I breathed a sigh of relief, he dropped news that he wanted to fast-track my promotion. That's amazing, I said, with a hint of a beam, but internally, I was indifferent. Sure, there were some aspects of my job that I found genuinely interesting, but as a whole, the whole career climb thing was quite unfulfilling to me.

But wins are wins, and to celebrate my success, I left the office early and made my way to a popular bar two blocks down the street. I frequented this establishment, typically for bourbon and Coke; it was almost always the only thing I could look forward to on Mondays. A co-worker introduced me to this place: Barry's Rum House, an upscale bar in the heart of gentrified San Francisco, where polished lawyers and well-heeled techies huddled, surrounded by homelessness and poverty. There was a seemingly endless juxtaposition here; when corporations talk about values, was it because of ethics? Or aesthetics?

Hard to tell.

I sat at my usual spot and ordered my drink. Apart from a half-eaten bagel earlier today, I hadn't eaten anything all day, and so I ordered myself a burger and some fries. Bar food isn't spectacular by any means—there was nothing special about the bun, nor the patty, nor the condiments nor style in which it had been prepared. It was simply a greasy-ass burger, and that is all it had to be.

"Mind if I sit here?" asked a man from behind me. I nodded, before taking a quick glance at him. Dressed in grey with black slacks and a Jeff cap, the man was otherwise brandished looking. Strapped to his waist was a fanny pack; for what purpose, I wasn't sure. It certainly wasn't for looks.

"How are you doing?" he asked.

"Pretty good," I replied. "And yourself?"

"Not bad. Not bad at all. Mind if I ask how's the food here?"

The question caught me off guard. I couldn't tell if it was a genuine question, or just an excuse for small talk. "It's alright," I said. "Nothing crazy for bar food."

"Fair, fair. Maybe I'll order some."

The man waved for the bartender and pointed at my burger, which the bartender intuitively understood as an order.

"I don't mean to intrude, but do you come here often?" the man asked.

"A fair amount, usually after work," I said.

"Ah, I see. Let me guess, you're an engineer?"

"Yeah, how'd you guess?"

The man burst out laughing. His laugh was so contagious that he even had me giggling before I knew what was happening.

"And what about you? What do you do?" I asked.

"Hard to say. I'm something they call a gig worker," he said and adjusted his cap. "It basically means that I hold a number of odd jobs around the city. Depending on the occasion, sometimes I'm a driver; sometimes I'm a bouncer; sometimes I'm a mover. Though recently, I have also been attending classes at a community college after work. It's never too late to learn, right?"

"Not at all. There's a lot to respect there," I said. "I really admire the determination."

The server arrived with his food.

"Would you like some fries?" he offered me.

"I'm good. Thank you."

I glanced at my watch. I had nothing else planned today, except maybe laundry, which I had put off from yesterday.

"Believe it or not, I'm currently here on a job," the man said.

"Oh, really?"

"I'm distributing flyers for this show happening tonight. It was one of those sudden, flashy jobs that popped up online, but it paid really well for such a specific request."

The man finished his burger, licked his fingers, and chugged his glass of water faster than most servers can pour it. Then, he reached into his fanny pack and pulled out a little pamphlet, which he passed on to me. The description was of a play a few blocks from where I lived.

"This seems...interesting," I said. I took out my phone and searched for any matching descriptions to the show. I couldn't find anything about it. "Thanks for the recommendation."

"And thanks for the company," he said. "If you'll excuse me, I'll be across the street distributing these. See ya." He stood up, adjusted his shoes, and left for the door. I could hear his departing footsteps on the pavement, and then on the walkway, then nothing more.

As I licked clean the remainder of my fries, I felt mildly perturbed with the whole thing. For one, I couldn't find anything on the web, and the venue listed was no longer available. It was quite possible that this was nothing more than a cheap marketing farce. This wasn't the first time I have been misled; I had a similar experience while backpacking in Thailand, where a mysterious man approached me with tickets for a show, only to deceive me into entering a brothel.

Wary about my previous incident, I shoved the pamphlet in my coat and downed my drink. Then, I left a generous tip and left for the door, timing my exit with the arriving buses.

The afterthought of laundry was still preoccupying my mind when I heard my phone ringing. This time, I took it right away, and I recognized the voice of the woman immediately. The same woman from Pizza Hut who called me yesterday.

"I see that you have been enjoying yourself," she said.

"Are you following me? Like I said, I'm not interested in your stupid pan pizza special. Don't make me call the police!"

She gave an audible chuckle. "That would be unfortunate, though I'm curious what you would report me for. Help me! A girl is harassing me over the phone with mediocre pizza! Oh no! How terrible!" She laughed. "Perhaps you're not used to a woman showing interest in you?"

I was exasperated by this point. When the hell did fast food chains get this persistent? I kept telling myself to hang up on her. Cut the damn line and get on with your life. But there was something about her brazen lack of etiquette that intrigued me; something about the absurdity of her specific words that pulled enough strings in my brain to make me want to continue.

"Listen," I said, "I don't know you. You don't know me. I'm perfectly fine with keeping it that way. Please stop bothering me. Or at least tell me what you want, please!"

"Are you sure you don't know me?" she asked.

"Clearly not."

"I don't work at Pizza Hut, but I do know who you are," she continued. "As a matter of fact, I know everything there is to know about you."

I said nothing, because there was nothing to say. The woman was clearly delusional.

"What if I could prove it?" she said.

"Prove what? That you know me?"

"Yeah."

"Okay," I replied, clearing my throat. "I'll play your little game. Where am I from?"

"Kuala Lumpur, Malaysia," she answered immediately. "Or more specifically, the town called TTDI."

That silenced me.

"Stop overthinking this." Her voice was notably more serious. "I wouldn't be calling you if I didn't have a reason to. Besides, you do know me—you just don't remember. Not that I can blame you for that. Go to the play tonight, you'll thank me later."

She hung up. With no outlet for my predicament, all I could think was that this was a ridiculous imbroglio.

Why was she so persistent? And aggressive? I had never spoken to someone so delusional and annoying. Yet, there was no denying the specifics of what she knew about me.

I took out the flyer for the theater. Somehow, this all was connected?

The pamphlet, as I began to unravel, read as follows:

4

THE LIFE OF BORIS - STRANGE
TALES OF A SHEEPMAN?

Once upon a time, there lived a man named Boris. Boris was not unlike any other man in the town; he worked a respectable job at an established company and was respectful of the law. He always paid his taxes and was a pleasant fellow to others. There was nothing inherently unkind about Boris, nor would he ever act out of adverse emotions, bar the rare instances that would call for it.

Boris was an explorer, an avid, insatiable explorer of human perception. Everything that was to be perceived was enriching; he would be overwhelmed with emotions as he thought about the wonders of imagination. Boris would cry at the sight of a lily, or laugh hysterically at the whiff of delicious grilled fish. He would sing songs on the streets, encouraging random strangers that walked by to accompany him. He liked all that he knew and was well-liked by all he knew. There was no end to what Boris could feel.

So it should come as a shock to many to see Boris, a man of passion and curiosity, take his own life. On the dreaded night that he did, news spread quickly, with many that knew him thrown into wild disarray and disbelief. He was the most joyful man they knew, they said. He was always spreading happiness, regardless of duration or distance, they said. His many lovers were stunned and disheartened; some of them spiraling into intense depression after, overwhelmed with sadness and grief. If Boris, the man heralded as the epitome of serenity, could take his life, then through what virtue would they stand a chance?

What they did not know is Boris's hidden secret—that he walked on two legs, spoke English, and enjoyed toast just as other humans do, and that he was also part sheep. Scientists still argue as to whether he was really a sheep. How was it possible for a man to be born half sheep? One theory is that, through a series of unorthodox prayers, he had been cursed by the devil, or through some haphazard medical complications, he was given a sheep's heart to replace his own. Such speculation, though understandable, would make little difference to Boris, for the fact was that he was irreversibly half a man and half a sheep.

Boris's life was thus a duality. During the day, he would do things as most humans do. He would make breakfast, go to work, watch a bit of television, and on some occasions, he would have a drink; usually a Cabernet Sauvignon. Then, at night, during his sleep, unbeknownst to anyone else, he would revert back to being a sheep. Boris was, of course, a smart man. He had no problems compromising to fit into society's mold, and he knew how to play the system. Yet, one thing that he had not understood was how to be happy with his human self and his sheep self.

Sometimes he would do human things, like prepare a plain bagel or participate in a video game conference. Other times, he would wish to just bask in sunshine and eat plain grass. This conflict extended to everything Boris did. For example, whenever Boris had some idea of going on a date, his sheep self would tell him: "Why don't you just relax at home and eat some grass?" A preposterous idea for a human, but perfectly acceptable for a sheep. Likewise, when in his sheep form, his human side would beg him to do something with his life, instead of lazing around and eating grass.

Such things were even true for the people around him. There was the camp of people who grew fond of Boris for his serious, ambitious human-self, and likewise, there were those who were attracted to him for the opposite reasons; the casual, indifferent personality borne by the sheep side of him. He had his work friends that would do serious, productive things with him (whatever that meant), and he had his relaxed friends that would hang around and do absolutely nothing.

Boris's relationship with others, thus, was no different than the inner strife within him.

It was not that the two conflicting sides were always at war with each other. On some occasions, the human and sheep side of him made peace with each other, and on rare instances do we see certain examples of them fortifying each other, echoing their duality as strength together. A compromise they would often make is to watch documentaries every Sunday night; entertaining enough for the sheep, knowledgeable enough for the human. But such cases, rare enough as they are, did not at all resolve their overwhelming differences.

You can imagine now how divided soul Boris must have had. Living at constant odds with himself, two sides fighting for control. Yet, many people, specifically musicians and artists, find themselves in similar positions. The pragmatic side of them sees life for what it is: survival, stable income, supporting a family. But they too have an idealistic, romantic perception of life. Perhaps to explore the facets of their talents? Or to engage in interests wholly for pleasure? Whatever it may be, they, like Boris, are forced into the same ruthless concessions demanded by life. Boris had the unique distinction of being half man and half sheep, but the conflicts he experienced were not exclusive nor uncommon. It was that all he thought and did with one half of his being was forever antagonizing and challenging the other half he so vehemently disagreed with.

Just as with others in history, the accumulation of such realities would eventually breach the level that Boris could bear, and so he would deem his life far too miserable to continue. There is an immense bridge that separates the thought of suicide from actual suicide. What remains distinctive in all suicides is that at some point in their life, either rarely or consistently, they find themselves in a highly susceptible emotional and vulnerable state; as if they are standing on the thinnest of ropes, and any movement one way or the other will be enough to drive them into their deepest holes— where light is destroyed, and the darkness vast and indefinite.

To understand Boris's suicide is to understand something crucial about ourselves. It may come as no surprise that we are fundamentally irrational creatures. We go about our day, relying on our instincts more often than our brains. This is not to say that logic is dunce, but perception and intuitions make for a more stronger conviction. Hence the power of narrative and the ongoing role it plays in our heads — to inspire, compel, induce, urge, sway. The salesman pitching a car to the prospective young couple looking to buy; the lawyer defending his client through a series of heartfelt anecdotes. We shape our lives through the accumulation of these accounts. What are humans if not a collection of short stories?

Logic is the sentinel that shows us the way we ought to reason; it remains purely subjective as to whether we follow these rationales. And so we are left with feelings, and how beautiful it is that we find meaning, aspirations, and desires here. The truth of the matter is that logic is simpler — logic requires an explanation, an absolute and finite answer that is tangible and coherent. Compare this to love; how does one describe the feelings of affection as your lover kisses you in bed? Or the warm, angelic comfort a boy receives from his mother? Logic is nothing but a shadow over the seat from which emotions reign. It would make sense, then, that one may act untenable when compelled by emotion, as with the tale of Boris.

Emotions are not just boxes we label, categorize, and stack as we please. Emotions are more sophisticated, more delicate. Like a drop of paint in an empty bucket of water, the color flowing within different shades and consistency. A purely logical perspective is nothing more than a confined one; it bars us from exploring the critical fabrics of interweaved interactions, and the possibility of something deeper.

There is no happiness without sadness; peace without rage; beauty without horror. Like in all theoretical *construit*, nothing quite captures the complexity and copiousness of reality; there is no convenient catalog of emotions which we can cherry-pick from, as much as we might want to.

To those that knew him, Boris was a happy, simple man that went about his day, doing what he could to make life just a little bit easier for everyone else. The truth is darker and more complex. Boris was anything but simple; he was complicated, torn by the spectrum of emotions that would encircle him every day. He had great talent at hiding from others the loathsome, inadmissible emotions that hung over his everyday life.

I must make clear that I have no right to call myself one who knows. This is, after all, just a story, and like every story, it is based on opinion, not fact; and if your views on this story are such that it is nothing but jumbled fiction from someone's imagination, then you are correct. Yet, reality is simply what one chooses to see, in the same way that we rewrite our pasts to shape our narratives and support the lies we tell of ourselves.

...TO BE CONTINUED?

5

It took me a while to collect my thoughts; to digest and consider what I had just read. It was true that my life was a meaningless mess—I had no compelling interests and was never proactive about anything that I did. The passing years had stripped me of my desires, a passion once burning now hiding in neglect. I had no motives; no responsibilities. If life had a taste, it was undoubtedly sour.

I tried my hardest to refrain from psychological introspection - it was now the time to shelve my reflections and get to the facts. There was a play, most likely related to the Life of Boris, that was important for me to attend, or so said by the mysterious woman on the phone and the stranger at the bar. The relationship between the two remained blurry, if there even was one at all. But this pamphlet; this story in my hand, was the only solid piece of information I had thus far.

I sped to my room and explored my wardrobe. Though I had no inkling for the type of occasion I should expect, a black coat with some dress pants would be appropriate for most events. I took out my razor for a clean shave, prepared my shirt, and dressed as I knotted my tie, putting on a dose of fragrance and taking a shot of scotch as I headed out for the show.

A couple of blocks away, I speedwalked to the supposed venue. The location was an interesting one: on the top of a hill in a lavish, upscale neighborhood right by the famous curvy "Lombard Street". I stood in front of a once-famous restaurant, which had been shut down a while ago as a result of a health scandal. The place had since remained unoccupied for two years; the eerie lack of activity around the area confirmed this fact for me.

Then, in the distance. I spotted a burly man loitering near an alley. He had a focused yet cautious look as I approached him.

"Here for the show?" he said. I drew my lips and gave a nod, which resulted in him coming closer and frisking my thighs. Was he expecting me to be armed? Satisfied, he then led me down a hidden path and gestured for me to follow.

After a short window, we arrived at a door of sorts. Here, yet another burly man greeted me. The two men stood in front of each other; they gave a simultaneous nod, and I was allowed in.

I was taken to a modified cellar of sorts. The place was dim but not dark. Inside, there were some others - a lady behind a bar counter; two men at a table smoking cigars. Though I received some looks, none of them paid any particular attention to my presence. The burly man showed me to my seat, at a table shared with another man.

I gave my thanks and took my seat. It was hard to tell from my angle, but the man seated across me was at least a few inches shorter than me.

The lady at the counter came over and whispered a few words to him - crouching so slightly as she did so - before returning to the bar in preparation for some cocktails. Not long after, the music stopped playing, and the lights dimmed further. The show, now starting, with the woman returning to the table with two bourbon old-fashioned.

A man came out from behind the curtains, and the loudspeaker above recited the story of Boris. There were other actresses and characters that came onstage as the narrator read the story line by line. It was hard to see this as an amateur play; the quality was identical to what I experienced on Broadway.

As the play ended, there was widespread applause from the audience, a few shouts of bravo at the very back of the room. The actors and actresses took a bow, some of whom I now recognized. Lin-Manuel Miranda, actor and producer of *Hamilton*. Sutton Foster, the actress who played Reno Sweeney in *Anything Goes*. What on earth were they doing here?

As I reflected on the sheer absurdity of what I was witnessing, the man sitting beside me plucked a cigarette from a case. He placed it in his mouth, and lit it with a rather fanciful tabletop lighter. He then gestured with his hands to offer me one, which I declined. At this point, most of the guests were heading out of the show, but the man sat firmly in place; he clearly had no intention of leaving anytime soon. Then, he took off his glasses as if to denote something, except that he was now directly staring at my face.

Out of awkwardness, I stared back at him. He wore round glasses and had a chiseled face — he looked somewhere between his forties and fifties. The black suit he wore was distinctly bespoke, and on his left wrist was a luxurious Patek Philippe nautilus watch. His entire appearance was meant to prove one thing: he was a man of obscene wealth.

I looked at the man as he looked at me, neither of us betraying anything. Neither angry nor calm, his gaze penetrated me as though he were running an audit on my soul. It was quite apparently just the two of us at this point, and the room was silent; silent in the same, ominous way one would feel before the start of battle. It was the somber, abnormal kind of silence. The dreadful type that would orbit around your ears and linger imperceptibly.

My head started spinning as the silent void slowly ate its way into my mental space. It would feel like a century later before words filled the air, by which time I was already in a psychosis state.

"A tragedy, isn't it?" he asked.

I cleared my throat; my brain was still rebooting. "Sounds about right."

He bit his lip, his eyes entirely concentrated on me. He did this for a minute or so before taking a puff of his cigarette. "An interesting one for sure. All that torment, the terrible distress as insight into one's worthless self? I can't imagine a story as real as it is dejecting. No power in the world could compel me to endure such a direct confrontation with my being. Yet, this is a story that we all share. What point is there in a story if it doesn't ram our skulls into the wall we call living? So that we would bask in unknowing bliss? We would be so happy if all we saw was happiness, but we need stories to strike us like disasters. How else would we learn?"

He noticed the wariness on my face, but continued to speak anyway. "People don't just die when their time comes. It's more creeping, more gradual. Inside of you, a timebox that withers, eating away at you. Worst, however, is the bearing of an untold story; how many Boris of the world may we find, if not for the coerced silence subjected to them? I had always thought these things to be an inescapable, unsavory detail of being human that is to carry."

The mysterious man went on and on with his thoughts on humanity, which I repeatedly acknowledged out of politeness. All the while, I was daydreaming of fermented soy noodles. How was it that I was still hungry? Maybe I was more restless than I thought.

"But enough of these abstractions! It is imperative that we speak with each other as honestly as possible. I do not wish to mislead you, and likewise, I hope that you see it is in your interest not to deceive me."

"Deceive you?"

"Don't play stupid with me, Mister Yam. Don't you know why you're here?"

I was confused with what the man was alluding to, but I took his question seriously. The easy answer was that I was bored and had nothing better to do. There was, also, the woman on the phone; I'm sure she had something to do with this. "I can't say I do."

"Very well. Let me tell you why you are here then—you know something. Something that you can't necessarily articulate but that you can feel; you have felt it your entire life. This inexpressible, inexplicable feeling that cannot be understood."

I peered at him, my lips swirling.

"Just like Boris, you are a prisoner, locked in chains to the complexity and unrelenting nature of existence. I'm sure you have heard the arguments against free will, some based on theology and others based on pure logic. Not that it's bad, but I'd go as far as to argue that such discussions are entirely pointless, and possibly detrimental to a person's inner peace."

The man flicked the tip of his cigarette and mashed it out, not even one-half smoked. There was a slight pause before he continued,

"Yet, these are just matters of the mind, and the thing about our mind is... Well, it's impossible to think of a perspective outside of the mind. After all, everything we experience in life goes through our mind, right? Not quite, because there's something else we're forgetting—the psūkhế, the soul. The reason why we focus so much on the mind and not on the soul is the simple fact that the soul is a lot less accessible. I mean, think about it. Twelve years of school, four years of university; so much information and knowledge condensed. And then boom, you're ready for the world. Except you're not, because throughout that entire process, only the mind is being worked on. What of *télos*? Nothing, zero. It's like developing your drawing skills without any of the flourishing color—what beauty of a life would that be? Do you see what I'm saying?"

I agreed out of courtesy, but I had no idea what he was talking about. Not that I couldn't understand the words he was saying, but it was impossible to decipher the overall meaning behind them.

"Society is only as good to you as you are good to it. I could say more; you should know that an old man like myself has nothing better to do than brood. But, alas, that is not the point of today," he said. "There is another, more compelling reason that has united you and I, Mister Yam, if you would be so kind as to indulge me a bit longer."

"Uhh...sure," I said.

The man pulled out a polaroid photo from his inner sleeve and set it on the table. Tints of color filled the air as it laid motionless in front of me. "The matter of interest here is regarding a certain photo," he said. "What do you know about it?"

I leaned forward to examine it. It was a picture of a man, alongside an assemblage of sheep. Right away, I recognized him—it was the strange, bald man from the train! There was no mistake about it, except that he looked considerably younger in the photo, and had masked his bald scalp with a hat. "I'm not quite sure what I'm looking at," I responded.

There was a slight, momentous pause. "I thought we were in agreement about being honest with each other."

"And I am being honest," I answered. "This is my first time seeing it."

"Even an unwashed carrot could fool me better," he said.

His analogy was a confusing one. What difference did a washed carrot make?

"Perhaps we have found ourselves on the wrong footing. Allow me to rephrase: do you notice anything odd about the photo?" he asked again.

I looked at the photo again, except this time, paying great attention to the little things I may have missed. The man was wearing a brown bucket hat, now normalized by Millennials as a fashionable accessory at festivals. He was dressed in plain gray pajamas; the picture was taken as though he had just woken up. Oddly enough, he was standing in front of an unusually purple house, amongst a sea of otherwise ordinary houses. On its front wall was a single, giant glass window; the kind of architectural layout one may consider futuristic. In the background, the sun was beaming and the sky pellucid blue. Without context, it was a weird but otherwise undistinguished photo —a man hanging out in front of a purple house with a random herd of sheep.

"I don't know," I said. "I truly do not recognize anything about it."

"Do you really think I'd be talking to you if I hadn't done my homework? I'm not that foolish, you know. Coincidences do not exist; the universe operates in absolutes. As Murakami states - what we understand as the present is simply an accumulation of the past; and taking it a step further, the future is nothing more than a set of conditions we ascribe to the present."

The man bit his lip and took a deep breath. "Nothing in life is fair, and yet, it is all the same. In this case, your immediate circumstances. How would it look if you continued deceiving me?"

"Are you threatening me?"

"That is one way of looking at it," he responded.

"What's the other?"

"A beneficial, mutual agreement between two parties."

"Alternatively stated - you're offering me a deal."

The man changed positions and leaned towards the back of his chair, crossing his legs. "Take a look at the photo again."

For the third time today, I stared at the photo, confounded.

"Make sure to look carefully at the man's brown hat," he said.

I squinted and brought the picture to the cusp of my eye, to the extent where my eyebrows were brushing against it.

"What do you see?" asked the man.

"Still nothing."

"Look closer."

At this point, only a sliver of air separated the polaroid from my cornea, but I noticed a little smudge on the top right of the photo, in the middle of the man's bucket hat. I was confused as to whether it was a part of the picture, or the result of some minor tearing from the film.

"Is that smudge supposed to mean something?" I asked.

"That's no arbitrary smudge," said the man. "That's the symbol of the winged sheep. Now, compare it with this."

The man motioned and took out a tobacco case. He plucked a lone cigarette and offered it to me. I took it from him and held it. It was a plain-cut joint with no brand, yet it was exquisite in its own right. There was a weight to it that was unusual for a cigarette, and engraved on the cigarette's butt was an emblem. An emblem of a winged sheep. The details were drawn with great care.

A winged sheep?

I shook my head and stared at it for a while. There was no mistake —it was a sheep. The exact kind of sheep in the photo; the exact kind of sheep carved in the box. My head began to hurt. This was all beyond me. Ever since the train ride at Berkeley, my grasp on things have been deteriorating. A kind of spell was being cast upon me. I did not know if it was a blessing or a curse.

6

"Just now, I asked you about your beliefs," said the man. "As long as what is real is defined by what's in our heads, what difference does the truth make? And this is only half of the story. What about our minds? Where each memory we hold is chosen and picked to conform to our personal narrative?"

"I'm not sure," I said. "To be honest with you, I'm not sure if anything you're saying is making much sense to me."

"You are a perceptive one!" he screeched, like how I'd imagine a calico cat with a thick moustache would howl. "These are all just theoretical discussions between you and I. As you might have observed, there is no causal relationship between theater, polaroid pictures, and sheep. Instead, there is an underlying glue connecting these seemingly separated things—an unfathomable constant set by the universe, if you will."

As soon as those words left him, an alternating shade of chill and secrecy swept the room. "Since you are seeking facts, allow me to indulge you in one." The man pointed to the photograph again and fiddled with his fingers. "I had a long and extensive dream revolving around lamb chops."

"You had a dream about...lamb chops?" I asked.

"That's right," he said with an utterly serious face.

His words defeated me, but I kept my composure. "I don't follow."

"Few can," he said. "It's not something that can easily be explained. Except that one day, I watched Gordon Ramsay reverse-sear a lamb chop, and had multiple dreams about it since. Mind you, it was miraculous; astonishing. It was unlike any piece of meat I'd ever seen. It had more character than a Tolstoy novel."

It was beyond my understanding where all this was going, but ignoring context for one moment, I did concur with his sentiments; it's no secret that I enjoyed a good lamb chop, especially one prepared oven-roasted.

"Seeing this," he continued, "I locked myself in the kitchen for the next twelve days to perfect the technique. I was trapped in an obsession; there was nothing I desired more than to master the cut of meat. But even on the twelfth day, as I got better at handling lamb, there was still something missing—"

"The lamb sauce," I interrupted. "You were missing the lamb sauce."

"Precisely. And not just any lamb sauce - chimichurri sauce. I'm talking about colorful, flavorful, Argentinian chimichurri sauce. Olive oil, vinegar, garlic, and red pepper flakes, infused with the beautiful lamb, dressed in green on a minimalistic plate. I was at the peak of my life—a kind of inexplicable pleasure would release itself whenever the meat came in contact with my tastebuds."

I nodded and nodded, like it was the only thing I could do.

"But, as you can imagine, the obsession came with a price: never-ending dreams about lamb chops!" he said. "They were all I could ever think about; the idea invaded all my headspace, every interaction of my thoughts. Soon, it became clear to me that I needed to end the infatuation, so I made a deal with God."

"You made a deal with God?"

"Well, not *literally*. I don't actually know if I made a deal with God. But then came a day where I went to sleep, and woke up after having a dream that wasn't about lamb chops. So, yes, it must have worked."

"I see." I gave a cough, but it didn't sound organic. The man's absurd dream added esoterism to everything in the room.

"Miraculously, though, this photo appeared by my bed right after. Inexplicably cryptic. And like a mysterious UFO sighting, not a trace elsewhere," he said. "Hence what you are seeing today."

Silence.

"So, according to what you're telling me," I said finally. "The photo here manifested itself into reality from your desire to not dream about lamb chops?"

"Precisely," he said. "It is not clear as to why it appeared in front of me. Nor is it clear as to how the photo was able to bend the space time continuum to appear by my bed. Nevertheless, the photo is here, and that is all that is important."

The man paused to take a sip of water.

"That still doesn't explain how I'm related to all of this," I responded.

Gently, the man took his right hand and eased the photo across the table into my peripheral view. "Care to flip it?"

I turned it upside down. The back of the photo bore a single line of profoundly black letters:

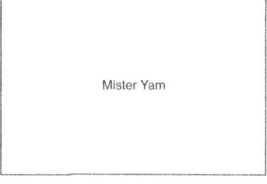

Mister Yam

My head started spinning.

"I don't understand," I replied. "This must be for some kind of sick joke."

"This is how you came into the picture," the man said. I was still staring at my name on the back of the photo. "As I said earlier, these seemingly ordinary events become more bizarre when put together. Like pieces of a puzzle that we have yet figured out. The question concerning you, of course, is the role you play in all this. Clearly, it was not you who sent this. But if not you, then who? And why would your name be used like this?"

I cleared my throat. I wanted to ask for a better explanation, but I didn't know what to say. None of this made any sense to me.

"There is more," the man continued. "While I was busy doing my research on you, I did some digging on the photo itself. Though I couldn't find anything about the man in the picture, I was able to get a timestamp on when it was taken. Some forty-three years ago. Most curious, don't you think?"

Forty-three years ago. Where had I heard that before?

"A mere coincidence," I answered.

"Maybe. As of right now, it's impossible to know. Rearrange the facts as you will, the correlation between these things are still a mystery."

"And why not let it remain that way?" I said. "Why not let it remain a mystery?"

"Because life does not work that way. Humans are not monotonous creatures; even if they were, I certainly am not. My curiosity has been piqued, and I demand an answer," he said. "Besides, aren't you interested in finding out your role in all of this? I'd imagine this would be of more concern to you than to me."

Undoubtedly, there was some truth to what the man was saying. Why wouldn't I be concerned about something like this? If my name was inscribed so casually like this, who knew what other false information was spreading out there?

"Going back to what I proposed earlier, allow me to make a deal with you—should you find this man and his sheep, I am prepared to reward you however you would care to request."

He took an even bigger pause and allowed the silence in the room to add more ambiguity to the already ambiguous atmosphere. "What if no such man exists?" I said. "What if this was all an elaborate piece of fiction?"

"Then that would be the end of that. You would go about your day as you do, and I will live with the consequences of a riddle unsatisfied." The man reached for his wallet and placed a stack of hundred dollar bills in front of me. "But until then, feel free to use as much of this money as you see fit. Should you need more, my secretary will be in touch. Any questions?"

"Your secretary?"

"I believe you have already met her. Any other questions?" he said.

"Not a question, but a comment," I said.

"I'm listening."

"This is, without a doubt, the most ridiculous story I have ever heard."

The man was about to say something, I could see it in his face. But an element of my comment caused him to hesitate, like he was searching his mind for something—like a drifting thought that once held him. Very slowly, almost imperceptibly, the man rolled his mouth.

He smiled softly. "Good luck."

7

I had always wanted to own a piston espresso machine, and so I bought one. Grabbing the portafilter by its wooden handle, I filled the fifty-eight millimeter basket with some medium roasted coffee beans, freshly burr-ground from Nicaragua. After some light tamping, I applied three bars of pressure on the lever for a gentle pre-infusion, gradually ramping up to nine bars. The few, noticeable moments of extraction produced two intense shots of espresso, contributing immensely to the flavors of the cappuccino I later whipped up.

Besides the Italian machine, I had also acquired a new pair of leather shoes from a bespoke cobbler, completely handcrafted. Thanks to the mysterious man's financial contributions, my old wardrobe was now entirely replaced, mainly with new clothes from different boutique outlets.

It had been a week since the encounter at the theater; the box from the bald man still sat on top of my desk. Though it remained an interesting spectacle in my room, there were no observable differences since. No strange dreams about lamb chops, at least.

When I switched on my television, the news recycled the same old stories: some war in the Middle East; protests and discussions surrounding wealth inequality. Usually, I'd watch these stories with measured interest—political discourse was something I enjoyed, even when I held unpopular views on the subject. But today, I was unusually removed from the happenings of the world; I saw these events as though they happened on some other, distant planet. The only thing in my world was a strong urge to relieve my back.

I headed to the nearby massage parlor and treated myself to a deep tissue massage. The experience, which I recognize as an immense luxury, dramatically enhanced my mood. It also rid my body of knots, even if only temporarily.

I had developed a cozy relationship with the therapist, having been her customer for almost a year now. "I can tell that something is troubling you," she said as she kneaded my legs. "Your body is stiff, and your blood flow is showing signs of irregularity."

"It's that obvious, huh?"

"Mhmm." She started working her palms onto my lower back with gentle force. She stretched my arms; a very audible pop echoed in the room as she pulled my forearm to her side. With two knuckles, she pushed against my spine from neck to waist—the crackling sensation of every vertebra perceptible as she went hand by hand.

The session ended shortly after. I left her a hefty tip and headed towards the pier, only about a few minutes' walk from here. Typically, there would be a lot more people going about, but I found myself navigating the shores alone.

I spotted an unassuming wooden bench by Fisherman's Wharf and sat on it. Seagulls come flocking to me—partly curious, mainly hungry. They seemed to have mistaken my shoes for food, and my laces for bread.

I took a piece of mango from my bag and tossed it gently to the ground. A few more seagulls flew in as they fought for a share of a bite. Basking under the sky, the Pacific Ocean was beautiful, as were the clouds, boats, birds, and bridges. The sand was glistening as the sun began setting; the Californian purple sky hovered over me as yet another reminder of the vast beauty surrounding the earth.

I headed down to the shore and bent over to brush the sand. The temperatures were freezing and the winds were gusty, but direction-less. I walked a few laps around the fogged-in beach. I took out my headphones and set it to shuffle; my playlist settled on Pink Floyd as the sea waves greeted my feet.

As I squatted on the sand, somewhere between sunset and nautical dusk, my phone rang. "The sunset today is especially beautiful, isn't it?" came a woman's voice.

"A lot of things in life are beautiful if you choose for them to be," I replied.

"You're quite the romantic, aren't you? Hmm, you must be popular with the ladies."

I said nothing.

I heard a soft chuckle. "No need to be shy," she continued. "Life's too short to be timid."

"Can you please just tell me what you want?"

"Oh, Mister Yam. I called you because I felt like talking to you," she answered. "Does everything have to have a goal with you?"

I let out a heavy sigh. "No," I responded. "But if I'm not getting a Pizza Hut coupon, then I don't see why I should keep talking to you."

"I know," she said. "Which is why I'd like to give you one!"

"Wait, really?"

"Yes. By confronting your mind."

Her meaningless statement dissipated into the sand like water from the ocean. "So, no coupon?"

"The more you take, the more you leave behind. What am I?"

"I don't know," I said. I also didn't know why I was still on the line with her.

"Footsteps. Footsteps left behind by you. The past that you are ignoring. The past that you are forgetting. Yet, you hide. Why?"

I looked at the beach. The stars were out in the night sky and glistening—ludicrous, not unlike the comments she was making. "You make no sense whatsoever," I said.

"*Of course I don't*," she said sarcastically. "But, no matter. I don't think you'd care much about me anyhow. No. I think you'd be more interested in knowing about the box you received. Am I right?"

That got me listening. "Go on..."

"A bald man, a box, and a book. What do you make of that?" she asked.

"Uhh...a terrible start to a joke?"

"Good one," she laughed. "But it could also be the start of something else."

"Like what?" I asked.

"Oh, I don't know. A mystery, perhaps?"

I crossed my arms and fixed my gaze upon the twilight beach, my phone now exactly at eye level. "That'd make a terribly lame mystery," I said.

More laughter. I could hear her breath next to the phone, her soft voice murmuring over the speaker. "There's more to it than you'd think, but saying it over the phone would be no fun," she said. "What about we meet? At one of the diners you frequent."

"How do you know about that?"

"It's my job to know," she said, monotone. "How does noon tomorrow sound?"

I took a moment to consider her proposal. First the theater and now the box; the woman was clearly not just a Pizza Hut promoter. She was involved, more involved than I imagined. But involved in what way?

"Okay, sure. But how am I even supposed to know what you look like?"

"I am twenty-nine years old," she said. "I'll have light mascara on, and I'll be wearing a white blouse."

Just like that, she cut the connection.

Wonderful, I thought. This woman would not give up!

I could not have said exactly what about the woman that I found so uncomfortable, but an odd sense of deja vu struck me as I repeated the conversion in my head. Why did I feel like I was forgetting something?

I woke up the next day and headed to the diner; there were three possible diners that she could have meant, but the establishment I was walking towards was the one I most frequently visited. It was, in my opinion, the best one—the service was excellent, the prices were reasonable, and most importantly, it brewed great coffee.

But before that, a pit stop—the pawn shop. In my bag was the wooden box, which I was hoping I could get inspected. I enjoyed the shroud of mystery it brought over my room, but it was causing too much of a distraction for me to let it sit idle.

Entering the shop, a lanky teenager with a baseball bat greeted me. He was engrossed with his phone, playing some kind of video game involving crushed candies. "What's up dude, how can I help you?"

"You guys sell jewelry boxes, right?" I asked.

"Oh yeah. Plenty of them. Let me guess, someone's getting married?" he said, still fiddling on his phone.

"Umm, no. I'm looking to have something inspected, actually."

He looked at me peculiarly and put down his phone. "Give me a second," he said, before turning around the desk and screaming **EMMA** to the back of the room.

One second.

Two seconds.

"WHAT?! I'M BUSY!" came a scream from behind a door - on the third second.

"YO! THIS DUDE HERE WANTS TO GET SOMETHING CHECKED OUT!"

I looked at the screaming, scrawny teenager. High schoolers had certainly come a long way with their enunciations.

"OKAY, TELL HIM TO WAIT LIKE TWO MINUTES," she shouted.

The guy turned around to face me. "Alright man, you heard her. Why don't you just chill out by one of the seats over there?"

I did as he suggested and took a seat by a fish tank. I waited for a while—for more than five minutes, but less than ten—before a woman with oval glasses emerged from the back room and peered over at me. "Hey, sorry for keeping you waiting. I was busy analyzing a coconut."

"A coconut?" I asked.

"Yeah. Do you know much about coconuts?"

I shook my head.

"They're really cool. Often overlooked though. They were first cultivated in India, and they're called *KalpaVriksha* in Indian literature, meaning a tree which gives everything you want. Because every part of it is edible—"

"Sis! Do you really have to bring up coconuts to every single customer?" the kid interrupted.

The woman told him to shut up. "Sorry, my brother's like four years my junior," she said. "Really immature. You know how teenagers are."

I nodded.

"Anyways..what can I help you with today?!"

I unzipped my bag and hauled up the box from the back panel. "You won't happen to know anything about wooden boxes, do you?"

She lowered her right hand and gently ran her palms over it. "Not too much, but enough. What kind of box is this?"

"I don't know," I said. "I'm not quite sure what it is exactly."

She rubbed her thumbs over the leather latch. She expressed some surprise at the lack of a keyhole, but it didn't seem to bother her. When she flipped the box on its head, the engraved emblem of the winged sheep was on full display, which she spent considerable time examining. She gave the box a knock, and a hollowed sound followed.

"I've never seen anything like it," she said, adjusting her glasses. She licked her lips and thought. "This feels interesting though. I can't say we're in the market for new purchases at the moment, but I might be able to make an exception for this. Do you have a price in mind?"

I told her I wasn't interested in selling. "Actually, I was hoping you could help inspect it for me. I'll pay for any price within reason."

"Inspection…" she mumbled. With her two hands, she aggressively shook the box left to right. It seemed as though she was waiting for a pattern to establish itself, but what kind of relationship could she infer from just sounds?

"When do you need an answer?" she said.

"Within the week, if possible?" I threw a random timeframe out there. "It's pretty important to me."

She pondered for a bit; her receding forehead expressed consideration at the idea. "Alright. What about this—fifty bucks for an answer within three days, which I'll lower down to thirty if you're willing to wait until the weekend. Which one would it be?"

Three days would be great, I told her.

"Okay, noted," she said. She scribbled down an invoice and asked for my contact. "I'll text you when I'm ready, but here's my number, in case you find out more."

I thanked her and stuffed the card in my wallet. "I'll be in touch," I said.

~

A few blocks away from the pawnshop was the diner. The place was hectic; there were about six different parties crowding at the entrance by the time I arrived.

I looked around for a woman with a white blouse, but as it turned out, I didn't have to.

"It's good to see you, Mister Yam," said a voice from behind me.

I turned to see her. Just as she said she would, she was wearing a white blouse, hidden under a gray cardigan. On her neck was a bright, pearl necklace, modest yet tasteful. I will admit that she was far more beautiful in person than her voice had suggested; she had a lovely build and knew how to dress. Her tone had a more comforting resonance than over the line.

"I'm surprised at how popular this place is. It's not even a weekend yet!" she said.

She could have been mistaken for a top of the line model; the subtle glares from the people around us provided evidence of that. I knew I recognized her from somewhere...

"After you, Mister Yam."

As we made our way inside, she invited me to sit at a booth by the corner. A waiter arrived shortly after, enquiring as to the state of our day and if we would enjoy some coffee. On her behalf, I said yes, because the coffee was delicious, and some caffeine would be enjoyable.

She searched through her purse and took out a little, printed booklet. The Life Of Boris—what else could it have been?

"What were your thoughts on the story?" she asked. "A sad one, isn't it?"

"It's a sorrowful story for sure; as I read it, it was as though my life was a blur, floating between the barely distinguishable seas of reality and fantasy," I said. "I see my life as a script I have written; every day, I grow more confused as to the role I have given to myself."

The waiter soon returned with two mugs, a coffeepot, and some condiments on a silver tray. "Can we please get two breakfast hash sets?" she said. "Over-easy eggs would be lovely." She was unimpeachably aware of my preferences.

"Do you know why I have arranged this meeting?" she asked.

"No. I can't say that I do."

I took a sip of my coffee. What was it about diner coffee that made it so good? Was it the ceramic mug? The triple-filtered water? The ambience? Probably all of the above, plus the novelty of it all.

"I once lived in Malaysia," she said. "For about three months or so. I was leading a project based out of Miri, Sarawak. Beautiful place, I must say. And the seafood! God, the seafood! The universal secret to a happy life lies buried somewhere in the steam crabs there."

She let out a laugh and opened a pack of sweetener, which she mixed into her coffee.

"Well, I must say that I did not expect to ever meet you again. Not that I did not want to see you, but rather, it was not within my imagination that the circumstances would align that we would meet like this. Yet here we are, and since we're here, I might as well tell you a few things about myself."

"Wait, hold on—"

"My name is Jess," she interrupted, ignoring me entirely. "I was born to a single mother, raised in a household with twelve others. I lived with my brothers, cousins, aunts, and uncles; such is the life of a struggling mother. For the longest time, the circumstances surrounding my father's disappearance went undisclosed. Whenever I would prod my mother, she would repeat the same story: my father left us on a Sunday, a week before my first birthday. He did not say why or offer any explanation, but he left a small wooden box for me, sealed, with no visible lock. My mother tried her best to break open the box, even to the point of employing a locksmith to help, but alas, it just would not budge, and so, she gave up and left it to me as I grew up."

"I took the tale for what it was and went about my life. Life was tough, distractions were abundant. Yet, there was deep conviction within me that made me push through; I would not fall into the same trap as my mother. Regardless of the outcome, I would try my very best, even if my best was mediocre. Such was the life I chose for myself."

"Despite all my efforts, I wasn't the brightest learner; far from it, to be completely honest. But I did well enough for myself and gained acceptance to a small college in the next biggest town. I embarked on this journey knowing next to no one, and while a student, I took classes in several different subjects. Unfortunately, nothing really stood out—I ended up picking visual arts because it was the only thing I wasn't miserable doing. Plus, it allowed my imagination to fly free."

I nodded, and took a sip of my coffee.

"But when I graduated, there weren't many jobs around. I, like every other aspiring fresh graduate at the time, was introduced to the job market at a rough time; the global financial markets were in a disaster, due largely to the subprime mortgage crisis caused by irresponsible leveraging. Lehman Brothers had just filed for bankruptcy due to their sizable gearing towards the collapsing housing market and low-rated mortgage trenches."

"I could go on forever," she continued. "The financial crisis of 2008 was a terrible tragedy of greed and irresponsibility. But the long story short here is that despite all the chaos, I still wanted to move to the Big Apple, so I persuaded a friend of mine to let me crash at her place in downtown Brooklyn."

She paused for a bit and swirled her coffee, her vibe rather dejected. "Truth be told, I hated my first few months there. Because of the volatile job market, I would spend most of my days on my laptop searching for a job, only to be rejected over and over again. It was a depressing experience for sure. Cold calls after cold emails, it would be about nine months of desperate inquiries before I would land my first interview; and even then, the pay for the gig was miserable! But I wasn't in a position to be picky. So I dug in and went to work, studying my hardest for the interview. Eventually, I would do well enough on the phone screening to receive an on-site interview, which then resulted in me receiving the job. *Hurray!*" she said sarcastically.

The waiter arrived with our food, mindfully respecting the conversation we were having. I scooped a generous amount of roasted potatoes into my mouth as Jess continued.

"I knew a scant few things about the job. It was with a creative design firm located in Manhattan, specializing in the illustrations of animals. Before I joined, there was a scandal some months ago with the CEO and a long history of sexual harassment. To digress just a bit, it's a shame that sexism and discrimination are still a thing in the workplace. What is it about corporate men and their lack of respect for women? Is it really that impossible to think without your pants in mind?"

She shook her head, then relaxed her back on her seat. "Thankfully, he was fired, and I was brought in as part of the company's ongoing efforts to improve diversity in the workplace. But unfortunately for the company, even a public relations campaign couldn't reverse the damage. This was especially true for our pre-existing clientele, who dropped us like flies as soon as the scandal went viral," she said. "Keep in mind that all of this was happening in the background as I was interviewing, so you can imagine how stressed out I was; even if I had passed all the interviews, would there be a job left for me?"

"Yet, miraculously, there came a day when a mysterious man reached out to the new CEO and offered him a deal he couldn't refuse. This man would pay the firm tenfold the regular rate on the condition of exclusivity. Though it was an odd request, it wasn't exactly unheard of in our industry, so the new CEO agreed, and a contract was signed. Of course, I only knew about this after I had joined on the first day. Can you guess what it was?"

I shook my head. "No idea," I said.

"Well, it turns out that the request from the client was simple—sometimes he would ask for copies of a specific breed of sheep, or a canvas detailing the different flock of sheep. It would always be something related to sheep. I knew next to nothing about sheep when I first joined, but it didn't take long before I could articulate every little detail about sheep—the scent glands on its face; the large, curling horns made of keratin; the soft, layered wool that coats its body. By sheer volume and repetition, I became an expert in drawing sheep.

And naturally, I developed an attachment to them, to the extent that I would no longer wear wool, or indulge in lamb."

"My illustrations grew better with every task, until one day, a year later, I was invited to meet the client himself. As you can imagine, I was curious; inquisitive. Not only was he able to afford the firm's services, but he did so at a premium rate for what I could only imagine being an unusual hobby. He was, without doubt, a man of unbelievable wealth, but his obsession with sheep was beyond my understanding, and so I saw the meeting as a chance to understand his intentions better."

I thought about what she was sharing for a minute. Why do I keep hearing about sheep?

"He invited me for coffee at a place in Midtown, apparently to discuss one of my more recent drawings. When I arrived at the shop, a man about my height waved at me from the back. He wore round glasses and was, in my opinion, extremely attractive for his age, which I guessed to be somewhere around his early forties. More notably, however, was his unbelievably shiny bald head. How on earth could someone look so outstanding with such an absence of hair? It was a surreal visual. He bought me some coffee and almost immediately brought up the work I'd done. Most of our discussions revolved around a specific illustration of sheep I did for the dorper breed from South Africa. To give you some context, dorper sheep are known for their well-muscled carcass and extended period of reproductivity. Like most sheep, they have wool, but unlike most, shearing was not a constant necessity. This made them an easy to care breed, hence their popularity as meat."

"A fascinating sheep for sure, I thought to myself. But really, dorper sheep are just about as cool as sheep could get, so surely there must have been something more. I was right, as he continued to press me about my design style, and the way in which I would detail the contrast between the darker shades of black on the sheep's face and the brighter tones of white on its wool. I told him that I based most of my sketches on images that I had found online, a handful of them being polaroid photographs. They outlined similar physical characteristics, with only light textural differences."

"As I went into detail on my methodologies, he pulled out a

picture from his briefcase: a photo showcasing a random assortment of sheep in what I imagined to be a ranch somewhere. Instinctively, I recognized the farmstead to be in Montana; it was where I was born, and also the place where my father disappeared. But there was something peculiar about the image—there was a purple house in it, and the sheep surrounding it had wings and colorful stripes of wool."

"I was astounded, of course. These were unlike any sheep I have seen. Mind you, I have been studying, capturing, and illustrating sheep for a whole year, and most sheep lie within some spectrum of black and gray. So imagine how marvelous and striking a sheep of such color would be! I shed a tear as I admired the picture, and as bizarre as the situation looked from afar, he stared at me as though my reaction was expected; as though there was no other way one could properly acknowledge it."

"When I was done crying, he then told me the reason for our meeting: it would be to depict and portray the picture that I had just seen in drawing purely through memory. Meaning to say, I would not be allowed to see or reference it ever again. The image was so sacred, he said, that he could not, would not, photograph, replicate, or manufacture copies of it; it could only be illustrated. And not merely any kind of illustration, he elaborated, but one done chiefly from imagination."

She paused to take more sips of her coffee, before continuing. I wondered where on earth this was all going. "So I accepted the task in a hurry and went away to work. There was something about the request that had spurred me. For one, it was difficult drawing something purely from memory, so I had to sketch what I could as soon as possible. It was certainly difficult at times to remember the details of the photo or exactly what I saw, but it was simply impossible for me to forget the way in which the picture made me feel."

"Initially, I drew the assortment of sheep as I had always drawn, except this time, with colorful wool and added wings. And with all my soul and passion, I drew. But as miraculous as the sheep was, I was no longer drawing it. No, I was beginning to imagine and visualize the most incredible shapes. I began capturing emotions I thought were lost in me. I closed my eyes and allowed my mind to operate unfettered. I don't know why, but I started laughing hysterically, and then immediately after, I would be weeping. Water was flooding out of my eyes like a waterfall. I thought about my family, reminisced about my friends. My entire life was transpiring in front of me as though I was witnessing an emotional melodrama of myself in my own show. And as I opened my eyes, the most unbelievable thing occurred. My sketch was no longer a drawing of a sheep, but of a key: a monochromatic bronze key!"

"I studied the key, obviously perplexed as to the why and the what. Like, a key, of all things? Well, a key only has two functions, to lock and unlock, so maybe this was some form of unconscious spiritual metaphor. But as I looked around my room, there was a faint, warm glow originating from my wardrobe, as though a part of it was illuminating. I looked into the wardrobe, and lo and behold, the glimmer came from a box; the box from my father I had kept for all these years!"

"I was, obviously, confused, but inquisitiveness and marvel got the better of me, and, well, it's impossible to describe what happened next, but basically, I took the key from the sketch and opened the box, as if I was giving purpose to something buried within me."

She smiled ever so slightly. "What happened shortly after would alter the course of my life; I would tell you, but there are certain meanings that would be lost forever the moment they are explained in words."

Having finished her story, she let out a deep breath and drank down her glass of water. It seemed that all that talking had made her hungry, as she began to attack all the eggs, potatoes, and beef hash on her plate.

As she ate, I was left deliberating for a few minutes. Was her box related to the box I had received? What was up with these strange, bald men? And why would she share such a specific story? I sipped on my now lukewarm coffee, further examining these absurd thoughts.

"I guess you're wondering about the what or why," she said, ending the silence. "To which I say there is no easy answer. It would be an unnecessarily long story, trying to piece everything like that together. And no offense to you, but it would be practically impossible for you to fully understand the meaning of the story unless you have been involved in that world itself."

She finished her meal and wiped the remaining food crumbs on her lips with the paper napkins on the table. The server rushed over to clear our plates—a subtle indication for us to leave.

I glanced at the window as I stood. There was a sizable line outside the restaurant at this point. "Before we go, there's something else you should know," she said.

Her eyes widened as she stared into my pupils, a more distressed look replaced the glee on her face. "You may have already noticed it, but I believe you are entering a chapter of your life from which there is no turning back. Quite a number of things will occur; many hard choices to make. What those choices might be I cannot say, and it is quite possible you will never fully understand the extent to which these circumstances are related."

There was a striking, ominous silence that followed as soon as those words left Jess's mouth; her eyes peered at me as if to say— please think hard and carefully about what I have just shared with you. "Of course, you are in no way responsible for the events that have transpired. But the past is the past, and the future—well, that's up for you to decide, isn't it?"

"Why are you sharing this with me? I asked. "Why do you keep bringing up this cryptic mojo about the past?"

With a single, considerable gulp, she finished the remainder of her coffee. "There's nothing else I can say at this time. That's strictly between you and him."

You and him?

Jess grabbed her handbag from the table and signaled for the bill. When the waiter arrived, she paid with her credit card and left an exceedingly generous tip, signed with an impeccably quaint signature one would expect from an artist. "We'll talk again. Though next time, circumstances will be different."

She then said her goodbyes, and disappeared.

Later that night, I laid in my bed wide awake. It was probably somewhere between midnight and dawn; not that it was distinguishable in the dark. This was my fifth attempt at sleep, but my mind was churning more than usual. I couldn't stop myself from thinking about Jess's story. The box. The key. The sheep.

Usually, I'd hear a ridiculous story like this and laugh it off. Maybe write it down somewhere and forget about it the week later. But the coincidence was uncanny; it was pestering me, like a hole in my shirt that was getting bigger with every passing day. Why did I feel like I was standing on the edge of a cliff? On the cusp of something bigger?

I gazed at the walls of the ceiling, shaking my head. There was something I was forgetting; something that I was not understanding. And there was nothing my mind craved more than speculating what was behind that door.

8

The past three days flew by quicker than expected. Christmas was approaching, and work was more or less idle; it was evident that everybody in the office was in full holiday swing. The bars were packed with locals and tourists alike. Popup clubs were being promoted everywhere, with alcohol sales in evident abundance.

I left the office early and went to my usual bar spot. To my surprise, a long line greeted me outside of Barry's Rum House.

I waited in the queue for a while, but as I approached the front, the bouncer I had now recognized a dozen times over apologetically turned me away, citing the bar's new provisional holiday policies— entry was set for groups of two or more only. "I know you're a regular, but my hands are tied. Sorry."

"No problem," I told him. Internally though, it was a different story. I was bitter, and a touch annoyed. My precious space was ruined, defiled by these party-goers who understood next to nothing of the brooding necessary for introverts like myself! I had lived my life in routine, enjoying the predictable schedule that would envelop my days. Now, with nothing else to do, I thought about heading home.

That was, until my phone started ringing.

"What's good, Mister Yam!" came a teenager's voice. It was the kid from the pawn shop. "How are you doing today?"

"I'm fine, thanks for asking. Hey, listen, is the box ready for—"

"Not so fast, Mister," he said. "I'm gonna have to verify something before we continue."

"Verify? Verify what?"

"I'm going to need to extract some basic information from you. Like, what kind of relationship do you have with sheep?"

"Excuse me? The kind of relationship I have with sheep? None whatsoever," I responded. "I think they're fluffy and cute, but that's about it."

"So, you don't have any special relationship with sheep?" he said.

"No! That sheep has nothing to do with me!" I said. "And nothing to do with you! You should learn to respect your customer's privacy in these kinds of matters."

"Hey, dude. I'm just really bored. I have homework to do, but I don't want to do homework."

"Fine," I told him. I wasn't about to get into an argument with a teenager, especially one that looked like he was from the Sunday baseball league. "Are you guys done with the inspection?"

"Let me ask her," he said, before placing the phone down. Through the microphone, some inaudible shouting was happening in the background. It seemed like this was something of regular occurrence between the two of them.

"Okay, she told me she has something for you. If you're not busy, you can come over and talk to her yourself."

"Like, right now?"

"Yeah."

I thanked him and hung up. God! What a nosy kid.

I felt water trickling down my forehead. A light drizzle from the clouds was ensuing, casting a gray hue across the Bay Area. It wasn't the heaviest of rain, but it was enough to cause a big scene on the streets. A few drops of water is all it takes for Californians to start evacuating.

I called a cab for the store—estimated arrival time was around eight minutes. Neither long nor short, I escaped into a nearby department store and waited in the shoe section. Leather loafers here were marked at a hundred dollars. I contemplated the source of these shoes. What South-East Asian country was exploited to make these?

Then, a honk. I ran outside and opened the taxi door. I gave directions to the store's cross street, which the driver acknowledged. If there was an underlying consolation from the rain, it would be the resulting lack of traffic—the driver sped through the road as though there was a military curfew in place.

Parking by the curb, I paid him and ran outside. By the time I was on the pavement of the entrance, my clothes were completely drenched.

"Holy crap, you're wet," said the teenager.

"Yes, and in the absolute wrong way," I said. "Could I borrow a towel?"

He disappeared to the back of the store and came back with a few beach towels. I layered them together and wiped across my face and chest. "Thanks. Where's your sister?"

"She's busy in the study room. I'll bring you to her when you're ready."

Study room? "Okay, give me a minute, " I said. For convenience's sake, I took off my shirt and squeezed the remaining water from it.

Once I was ready, he led me through the shop's display cases, and then to a door, which he knocked on." Yo, sis! He's here."

"Come in!" she said.

The teenager pulled the door open and gestured at me. "After you," he said.

I walked in. The first thing that came to view were the coconuts plastered on the wall. It wasn't a stretch to say that there were coconuts everywhere; the shelves surrounding the room were filled with at least a few dozen groups of coconuts. Even some of the furniture, like the stools and tables, had makeshift elements of coconut in them.

"I've got King Coconuts; Macapuno Coconuts; Malayan Dwarf Coconuts—name me a cultivar and I probably have it somewhere," she said. "Though it bothers me how much space they're beginning to take up." She was seated behind a desk, busy fumbling with a magnifying glass on a dried husk. She wore a gigantic white lab coat; the sleeves were twice the size of her head.

I gave my glasses a quick wipe with my shirt. There were a number of coconuts on her table, some of which had their shells drilled open. They had different colored labels, though it was beyond me how they were physically distinguishable at all.

A collection of lab equipment, namely beakers and burettes, were organized towards the back-left. It seemed as though they were part of an analytical workflow. "Do you mind me asking why you have a lab setup for coconuts? In a pawn shop of all places?"

"It's quite an arrangement, eh?" she said in a proud voice. "Honestly, I'd love to tell you more, but I signed a non-disclosure agreement a few months ago. Stealth startup kind of business, you know? Can't be giving out company secrets like that."

"Um, yeah, I guess." A bunch of Silicon Valley slang; such things meant nothing to me.

"Anyway, thanks for coming on such short notice," she said. "The nature of my work makes outside research a bit difficult, but I was able to locate a record of your box through my university's archive."

"Boxes...have archives?"

"Well, yes and no. Not all of them have registrations. Think of it as an ISBN, except for box collectors."

The technicalities confused me, but if what she was saying was true, then I'd at least have a north star to work with. "Were you able to find anything useful from it?"

"Somewhat," she said. She then glanced a look at her brother. It was only a brief stare, but I recognized the sibling's reaction; he understood it as a request to leave.

Once he was gone, she locked the door and walked over to a sealed cupboard. "Apologies, safety precautions. What I'm sharing with you is technically illegal since it was proxied through the university, so we have to keep this on the down-low. Are you following me?"

"Yes," I said.

"Okay. So, the first thing you might want to know is location. The box was first registered some forty-seven years ago in Berkeley, California. Unlike most other antiquities, however, the transaction list was missing."

"Transaction list? What's a transaction list?"

"It's the list that holds the record of all buyers and/or sellers," she clarified. "Usually, the price of an object is derived from its previous resale value. For all things collectable, this is a pretty imperative process, since a written record of a previous, prestigious owner could increase the value of the item. Having said that, it's difficult to overstate how difficult the past few years have been for the antique market. The foreclosing of shops across the country would at least contribute to the idea that *some* of these records would disappear. And—"

"Long story short," I cut her off, "you're suggesting that we have no record of who the previous owner was, right?"

"*Kind of*," she said after a moment. "Though there aren't any specific breadcrumbs for us to follow. There was some recent activity spotted on this specific record."

Recent activity? I hadn't the vaguest idea if these words were jargon or literal definitions. "What do you mean by 'recent activity'?"

She reached under her desk and pulled out a piece of paper. "Just three weeks ago, a page of numerics was attached to the record," she said. "Have a look for yourself."

47°27'22.3"N	112°43'11.3"W
_ _°51'11.5"N	130°_ _'19.5"W
43°_ _'35.2"N	_ _ _°57'23.4"W
_ _°20'56.3"N	_ _ _°32'42.8"W
46°13'_ _._ _"N	109°_ _'71.2"W

I stared at the random mismatch of numbers a couple times over. "I don't really understand what I'm looking at," I told her.

"Me neither. Call it a juxtaposition of sorts, but numbers have never really been my thing."

I skimmed over the figures again, except this time with my phone. According to the various internet search results, it seemed as though the numbers displayed here were latitude and longitude points, coordinates, paraphrased in the DMS format. But the list was clearly incomplete. "Where are the rest of the numbers?"

"No clue," she said. "Whatever it is that you've gotten yourself involved with, it's quite a mess. On a separate note, however, I was able to better understand the logo inscribed underneath."

"The sheep logo? You're talking about the winged sheep inscribed at the bottom, right?"

"Yes. I uploaded a photo of it to my university's pattern recognition search engine and was able to locate a source: it was the work of a student, from an undergraduate art class in San Luis Obispo. I'm not sure how helpful this would be to you, but you could connect with the artist that drew it."

"Sure, what's the person's name?"

From her lab coat's pocket, she took out a notebook and squinted her eyes. "I might be butchering the pronunciation, but according to my notes, it's...Lorenzo de' Medici. Sounds Italian. Does that name ring any bells?"

I looked at her with my jaw wide open. If I could transmogrify into an ostrich, I'd bury my head into the ground. "No way," I said. "You're kidding with me, right?"

"I wish I was, but no. That's the name on the record." She handed me a few copies of the page, before returning to her desk. "Judging by your reaction, I'm assuming you know this person? Whatever it might be, all of this is out of my pay grade. I'm going to have to return to my coconuts now."

The winged sheep was Lorenzo's drawing? How was that even possible? It was hard to articulate the turmoil within me. I felt like somebody had pierced a hole in my skull and mashed the inner cortex of my brain.

"Thanks for your help," I said, after regaining some composure. I handed her the payment of fifty dollars, which she graciously accepted.

"No, *thank you.*"

She guided me to the exit, then faced me, "Mister Yam," she said, grabbing me by the arms. "I wish you the best in your future endeavors. And, please, don't forget to take the box with you."

Which I did not forget to do.

9

I returned home and made preparations for an early dinner. The phone rang a couple of times, but I ignored it. I found a few pieces of mail in the mailbox—two credit card invites and an auto-insurance notice. I went into the kitchen and stared at the clock, watching the minute hand flip from 4:19 pm to 4:20 pm. Then, I changed into a pair of sweatpants, walked into the kitchen, and fried some eggs.

With the yolk still runny, I ate over the countertop. My eyes were tired, but I couldn't help but contemplate the predicaments I had found myself in. Lorenzo, my dear friend from the career fair, was somehow involved with this ridiculous box business. Was it a mere coincidence that his drawing was being used? No. Probably not. The unlikely chance of coincidence was uncoincidental in itself.

I sighed, and stared at my pathetic excuse of a sunny-side-up egg. Could it have been an elaborate setup by Jess? If I asked her directly, she'd probably dance around the question, and give some nonsensical response, like: "It'd be a waste of time to spell this out for you, so why don't you continue whisking your eggs and go about your stupid day."

I went into the restroom and washed my face. The migraine from earlier today had only grown worse, not helped by my less than appetizing lunch. I took a shower and attempted to think of something else, but my mind would not yield; some corner of my brain was pushing hard for more.

Sheep—that frustratingly cute derping fluffy animal. How was it so fat and delicious? And why did it decide to haunt me like this? I sat down on the couch and rubbed my eyes. Chimichurri sauce aside, the other pressing question I had was Lorenzo's connection to all of this. Did he also have a dream about Gordon Ramsay?

Pulling out my phone, I decided to give Lorenzo a call. That was the only way I could confirm my theory for sure. He'll probably find the question funny, or maybe downright ridiculous—but I needed some answers. Worst case scenario, we'd laugh it off.

I waited a few seconds before my call was picked up. When I heard a click, I opened: "Hey, man. This is going to sound really random, but can I ask you something about a drawing you did back in college?"

I waited for a response, but I heard nothing. There was only silence. Dead silence.

"Hello? Can you hear me?"

Still Nothing. Nothing but crickets.

"Hellooooo...." I continued. "Cannnnn youuuu heaarrrr meeeee..."

It took about a minute before an exhale was audible. I could sense there was light breath by the microphone; but still, no official words from the other line. "If now isn't a good time, I'll call you back tomorrow—"

"Wait!" came a girl's voice. It was probably the softest voice I have ever heard. "Who is this?"

"This is Mister Yam, Lorenzo's friend. *Who are you?*"

"This is Mary, Lorenzo's sister," she said.

"Mary? This is Mary?"

"Yes. Sorry for leaving you hanging. I wasn't sure who you were."

"No worries," I said. I knew of Mary through Lorenzo, but this was my first time ever speaking with her. "How are you doing?"

"Umm, I'm okay."

"Is your brother around? I was hoping I could speak to him for a bit-"

"He's not available right now," she interrupted. There was a trace of insecurity in her voice; the kind you get from someone who lies poorly.

"Well, umm. Could you tell him to call back then?" I asked.

No immediate reply. It was quite a frustrating experience trying to talk to her, but the same could be said about my friend. Perhaps it was a trait that ran genetically in the family?

"He's really busy..." she said, after some time. "And he won't be free anytime soon."

"Oh."

"Yeah, I'm sorry."

"If that's the case, then could I at least drop him a note?" I said.

"I wish it were as simple as that."

"I beg your pardon?" She didn't respond to my comment, and remained silent for the longest time. What was up with the crypticness?

"Hello..?" I mumbled.

More silence.

"I know this is a terribly sudden request, Mister Yam, but would it be possible for us to meet right now?"

Now it was my turn to shut up. "Excuse me?"

"You live in the city right?" she asked. There was tension in her voice, followed by disembodied breathing. She sounded stressed.

"Yes I do, though could you please tell me what's going on?" I asked.

"It's better if we talked about it in person," she said, with measured urgency. "This has to be strictly between you and me."

"May I ask why?"

Instead of answering, she gave me directions to a subway station a few blocks away. "Wait for me at the billboard by the entrance. I'll be there in fifteen," she said. Without any warning, she hung up.

Just great, I thought. Did Lorenzo get into trouble? I didn't know the answer. Hell, I wasn't even in the mood to speculate. I gave up trying to think. If I had things my way, I'd be watching CNN's evening commentary while chomping a glazed donut.

Per her instructions, I arrived at the station. The gate area looked a little odd, and the people passing by had an unnatural, fictitious look to them, as if all the lingering excitement in their life had been sucked and swept away.

I leaned against the wall by the billboard, staring at the crowds of people going about their day. I tried searching for Mary, then realized that I had no idea what she looked like. Anyone could have been her, I thought. But I had no problem waiting. To be frank with myself, what was I going to do, if not this? Soon, the holiday season will begin to wind down, and the flowers will bloom for the arrival of spring. I'd go on with my routine, doing the usual mundane things in a predictable manner. At times, I would find joy in these things, like showering after a hot day, or drinking a cup of fresh coffee in the early morning. But there was no deeper meaning behind any of it; life was lacking, in a lactose intolerant kind of way.

"Hello," came a voice. It was spoken so softly that it was a miracle that it was discernible at all.

I turned around to see a young woman. She wore a cap and an oversized sweatshirt, and accompanying her baggy joggers were a pair of pearly white sneakers. If her goal was to appear as relaxed as possible, she had nailed it to a tee.

"Hello," I said. "You must be Mary."

"Yes, and you're my brother's friend, right?"

I nodded. "Let's cut to the chase: did something happen to Lorenzo?"

She stretched her arm and took a long, deep breath. "He's gone," she said, in a surreal voice.

"Gone?!" I said. "What do you mean he's gone?"

"Like. 'Gone' gone."

"He went missing?"

"Yeah," she answered. She then gave the edge of her upper lip a little bite. "He's been missing for a few weeks now!"

At this point, Mary took an audible deep breath. She then glanced at her phone as I processed my shock. "I'm sorry..." she mumbled, in a somber voice. "A lot has happened in the past twenty-four hours."

"Please don't apologize," I said. "Could you tell me more?"

"Sure. But before that, let me provide you some context—as you know, my brother was never a fan of technology. Within the family, he's had a history of undertaking these periods of social isolation where he would live like a nomad. No phone, no internet. No nothing."

"Right," I said. What she said was true; Lorenzo was infamous within our friend group for never responding to our text messages.

"Yet, usually in these periodic waves of technological isolation, he'd reach out in no less than a week, mainly to reassure us that everything was okay. I don't think he had ever ghosted us out of malice, but last week marked the first time ever he's exceeded a month in his blackout silence. So, naturally, we started to get worried. Like, what if something happened?"

I nodded.

"It was around this time that my parents started freaking out, which also caused me to freak out. The first thing I did was to stop by his house and make sure he was okay, but he wasn't at home. Then, I tried calling his girlfriend, only to realize that they had broken up quite some time ago, so no luck there. It was only when I revisited his place the second time earlier yesterday that our deepest fears came true—he never came back home! His housemates, when we spoke to them, just assumed that he was living with us. How stupid are they, really?"

She paused for a few seconds to reclaim her breath. "Obviously, things got really serious after this. Like, my mom started acting hysterical, and my dad wasn't doing too well either. We filed a police report and did a search through his room; and the house, and literally everything else. We met the detective assigned to the case, and even sat in on his interviews with the housemates. But seemingly, they're all just as clueless as us. There was no motive. No traces. Just a disappearance into thin air!"

I stood in thought for a few seconds. The last time I saw him was about a month ago. He had Vietnamese noodles for dinner after. It was also roughly within the same week that I received Jess's phone call at Berkeley.

"We were told to keep this on the down low, pending the investigation results. But since you called, I'd figure I'd tell you as well," she said.

71

I had no words to offer her, except my deepest condolences. "I'm really sorry about what happened," I said. "Did he leave any notes? Or messages?"

"None that we could find. And searching through his emails, there was no indication of this whatsoever."

"What about plans? Or trips? Did he mention anything about traveling?"

"There were talks of a family trip to Vancouver, but it was just a floating idea. Nothing concrete had been developed yet," she said.

I shook my head. If Lorenzo had run off with a girl, he would have definitely told me. "And his housemates? When did they last see him?"

"Saturday morning, also around a month ago. He was last spotted preparing coffee in the kitchen, as per usual according to them. He had also mentioned about going on a job later that day."

"Okay, and there was absolutely nothing else?" I asked.

Mary reached into her backpack and pulled out a small book. It had a leather honeycomb cover. "My brother had a diary stashed under his bed. The detectives made copies of it, and we did a full run down through it, but we couldn't find anything unusual in it."

She opened the book and swiftly flipped through the pages, before passing it to me. "You're welcome to look through it though. Maybe you'll find something we missed."

I took the journal and shoved it in my pocket. Lorenzo had never once occurred to me as the type to jot his thoughts down in ink. He had always struck me as someone more open, someone less reserved; someone who would talk rather than write. Maybe this was a side of him I had not yet discovered.

"Anyhow, we're organizing a walk around the neighborhood with the police tonight. We'll be searching the parks and distributing flyers across the city. You're more than welcome to join."

You are, of course, in no way responsible for the events that have transpired. But the past is the past, and the future—well, that's up for you to decide, isn't it?

Was this related to what Jess had shared with me? The more I thought about it, the more certain I was. She, and the bald man and the box, were somehow related to this. I couldn't put my finger on what it was exactly, but the correlation was no mere coincidence. Live an adult long enough and you get this tingling sixth sense, this unassailable feeling when something's not right. No concrete evidence to work off of, but a strong hunch that there was more here than was being said.

"Sheep," I said to her, the thought of the animal suddenly manifesting in my mind. "Did he mention anything about sheep?"

She shot me a startling look, like she wasn't expecting those exact words to come out of my mouth. "Ummm... Well... Many months ago, he shared a drawing he did of a sheep. But that was it."

"I see."

"What's sheep got to do with my brother though?" she asked.

"I have no clue," I said. "And I sound like a lunatic for even bringing this up, but on the off chance that I'm right, there's something else I need to follow up with. I'll call you if I find anything useful."

"Okay", she replied, a few tears sliding from her eyes. Her hands were beginning to shake as she cried quietly. I reached out for a hug, by which she was uncontrollable sobbing. Both our clothes were soaking wet when she finished crying. "It's getting dark. I should get going," she said. "Mom's gonna be upset if I'm gone for too long."

I stood there and watched her depart on the BART train. After she was gone, I felt an undeniable emptiness inside of me—a helpless kind of feeling like that of a puppy left abandoned on the streets. I tried my best to remain composed, but a torrent of tears overwhelmed me as I walked back home. I felt the darkness begin to wrap itself around me, until there was nothing left to see.

I slept terribly that night. The room was cold and stuffy, to the extent I could not leave the windows closed; yet, if I opened them, the ghastly sirens of a hasty ambulance would fill the noise. Everything that had happened to me, as strange as it was, had been innocuously irritating at worst. Up to this point, this had been the kind of story you would share at a birthday party—the kind that may gather some weird looks and chuckle. But the disappearance of my friend was hardly laughable. The rings surrounding these events were different now. They were more serious, and they bothered me considerably.

Glancing at myself in the closet mirror, my face was as expressionless as it was unreadable. Had my friend decided to flee from society? I couldn't blame him. Truth be told, I couldn't remember the last time I was genuinely happy in the city. Like most people, I did a good job of convincing myself of all the permutations of opportunity that existed here—networking with successful entrepreneurs; hustling my way to fortune. But outside of the initial optics, I had no desire to do anything, no desire to be anything.

I plumbed back to the depths of isolation. My body was withering deeper into my sheets. Images I held in the past took power like never before, manifesting themselves into different shapes and sounds. With my arms raised, I tried to grasp them. Where have you been, my dear memories? Why did you abandon me?

I swam through more of my memories. I saw friends whom I was ashamed of seeing; thoughts and feelings I no longer recognized. I was an unfamiliar stranger, trying to relate to a variant of me that no longer existed. I thought about my parents, who had sacrificed, compromised, and invested their entire lives so that my sister and I could have a better life. I never took their love for granted. I had always worked hard; I never stopped short of recognizing the opportunity given to me. I had done everything asked of me. Yet, an overwhelming dread of meaningless, confusion, and loneliness surrounded me; of inexpressible emptiness and void which fell on me.

I could hear the acceleration of my heart. Was I leaving my body?

I was leaving my body. I was flying somewhere else.

I pictured my mom's home cooked chicken to regain a measure of calm. But defenseless and vulnerable, my mind was drifting further and further from my body.

My mind was taking me somewhere, somewhere far.

$\sim$

I arrived at a house. I did not know where it was, or if it was even real, but I laid in front of its door, already half opened. When I peered within, there was a long corridor, lined with candles. The light was dim, but it was there. And towards the end, there was a slightly stronger glow.

Very slowly, I dragged my legs and felt my way across the hallway. I was careful of my every step, so as not to disturb the candles. At some point, I reached the source of the central light. Embers were lingering from an altar, with sparks flickering from recently burnt wood.

I stood by the flames. I soaked in the warmth and listened. Usually, even the quietest of libraries would have notes of sound; but here, outside of the fire's crackle, there was nothing else audible.

To my left was a bookshelf. A collection of Tolstoy, Jung, and Proust were shelved in succession, in which their stems were facing outward. The crevices in the rows permitted some light to escape between them.

On my right was a door. It had no knob, no lock, no hinges, no handle, no nothing to grip. The top and bottom were so perfectly flushed within the frame that there was no possible way of jamming it open. Some familiar light lay behind it.

"It won't open for you," said a monotone, unrecognizable voice. "Not yet, at least."

I turned around, but there was no one there. The voice had no visible source. It sounded like something from another reality—one that existed here.

"The fire died a while ago," it continued, "and it'll be awhile before it burns again."

Fire? What fire? I looked at my hands above the flickering embers, and then at the floor. I was confused, and sad; yet, I was not afraid. I knew there was nothing to fear.

"You never had to be scared. We were always here for you."

In the dim light of the fire, I stood to face the voice. There, in the embers, it was looking at me as I was looking at it. "What is this place?"

"This place? This place is what kept you from forgetting," it said.

"Forgetting?"

I began recalling parts of my memories. When did I lose my motivation? My happiness? With my sorrowful voice, I poured out my soul. How I went far by the standards of many, but also went nowhere. Did nothing. Built nothing. Meant nothing to those around me. Meant nothing to those that cared for me.

"You never had to be scared," the voice assured me. "You never had to run away."

Run away —I thought I understood it, but I didn't understand it at all. The words were too vague.

"I don't get it. I don't get any of this."

"You brought us here," it said. "Don't you remember? It was to keep you from forgetting."

I shut my eyes and breathed a sigh. "None of this makes sense."

The voice didn't answer, and I didn't know what else to say. All at once, the walls around me started sundering. The floor was quaking, the air simmering; I couldn't tell if the world around me was collapsing, or if my perceptions were combusting. Either way, I was struggling to find my breath. The strength from my body, escaping. My mind and body were separating, floating in some eternal darkness.

I surrendered myself to the overwhelming forces enfolding me.

I was dying, like everyone else cursed with existence.

The full light of day was shining outside my window as I woke up feverish and drenched in sweat. A burning sensation festered in my throat, carrying its way down from my mouth to my lungs. Next, I realized that I was completely naked, my pajamas scattered across the bed.

I had no outlet for my confusion but to pee, so I went into the toilet. Afterwards, I went into the kitchen and poured myself a glass of orange juice. I'm not a nutritionist, but surely, vitamin C must do some good? Feeling hungry, I also prepared myself a bowl of cereal.

I turned on the television in the living room. A political commentary regarding Donald Trump greeted me. I ate my cereal and immersed myself in the episode; they were discussing his authoritarian tendencies, and attachment to hypocrisy. It was still perplexing to me how America elected a reality TV star to the presidency. Why would anyone vote for Mango Mussolini? Was the electoral college to blame for this? I had yet heard of a good defense on its behalf; the numbers simply didn't make sense. Similar to the numbers I'd received at the pawn shop.

From my wallet, I pulled out the list. The first row was the only row that had coordinates written in whole:

47°27'22.3"N	112°43'11.3"W
__°51'11.5"N	130°__'19.5"W
43°__'35.2"N	___°57'23.4"W
__°20'56.3"N	___°32'42.8"W
46°13'__._"N	109°__'71.2"W

(47°27'22.3"N, 112°43'11.3"W -- the format of these figures roughly translated to degrees, minutes and seconds.)

Turning on my laptop, I typed these coordinates into an internet supported map interface. The results were as follows -

"You are currently about 1,102 miles from Helena, MT. Driving by the I-80 E, your estimated arrival time is approximately 16 hours and 22 minutes."

Helena, Montana? I thought about it over and over. What a random place - Lorenzo didn't strike me as the type to venture to a state like this. I knew he liked the outdoors, but this was a different kind of "outdoors." The mountainous state wasn't someplace you could easily integrate to. It was a remote region, in a very remote corner of the United States—society there wasn't anything like society here. And the swath of wildlife there was intimidating; unforgiving even.

But nature aside, it wasn't too far-fetched of an idea for him to go there. Logistically, it was only a two day drive away from California, and if his goal was to isolate completely from high-tech society, then that would be the perfect place.

I pulled out the diary that Mary had given me. The front cover of the book carried no name; its leather corners were well kept. Though it showed signs of wear and tear, it was in otherwise mint condition.

I skimmed through his diary entries and got a glimpse into Lorenzo's thoughts. Curiously enough, a sizable chunk of the diary was torn out. In the absent pages' place was a polaroid photo, which fell down to the ground.

I picked it up from the carpet and brought it closer.

What the hell?

I sat up and looked around. Again, this damn sheep! How had such a thing escaped the attention of the detectives? I put on my investigative shoes and attempted to theorize their perspective, but envisaging about it only confused me further. Perhaps they had deemed it of no value? Come to think of it, why wouldn't they? It would be absurd to try and derive anything meaningful from this animal.

Regardless of how silly I might sound though, it was important to inform Mary and the police my beef with this sheep.

Pulling out my phone, I called her number and waited for a few seconds.

> The number you have dialed is not available. Please try again later...
>
> The number you have dialed is not available. Please try again later...
>
> The number you have dialed is not available. Please try again later...

After five more tries, I gave up. She could have been busy talking with the police. Or maybe she wasn't near her phone? I was increasingly befuddled. Something was wrong; something was missing. The bald man from train had something to do with this; that I knew for sure.

Okay, calm down, I said to myself. I stood up, switched off the television and paced myself across the living room. I did twenty push-ups and twenty jumping jacks. I couldn't look at these events as a whole. I needed to unravel them slowly.

When one goes to KFC, what's the first piece of chicken that gets picked from the bucket? The breast? The thighs? Crispy and delicious, of course it was the golden piece of drumstick. So, what was the drumstick of my situation?

Nothing. There was no tender drumstick here. Try as I might, no matter how many times I redrew the lines, the same shape would manifest itself—a black hole. An intangible void of the things I did not know. The thought of it depressed me, and made me hungry. So much so that my toes started tingling.

Wait, that didn't sound right.

My foot felt funky. It could have been the cold, I thought. But I was warm. Very warm.

Was it my phone then?

No. Something else, my gut told me.

I sat back straight and placed my hand on the coffee table. There was a very slight vibration that persisted as I pressed my palm against it. As I stood up, I felt that same resonance quiver throughout the air, delicately shimmering around me and my ears.

I closed my eyes and focused on my breath, magnifying the senses within me that first noticed the subtle movement. I could hear the red blood cells flow as they circulated throughout my body; the pounding of my heart so resounding that it flushed out all other thoughts. And in between all of that, I could feel it's warmth - a faint power was revealing itself to me; traces of stardust inviting me to follow.

I pursued the mystical trail and was led back to my room. On my desk, a rectangular object was glowing. The light was so illuminating, so prevalent that I had to shield my eyes. There, in front of me, was the box. The luminous object was my box.

I blinked my eyes twice. I blinked my eyes thrice. Lights were glistening across the room like constellations in the Gobi desert, the contrast of it all substantially pronounced in the dim room. A field of gentle light was enveloping my hand as I guided my hand around the box. It was a jewel, a piece of magic. No object on earth could produce such perfect light.

The temperature now beginning to swelter, whatever pockets of darkness that lingered were swept away in a grand motion. The subtle nuances of life revealed themselves to me—the grass that grew by the pond, the high tides and low tides caused by the gravitational pull of the moon. Whatever immediate worries I had were gone; my stream of thought muddled in the veins of the energy orbiting the object.

I worked on the box, top to bottom, repeatedly trying to open it. But such a concept did not apply to this thing; there was no physical way of opening it. From a logical standpoint, it was impossible to describe. And yet, it was also the most beautiful thing I have ever seen, as if the universe had been consumed by pure, un-tainted light.

Slowly and steadily, I tried to disengage my hands from the box, but my movements were being paralyzed; the glowing object was demanding attention from me. It was conveying a message to me - being alive, in the midst of the world, with every experience flickering through my eyes. It was telling me about the world I was in. The world I needed to leave behind. The world I needed to rediscover.

The glow from the box gradually diminished, the emitted light retreating back within it. It wasn't long before the rectangular block returned to its original, unassuming state.

PART II

10

I made a mini-itinerary for myself and started gathering my bags. Outside of the box, a few clothes and some toiletries, I packed as light as possible.

Montana, Montana—east of Washington and north of Wyoming. The longer I stared at the map, the more confused I was; what did the rugged, western place have to do with any of this? The state—known for its grassy plains and considerable real estate—had one of the country's lowest population despite also being the fourth largest state. It puzzled me that Lorenzo would run away to a place like this. If it were somewhere like Paris or Tokyo, I'd at least somewhat understand. But Montana? Really? It seemed like an unremarkably boring place.

I searched my room for a pair of thicker socks. Bordering the south of Canada, I should expect no less than freezing cold weather upon arrival there. Ideally, I'd replace my San Francisco clothes with something more appropriate; something that didn't scream California. My warm, parka jacket from Uniqlo would serve me well— granted, frostbite in the snow had an inviting ring to it if you didn't know what it meant.

After calling a cab, I began drafting a note to my manager and coworkers about a crisis I had to attend to. *Medical emergency* was the excuse I used.

I reread my message a few times over before sending it over. About five minutes later, my boss responded. "Duly Noted," he wrote. Not a word more. I expected nothing less from the straight-edge man that he was.

Bringing my bags to the living room, I took a seat on my ottoman couch. I tried to think, but I couldn't focus on any singular thing. All that came to mind, insistently and repeatedly, were the profusion of events since my phone call with Jess. I had deep suspicions that the task given to me at the theater—to find the bald man—was somehow connected to Lorenzo. For what reason? Who the hell knows. I had no hypothesis; just a hunch and a box.

Staring out the window, I spotted a yellow cab parked illegally in front of my doorway. There were two successive honks. It sounded so personal that it must have been for me.

I took a few last sips of water before leaving. I threw my belongings in the cab's trunk and gave directions to the Oakland bus station.

Thick gray clouds were hovering over us when we arrived at the station's entrance. Those in the Bay Area had a name for the perennial, omnipresent fog—Karl. Karl the Fog.

Bags in hand, I gave the driver a sizable tip and marched towards the electronic kiosk by the gate. A selection of exactly one option was offered for the journey up to Helena—thirty-six hours on a double-decker coach bus.

I warily accepted the ticket, but declined the "addon" meal option without a second thought; five dollars for chips, especially Pringles, was completely unacceptable.

As I stood in line, I was surprised with the size of the crowd. Public transportation isn't really a thing in the United States—most people either drive or fly to Montana. Yet, there was a large number of people waiting to board.

I took out the ticket and studied the schedule, scanning for an explanation. There were a number of pit stops planned along the route. Most were direct, but some had detours, including a few at Lake Tahoe. Suddenly, the crowd made sense—they were mostly tourists heading to ski. When was the last time I saw snow? Maybe a decade ago, when I was last a kid. California's certainly a bubble.

The line moved quickly. It only took a few minutes before my hands were resting on the door's entrance. I found an empty seat somewhere towards the middle-left. I was surprised with how spacious the whole vehicle was. Given my experiences with busses in America, I expected an aged, unremarkable interior; it was anything but, as noted by the fresh carpeting installed on the walkways.

Adjusting to my seat inside, I turned off the air conditioning on the top panel and prepared for a nap. I took out a blanket from my bag and wrapped myself like a toasted quesadilla. I was hoping for some warmth, but an invading image came to mind instead. It was a sheep; the strange, recurring animal of my life. For sure, there were a lot of things I didn't understand at all. But what was it about this fluffy, unassuming mammal that decided to preoccupy me? Was this long-awaited karma against me for enjoying mutton curry?

I swung the curtains open and rested my head against the window. The cloudy overcast of the bay area served as my backdrop as I went to snooze.

I woke up to the sight of snow, and shortly after, to some disorderly commotion on the bus. A sizable number of passengers were in the midst of leaving; a careless few were swinging their ski goggles recklessly, waking and disturbing the other passengers seated. If I had to guess, we were pit stopped at the entrance of a ski resort somewhere in Tahoe.

I shut my eyes, opened them again, and looked at the hands of my watch. About six hours had passed since I undertook my nap. The thick, silvery clouds from over the mountains were hovering on top of us as a reminder of the impending ski season. Most resorts here begin receiving customers after the Thanksgiving holiday weekend, but it's only around Christmas where business really takes off.

I didn't care much about winter sports, though, especially as my stomach was growling. It seemed as though I had left in such a hurry that I had completely forgotten to eat! I searched my bag for some beef jerky to munch on. Usually, I would take the first few bites and find the meat a touch too salty, but I had recently developed an affinity to the lingering hints of applewood smoke.

Once the bus driver returned, he revved the engine and departed the resort. The sky was sullen, and then inducing, all depending on the angle. No doubt, a storm was beginning to unravel as the bus headed down the freeway.

Tap. Tap. Tap. Tap. A million miniscule taps at once.

Enveloping the bus was a mindful stillness, brought upon by the gentle raindrops falling from the sky.

Ah, the wonders of nature.

I unbuckled my seatbelt and made my way to the restroom at the back. The other passengers I could see in my walk were sunk back in deep sleep—I'd imagine that they were in a transient state similar to that of yoga. None of the usual background noises were audible as I took my leak.

I returned to my seat and let out a big sneeze. I looked up at the ceiling of the vehicle, then stared out the window for a while, then shifted my view to the ceiling again. The air felt ominous. Something was coming towards me. Not a creature though.

Thirst. I felt thirsty. I searched my bag for a bottle of coconut water and chugged it. The natural electrolytes did well to hydrate my dry mouth, but that wasn't enough; my body also craved rest. So I fell asleep a few times and woke up at random. Whenever deep sleep was about to arrive, I would wake up unexpectedly to a bump in the road, and whenever I was trying to stay awake, a wave of drowsiness would hit me.

On the fifth iteration of this loop, I woke up to beautiful pine trees and stunning maroon lakes. Straight ahead was the forest—rays of light from the late winter sun were glinting on the debris encompassing the road. From some distance away, I could also see the snow-capped mountains. I'd never imagined that nature could be so large and untamed. The only wildlife I have really interacted with were the cosmopolitan types, like trimmed bushes at a city park. But the ones here—the ones in view—are totally different, bigger. It was as though they held some kind of deep and astrological power.

The sky pressed thick and intimidating upon the bus. The intensity of the storm was now palpable, the wind pushing and pulling from every angle. Swoosh, swoosh—like a washing machine. Each motion was like a massage across my whole body, cycling through from head to toe.

Searching for the lever directly below my seat, I adjusted my seat back. It only took a few minutes for me to fall asleep.

⁓

It was a little after eleven that I woke up to the bus driver's announcement, fifteen hours after we first left: "A very good morning to all aboard! I hope the drive has been smooth thus far. We're about an hour's drive away from Idaho Falls, where we'll be stopping for a quick lunch break. There will be no pit stops after this, so please make sure to grab some air, buy some snacks, and do whatever else to make this ride more comfortable for you."

I drew the curtains back and let out an audible yawn. The sky was crystal clear, but traces of water droplets from the rain were still perched on the windows, like fresh wounds from a battle. The storm must have just stopped.

I took out a piece of tissue and wiped the accumulated gunk around my left eye. A quick skim around the vehicle revealed a significantly emptier bus. There were only four other passengers, two of whom were a couple, most likely in their mid-forties, and evidently tourists—the 'I love San Francisco' shirts gleamed with neon colors. The other two passengers were enigmas, both sitting in different seats towards the back. The lighting in the bus made it difficult to tell what they looked like.

Not long after, the bus pulled off the freeway and came to a halt. We had stopped next to a ranch and a convenience store. Upon exiting, the bus driver was warmly received by one of the shop owners. The familiarity of their interaction indicated that they knew each other well—this was evidently a regular stop on the route.

I hopped off the bus and did a little stretching. Immediately, I was struck with how crisp and refreshing the air was; it could have very well been packaged and sold as its own certified medicine. But more miraculous was the landscape around me—snowy mountains and radiant hillsides showered in sunlight.

Hands over my head, I stood speechless. A beautiful view in a beautiful season, during noon, in the afterthought of rain. Where was such beauty in my life? Why was I only noticing it now? Not just beautiful though—the mountains towered over me like they were breathing, alive and soulful. They were watching me with keen interest, anticipating my next step. They know what I have done; they know what I'll do. There was no fooling them, nature was in charge here.

"They're beautiful, aren't they?" came a voice from the bus. A young woman emerged down the stairs and walked towards me. "Skyscrapers in the city stand pale against these mountains," she said. *"For most of history, man has had to fight nature to survive; in this century, he is beginning to realize that, in order to survive, he must protect it.* Have you heard that saying before?"

"No, "I responded. Her voice sounded a little groggy, like she had just woken up. She was equipped with a fur coat, and underneath it, a long-sleeved jumper with boxed patterns— colors alternating between red, green and blue. It was a striking piece of fashion, but more bizarre was the fact that I found her familiar. Where had I met her before?

"Where are you from?" she asked.

"San Francisco," I answered.

"Oh, that's funny. So am I," she said, before letting out a tired yawn. "I keep forgetting how long of a trip it is."

"Mhmm," I mumbled. As soon as I made those sounds, a realization hit me. The geeky girl from the pawn shop! That's how I recognized her! With her whacky clothing choice and deep husky voice, there was no doubt in my mind that it was her.

"To be honest with you, I'm not a big fan of the countryside," she said. "It's cold, and boring; and nothing is accessible here at all. But…"

"But..?"

"I guess it's just easy to fantasize about it when you've been away for so long."

"Distance makes the heart grow fonder?" I prompted.

"Yeah, something like that."

Now that she stood directly in front of me, I wasn't in the mood to say much more. Her presence in itself was perplexing enough, and though I was unquestionably curious about the how and why of seeing her here, I didn't need to add more questions to my trip. Stuffed in my mouth were already more treats than I could chew.

"You know, I met a guy recently who looked just like you," she suddenly observed, as though it had just occurred to her. Her eyes were keenly scanning my body. "I can only vaguely remember, but he had a really unusual name."

"Oh, really? Unusual how?" I asked.

She frowned. "It was unbelievably stupid. If I recall correctly, he was named after a fruit! Can you believe it?"

I shook my head. Though I was typically indifferent to insults, it was hard for me not to find that particular reference offensive. "My name's not stupid!" I said. "Also, yams are vegetables, not fruits."

Her face turned blank; her smile cratered into the ground like raindrops. "Well, shit! I'm sorry. No wonder you looked so familiar," she said. "You were at my shop, weren't you? You and your strange sheep cult."

"The sheep's got nothing to do with me!"

"*Of course not...*" she said. "Anyone with the first name 'Mister' is definitely in some sort of cult. I bet you're in one of those flat earth cults too."

"Flat earth cults?"

"Flat earthers. Haven't you heard of them? They're the wacky conspiracy folks that believe that the Earth is flat. That all the satellite photos of Earth as a sphere were fabricated by NASA and the US government."

"Nope. Never heard of them."

She rolled her eyes. "Have you been living in a cave? Don't you ever go on the Internet?"

I shook my head, slightly embarrassed. "Not usually," I said.

"Anyway," she continued, "what I'm really trying to convey is that you're really strange. And seeing you here is tripping me out a bit, that's all."

"The same can be said about you!" I responded. She was right though; the coincidence was uncanny. "What brought you here?"

"I'm from Idaho. This is my home. And you?"

"Um...I'm here to taste test olive oil," I said. It was such a terrible lie that I almost choked on my own saliva.

"Hahaha!" She burst out laughing. "What kind of whack-ass job is that?" she asked.

"It's not as weird as it sounds," I answered. "Anthony Bourdain used to do it all the time."

Hmmm, her eyebrows said as she gazed suspiciously at me. "I don't believe you one bit, but I suppose your business is your business," she said finally. "But, anyhow, I'm hungry. Wanna grab a quick bite inside? Bus doesn't leave for a while. We've got time to kill."

I looked at my shoes. I tried to think of an excuse, but my stomach wouldn't cooperate. It was seriously considering her suggestion, consumed by the prospect of a savory ham croissant, or the suitable Italian alternative—spaghetti *Aglio e Olio*. "Food does sound pretty good," I said.

We walked into the ranch, which coincidentally had its own mini restaurant tucked inside. A brief glimpse at the menu revealed a favorite of mine—pan-fried pieces of beefsteak, coated in flour and served with a generous pour of peppered milk gravy, otherwise known as chicken-fried steak.

We took a random seat at a table. There were no other guests, resulting in the sole waiter being uneasily attentive to us. "Would you folks like to start with water?" he asked.

She nodded her head aggressively, which he quickly acknowledged.

"I can't recall the last time I ate here," she said.

"You ate here before?"

"Yeah, though it's been a while," she remarked, smiling softly.

The waiter arrived with our waters and took our orders. He was impressed with my inclination towards chicken-fried steak, but remained neutral on her choice of Caesar 'blue cheese' salad. "Hey, I have a question about your job."

"Shoot me."

"What does one look for when tasting olive oil?" she asked.

Was that an earnest question, or was she just calling my bluff? "I don't really know what to tell you."

"Isn't it your job to know?"

Checkmate, atheist. "Well....there are usually three basic categories to consider when tasting olive oil - delicate, medium and intense. Similarly to wine, the distinctiveness is subtle; there is a wide variety of flavors and aromas to detect. And also similarly to wine, the olive oils are kept in barrels, away from oxygen and light so they don't become rancid—"

"Wait," she interrupted. Her face, slightly in shock. "I meant my question as a joke. You're not actually here to taste olive oil, are you?"

"Uh..." I glanced down at my shoes and thought over my response. Of course I wasn't here for olive oil, but what else could I possibly tell her? That I came here specifically to find my missing friend, based on a box from a bald man and some strange tales revolving around sheep?

"No," I answered finally. "To be honest with you, I'm heading to Montana."

She gasped. "Montana?! Did I hear that right?"

I nodded.

She doesn't say anything, mulling over this fact for a while. Meanwhile, the waiter arrived with our food. "So, care to explain what the hell you'll be doing in Montana?" she asked, when she spoke finally, scarfing her salad.

"I have no idea," I said, which wasn't even a lie. "It depends on how things go. I'll think about it more when I get there."

"Why Montana then? Of all places?"

Instead of replying, I sliced a sizable hole through the center of my chicken's crust. The batter had kept the exterior crispy, but more importantly, the trapped moisture that resulted from the layer had created an utmost juicy profile of meat.

"Why not?" I rebutted. "I've never left the city before, and rural

America sounds interesting. I'd figured it'd be cool to try something new."

She chomped on her salad, shaking her head silently. I had no idea if my answer was even remotely believable. "First the sheep box, and now this?" she remarked. "You're a hella weird dude. Perhaps the weirdest dude I've ever met."

"I'm not so weird to me..."

∾

We finished our meal and headed back outside. The bus was fully running and preparing to depart.

"Emma," she said, removing her suitcase from under the bus. "The name's Emma—Emma from Idaho, if that's easier to remember."

"Emma from Idaho," I repeated. "Has a nice ring to it."

"*I know,*" she said. With deft movements, she unzipped her suitcase and threw her handbag in it. "So, what are you going to do now?"

"I'll go back on the bus, not that I have much of a choice" I answered. "And you? I'm guessing you're heading back home now?"

"Yep! This is my stop." Emma took a lengthy pause before continuing, "It could be yours too, though."

I nodded, but quickly shook my head as her words finally registered with me. "I'm sorry what? Say that again?"

"You said you wanted to check out the countryside, right?" she continued. "Well, you should know that you're not gonna gain any perspective on that bus."

"Uhuh...meaning?"

"Meaning! You should get off that bus and join me!" she said.

"Join you? Join you where?" I asked.

"In my truck, *Mister Yam.* God, how dense are you?"

Her offer caught me off-guard completely. This was not a development I was expecting at all. "Are you being serious right now?"

"I'm one hundred percent dead serious," she said. "If you genuinely want to experience the countryside, I'm the best bet you have for something truly authentic."

"Uhhhh…"

"Stop. I don't want to hear those annoying sounds," she said. "Just come! It'll be a quick day trip around. I could always drop you off at the bus station tomorrow."

I thought it over for a bit. "I'm not sure if that's a good idea—"

"Okay, whatever," she interrupted. "My truck's parked in a shed nearby. If I don't see you back here in a few, that'll be that." Emma paced off with those words.

Just great, I thought. My trip, already haphazard on its own, was just presented with a big detour. But as random as Emma's suggestion was, I couldn't honestly claim with confidence that I was uninterested in her proposal. There was nothing I knew about the countryside; and if I was truly serious about locating my friend, I needed to familiarize myself with the area - to ground myself with the reality here.

…

Alright. Screw it. Why not?

I searched for the bus driver, who was enjoying himself with a can of Pepsi by the wheel when I found him. He gave me a few weird looks as I informed him of my decision to leave, but was otherwise indifferent when I took my luggage from the bus. "No refunds by the way. You'll have to call us again to rebook."

I nodded and brought my stuff to the road. At this point, Emma's truck was revved up and waiting by the curb. "There's a tall peak I know of where we can see the sunset," she said, about an hour's drive away from here. "Wanna check it out?"

"Sounds great," I said. I opened the back seat door of her truck and tossed my belongings there. Then, I entered the vehicle through the passenger seat and equipped my seatbelt. The audible click caused Emma to immediately rev the engine, and we blasted off on the road. Within just five seconds of driving, she was at the speed limit.

"Do you always drive this fast?" I asked her.

"Depends how I feel," she said. Judging by her tone, she wasn't joking.

As we covered more ground, I couldn't help but notice the vast potato farms dominating the land. My observations were confirmed when we passed the potato museum in Blackfoot, some thirty miles south from where we just were. "As you can tell, there aren't any skyscrapers here," she said. "Lots of farms though."

After a few minutes' drive, the road quality increasingly deteriorated. The road narrowed on both sides. Emma was forced to slow down considerably. "Don't worry, this is the worst it gets," she said. "Most of the mud is frozen by now."

Her reassurance was completely nullified as we continued driving under these conditions. Each turn Emma took developed into an edgier angle. At some point during the drive, the road started curving.

I held tight to the seatbelt as my butt began sliding left and right. I'm nervous, I told her, but all she did was laugh back. "Relax, Mister Yam!"

"Could you remind me what we're trying to see again?" I asked.

"Patience," she answered, remaining unhelpfully vague. There was a hint of snicker in her voice.

"I think you're teasing me."

She shook her head. "Good things come to those who wait."

It was hard to believe she was right at the time, but then I saw a slick, tall mountain in the distance. At first, it greeted me as no bigger than a thumbnail; but then it grew, and grew, and grew. Soon, I could observe all its details—towering guardians of granite, spattered with a trail of past unsuccessful climbs. The mountain stood powerful and tall, unforgettable as a birthmark on the crust of the earth. A shroud of clouds was guarding its peak. You could tell it was covered by a tremendous amount of snow.

"Wait until you see the best part," she said.

In the mountainous terrain, snow was all around us. Even with the windows closed, I could sense the howling wind I was being protected from. Swishing and swirling was the word of the road; unrelenting chaos, its motto. "I don't understand how you don't get nausea from driving like this."

"Ha, I'm used to it," she laughed. "Besides, it's worth it for the view."

We continued our drive up the mountains, as though we were climbing them physically in the luxury of our seats. As uncomfortable as the road was, it was a modern marvel that we were even able to do this at all.

When we finally arrived at the top, I exited the car, speechless.

How long I spent surveying the scene, I didn't know. The clouds that hovered thick and foggy over us were absent of everything but unadulterated white. The landscape shook me, as did the trees, snow, and smell. Though it was freezing cold, I closed my eyes and felt my forearms loosen; the stress in my muscles took an extended vacation to the Bahamas.

"Pretty sick, huh?" said Emma.

"No kidding..."

"It's a whole other world," she continued. "Not that I don't love civilization. I just like nature a bit more."

"Wasn't there that quote by Dante—"

"*Art imitates nature as well as it can, as a pupil follows his master; thus it is sort of a grandchild of God,*" she interrupted. "He says it a bit too dramatically for my taste, but it gets the point across."

I thought about it for a minute. I wanted to respond with a pop culture reference, but my mouth refused to cooperate. I couldn't stop staring. "I've honestly never seen anything so remarkable," I said. Bending down to the roadside, I scooped up a handful of snow and examined it. "Snow had never occurred to me to be more than...snow."

Emma chuckled. "It can be whatever you want it to be. It's all just a matter of perception, right?"

"Yeah, I guess so."

Standing by the road rails, Emma began taking pictures with her phone while I strolled along the edge. I stopped and looked at the mountains at times. Miraculously, when I stared long enough, I could feel my friend Lorenzo. There was an unmistakable feeling to it; my thoughts about him were buried in some deep, hidden place. Something about this place carried his essence, except that place was somewhere close to me.

"So, why did you leave?" I asked, ending the silence.

"What do you mean?" she asked.

"It's so beautiful here. Why did you leave Idaho?"

"Well...it's not all roses here." She returned to her truck and came back with a cigarette. "The city's got pretty cool perks."

"I see."

Taking small puffs of tobacco, Emma began looking at me with measured intensity. "You didn't grow up in a religious household, did you?" she asked, out of the blue.

"Not really," I answered. "My parents were pretty agnostic."

Silence.

"Do you know much about Mormonism?" she continued.

Outside of the satirical musical comedy *The Book of Mormon,* I knew very little else about the religion. "No, I can't say that I do."

"Gotcha..." she mumbled. My answer had clearly struck a chord with her.

"Why?"

"It's...don't worry about it," Her mouth closed shut, but her body language said otherwise.

So I pushed her. "Don't leave me hanging. I'd really like to know," I said.

Emma doesn't respond immediately. Through her eyes, I could see shelved thoughts and buried emotions returning to shape her face. "It's a long story. I'd rather not get into it right now," she said, after some considerable hesitation.

"Please," I said, carefully regulating my words, "it would mean a lot if you could share your story with me."

She peered at me. "Really now?"

"Yeah!"

I watched her blow cigarette smoke into the air, dissipating as soon as the wind pushed it away. She continued doing this until there was no more cigarette left. "What would you like to know?" she asked, finally.

"You brought up Mormonism. Were you involved with them at all?"

"Yeah, I was. For about eighteen years."

"Eighteen years?!"

"My entire upbringing was religious." She coughed a few times before continuing, "If you really want to know the details—I was born and raised in a small town you've probably never heard of, some thirty miles away from here. I grew up as part of the Church of Latter-Day Saints, also known as the Mormon church, before fleeing the state with my brother five years ago. I drink milk by the cup, my blood type is O, and I like to brush my teeth in the shower."

I looked at her in disbelief. "You ran away from home?"

"That's right." She touched my shoulder, then leaned her head on it. "It's a shitty story, I know."

"I'm sorry, I had no idea."

"Nah. Don't apologize," she said. "But don't be surprised either. It's not uncommon to hear of people running away from the church, just so you know."

I nodded. Her comment surprised me. "What do you mean by that?"

"Are you sure you want to get into it right now?

"I really don't mind," I said.

"I can't promise you it'll be a happy story."

"Only If it's fine with you."

"Alright," she said. "Let's go back inside then. This might take a while."

Returning to the truck, I adjusted my chair and listened to Emma's story.

11

EMMA'S STORY

To be a Mormon is to idolize the quintessential American way of life: to be a good neighbor, to treat others as you would like to be treated. On the surface, these are wonderful things, and why wouldn't they be? An organization that values responsibility, respect, and good work ethic should be highly regarded and even celebrated, amongst other things. For the longest time, my family had shown me this life and had taught me this life; to the point where each and every virtue would be engraved into my fiber, only to come out later as rehearsed recitals for our church leaders.

The thing about religion is that it is so well-packaged, so fine-tuned, that from above, it would be considered too good to be true, but while in the midst of it, it shapes itself to become the only truth. I believe now that my family were victims of this, and had chosen to ignore the bright, flashing signs that were inconsistent with the church's way of thinking. They would doublethink ideas when it served them, and when it didn't, they would conjure a tautology, filled with impenetrable narratives as a way of reminding themselves that this was the invariable and absolute way of living. After all, what is a life without ideology?

Leaving Mormonism was, in a way, a decision to kill myself—to purge and oust everything I had associated life with. It's been five years since I left the church, and yet I remember every interaction and decision that led to that moment as though it were hanging over me. The easiest part, of course, was unconvincing myself that God was real, and that God was good. As a matter of faith, it was merely a matter of believing versus not believing, and I picked the latter. Not that I couldn't accept the idea of a deity, but rather, I had rejected the deity depicted by the Latter-Day Saints. The harder part, of course, had nothing to do with the man in the heavens, but everything to do with my family, the relationships I held, and the fanatical zealots on the ground, who, to this day, continue to mislead and manipulate others.

The seeds of my rebellion started when my father came home one day, pestering me about a boy I have been seeing. Amongst Mormons, premarital sex is as bad as it gets, and though we did not have sex, we did many other things, and my father was unhappy with the promiscuous nature of our relationship. There were a couple of other incidents before that, like the one time I brought up the idea of studying out of state in California at dinner, when I was scorned for "trying to be liberal," or when I brought home a latte from Starbucks and had a problematic episode with my mother for drinking the devil's nectar. As my mom would say: "Do you want to go to hell, Emma? Every sip of caffeine brings you closer to Satan."

To be clear, I loved my parents, and my annoying older brother in the same universal way that most humans do. But it was also complicated by the fact that what I most despised about them stemmed from that same love, twisted and exploited by the church.

For years, I had been harboring doubts about the faith, and the church, and the influence it has had on my family. These doubts were small at first, and would come from natural inquisitiveness. Like, for example, did I believe in evolution? Or did I agree with the faith's view on marriage? I would presume these questions to be healthy, even necessary, for the church to strengthen and reinforce their positions. Instead, I was incriminated as a doubter and sentenced to correctional lessons for my behavior. The church had robbed me of many things, but most painfully, it had stripped me of my curiosity. Still, to this day, I struggle with this.

Nevertheless, I grew up as a good religious girl. I was obedient at school; I read the Bible twice a day; I went to church with my family. I was doing everything that was asked of me, the last thing I wanted to do was cause trouble. But ever so slowly, my soul was dying. I had become so good at feigning happiness that I had forgotten happiness itself. I had become so good at subscribing to my family's needs that I had sacrificed and immolated the voice within myself. I had become so accustomed to living a life of what should be, that I had lost the very things that made me. I would wake up in anguish; desire was an alien concept, no longer a feeling I understood or was capable of. And if the exhaustion and despair were not enough to numb me, then I would find myself ashore, beginning again in the cycle of misery.

I soon lost my appetite; my survival instincts withered. Day by day, I ate less and less, until it had gotten so bad that my parents, who had hated the notion of doctors, were forced to take me to one. And so they did, driving me to the closest one where I was given scheduled feeding therapy, and later, diagnosed with severe depression. The psychiatrist evaluating me told my parents that he could see the creeping evaporation of my life.

What life? Whose life? Here I was, in the land of the free, so dejectedly confined into this meaningless life. Day by day, I took my antidepressants, and yes, my pain went away, but so did everything else. As I went to school, the boys and girls of my class took turns bullying me, harassing me, stealing from me. They would take my lunch and shove it down the trash, vandalize my locker, accuse me of things I was incapable of doing. Not that I cared, because I was a robot, incapable of feeling, incapable of joy. For everyone that you know, that you love, to curse you and to scream obscenities as though your existence was a catastrophic mistake—the absence of love challenges your biological will to live like no other.

So, yes, life was terrible. Indisputably terrible. Whatever points of happiness that reached me would eventually resolve into some kind of forsaken trouble. Yet, despite this, some hidden part of me wanted to push on, with a lingering hope of a light at the end of the tunnel. This frail, vulnerable string was what I clung onto when I graduated high school and enrolled in the nearest community college. Such a thing was easier said than done, but there was no alternative for me: it was either I suffered doing nothing, or suffered while pushing forward.

My family, all the while, remained utterly ignorant of my mental state; it was much easier for me to fake religious devotion than to fight and argue constantly. To them, I was still a relatively good church girl, living and experiencing the joys of Mormon life. No problems, they thought. After all, everything in their life was good. For example, there were talks within my neighborhood about my oldest brother's recent accomplishment; he had just served a Mormon mission in Brazil, and had met his fiance while preaching. Though more significant for men, serving a mission is essentially a rite of passage with the church. My brother's recent trip had made him something of a local celebrity in our town, to the extent that I was treated more favorably solely because of my association with him. It was a strange feeling, not being loathed. Things were better, flowers were prettier. And despite how artificially senseless it was, people were nicer.

Meanwhile, in college, I enrolled in a cultural geography class to satisfy one of my general electives, which would serve as one of the two most life-altering events of my life. To describe just how important this class was: suppose a person to have been born colorblind, and to have become acquainted with all the different colors but red. This person is incapable of seeing red, which is a rather inconceivable thought, given how commonplace a color red is. And it isn't just this person's inability to see red, but also all the possible interactions that would result from red, like orange, or violet. Now, miraculously, imagine that this person, out of thin air, was able to see red. What would it mean to them?

If my life had been that of the colorblind person, then that class was the catalyst for my eyes. For the first time in my life, I saw the world as it was: vibrant, exciting, and full of mystery. I learned about the different cultures in practice, and grew to appreciate the different ways of life in the world—the idyllic, passionate romanticism of the French; the minimalist, reticent lifestyles of the Japanese. The beauty of linguistics showed itself to me: how different tones can translate into different expressions, and how certain propositions could elevate a sentence completely. I would close my eyes in lectures and picture the bustling streets of Bueno Aires as Argentina was being described to me. I was addicted to learning; addicted to the idea of a life beyond these fictitious walls.

As such, every day after class, I would come home, perform the pious scene I have been routinely acting for my parents, and lock myself in my room. It was my sanctuary of sorts, possibly the only thing in the house I did not despise. It was a safe space of mine and mind; a fortress of my own making. In this castle, I would unpack my bags, read, and lose myself to fantasy—to places depicted in text, and to images captured and painted. I would go through my books like numbers on a checklist, swimming through interesting thoughts and momentous considerations. It was all I could do; it was all I wanted to do.

Did this solve my misery? There was no way I could answer that question. The question itself seemed impossible. Yet, in the midst of summer, at seven pm on the evening of the nineteenth of June, something miraculous happened. While I was reading my geography textbook, light from the stars shot down through the crevices of my window, shimmering its way onto me like some kind of celestial revelation.

At that moment, light was everywhere. Floods of brightness occupied every inch of the space. I could see everything; I could see more than everything. Physically and figuratively, there was a tactile sensation to everything around me.

Everything cold and dark had dissipated as starlight brimmed around me. Even the pain was swept away, and warm and gentle light took its place. I looked into the dazzling light as it confronted me, in vision of the things I had dreamt: a life in which I was independent, a life in which I was in pursuit of love, and adventure. An intense bliss swept my face. A phrase I could not stop repeating echoes in my head: "I can and I will."

I can and I will.

Then, the light faded as suddenly as it had arrived. The normal state of things returned. But the light was not without a message. I could grasp its meaning: actions are what differentiates dreams from reality—I am the master of my fate, I am the captain of my soul. There and then, I knew I had to leave.

"I want to serve on a mission," I said to my ward.

He stared at me in disbelief as I told him of my plan to serve the church. I was selfish in a way, helping these guys promote the faith I so hated, but my desire to see the world would put a pause on whatever moral doctrines I held.

"I must admit that this is surprising, Emma, but I'm happy that you have decided to play your role in God's world."

My parents were undeniably jubilant after I informed them of my plans. I would undergo training at a nearby missionary center, where I would learn how to smile and converse in the way of the ideal Mormon. The mission itself is pretty involved, with long hours, six days a week. There would be dedicated time for scripture, with the rest of it being training, mainly on door to door activities like spreading the teachings of Joseph Smith and the Book of Mormon. I didn't have a say in where I would be located, nor the people I would be joining; the church would decide it entirely and anonymously. Perhaps the most ridiculous part of the training was the companionship program they enforced, where they would have someone follow me twenty-four hours a day, as I ate, dressed, and studied. As the ward would say: "Your companion is there so Satan can't win."

As demanding and involved as the training camp was, it didn't take me long to recognize the pious exemplar that was expected of me. Regardless of how I felt, I would have to grow comfortable in advocating for the faith, even if it meant lying about polygamy, or Gods in embryo doctrine, or Joseph Smith and his gold plates. In other words, like a Method actor, I would have to get good at compartmentalizing my persona. And Mormon missions are rarely about finding new converts. The point or essence of the mission is for young people to invest time, sweat, and energy into a cause - that they become the very stories they preach. When the Elder or Sister returns from the mission, what else is there to do but defend the investment he or she so desperately worked for? The true converts are not the ones you find, but the ones that served. The final step in a lifelong conversion.

～

I was pouring myself a bowl of cereal when I received a call from the mission president: "Emma, what do you know about Mongolia?"

Mongolia? I have read stories about it but knew nothing else. I grabbed my textbook, searched for a map and as I directed my fingers to Mongolia, I stared at it in awe.

"Mongolia is a place of staggering extremes—a landlocked country featuring some of the harshest winters and pleasant summers. Yet, it was also here that the most magical thing occurred. As you may recall, a revelation that was deeply staunched by Joseph Smith was to 'lay the foundation of the church and bring it forth out of obscurity'. What better manifestations of these words are there, if not to describe the wave of Mormonism in Mongolia; perhaps the most obscure and isolated place in which the church was found?"

"Congratulations, Emma. Your mission starts in Ulaanbaatar."

EMMA'S STORY, CONTINUED

Waking up to the bustling sounds of live chickens being chopped in the morning market; to a language so unfamiliar that you would deem yourself on a different planet. I made no attempts to capture such alien feelings. Yet, it was exactly this experience that greeted me as I arrived in Mongolia some twenty-four hours ago.

The plane ride was awkward and wearisome, but the enthusiasm that came from my first time traveling more than made up for it. Coincidentally, it also helped that I was with a group of other Mormons, congregating on this new land. There was myself, my training companion from Idaho, and about a dozen participants from the different states across America.

From the airport, we crammed onto an un-labelled, rustic bus with no seat belts. Then, vehicle in motion, we fought against the chaotic traffic, with every pothole perceptible. It was an uncomfortable ride bar none, but we were told to expect such "unpredictable" conditions. Mormon doctrine, after all, was to accept, not question; the ones chosen for this trip were exceptionally good at that. Hence, we sat quietly and accepted our fates.

Uncovering the windows would lead to the view of an unfamiliar haze of brown, which coated the landscape from cloud to soil. On the road, there was a seemingly unofficial right-of-way hierarchy being observed. They all seemed to follow one fundamental rule: the bigger the vehicle, the more priority it had. As ridiculous as such a concept was, it explained our bus driver's fanatical driving as he plowed along the road with no regard for anyone else.

Once we stepped outside, we stood on a land unrecognizable. Ulaanbaatar is Mongolia's only major urban center. To put that in perspective, about half of the country's entire population lived in the city. It's disproportionately industrialized when compared to the rest of the country. Despite this, there were audible gasps from within the group as we walked through the city.

We looked at the Mongolians in fascination as they did with us; to the sights of kids playing unsupervised across the roads; families dining on tiny stools by the gravel floor; unchecked livestock roaming the sidewalks. Streets, shops, and people were unlike anything I'd ever seen. Culture shock would be appropriate, except that it was more than shock. It was excitement, excitement of a variety I never imagined before.

There were no visible signs on the streets during our walk; no cross street markings of any sorts. It was truly as though the Mongolians just intrinsically knew where to go! But, miraculously, we found our way to the hotel. It was located somewhere close to the main highway, but was also secluded enough as to spare us from the hustle and bustle of the city.

The building itself, however, was unlike any hotel I had ever seen. It was a bland piece of dystopian construction; a purely functional rectangle that made no efforts to conceal its utility. I couldn't tell if it was a matter of taste, or if Stalinist architecture was just downright terrible.

"Listen, everyone," said the mission leader, as we entered the reception area. "Try to get some sleep tonight. If you can't, don't worry too much about it—jet lag is a real thing. Your body will take a few days to adjust, especially after a long haul international flight like the one we just had. Meanwhile, it is absolutely imperative that we stay put in the hotel. No one is allowed to go outside, or wander anywhere that isn't part of the schedule. We are in a new country, very far away from home. The rules and norms are different here; the last thing we want is for anyone to get hurt. The front desk will have your room keys ready for you, and you'll find basic amenities already provided. Should you need anything else, we'll have counsellors on standby in the lobby, ready to take your any question. In terms of logistics, there'll be a meeting with the president tomorrow, where we'll be introduced to the city's bishop and some of the local missionaries operating around the area. Wake up call will be eight a.m. sharp."

~

When I woke up, my head was fuzzy, restless even. But being able to sleep was in itself a victory, as indicated by the droopy eyes and fatigued faces that dominate the other Mormon participants that were gathered in the lobby.

Once a headcount check was conducted, we exited the building and waited for the bus. There weren't any clouds that morning, just a cobalt-blue sky; the sun, gradually scorching my pale skin. But thankfully, the bus—that of which was now an upgraded, luxurious coach ride—arrived shortly after.

Unlike yesterday however, the bus ride was brief, and we arrived at the venue—centrally located in the middle of the city. From the outside, it stood stereotypically with the other generic, corporate buildings. But a step inside dispelled any impressions of that immediately. An extensive lobby greeted us: granite walls and fancy carpeting filled the room, and with it, an assortment of Christian relics and colorful decorations. It was already luxurious in every day's standards, but to see such intemperance transplanted in Mongolia made the contrast all the greater.

A massive portrait of Christ gawked at us as we stood in anticipation of the president, who welcomed us shortly after. He was an American man who wore round glasses and a three-piece suit. He looked as though he was in his early forties—some evidence of graying hair was palpable towards his occipital bone. Accompanying him was an Mongolian man, who in contrast, was dressed rather unremarkably if not for the bucket hat he wore. An odd choice of clothing, I thought.

"It might strike you as a matter of curiosity, how our story started here," said the president. "For that, we can thank Elder Brough, who brought forth the inception of the Latter-Day Saints in Mongolia! It was he who first traveled to Mongolia for a hunting trip; as he saw the land, he fell in love with it and the Mongolian people that walked it. Elder Brough swore to return after his trip, and when he did, he brought alongside with him six other missionary couples. And so began the foundation of our church here."

"Thanks to their efforts, we were able to grow and establish ourselves in Mongolia—just two months ago, our ten-thousandth member was baptized! Such an achievement, though miraculous in its own right, was much owed to the hard work and persistence demonstrated by the founding fathers. Now, we are here to aid in that mission: to spread the word of God to the beautiful Mongolian people, so that they may be inspired by the gospel as we were."

Our mission, in essence, was to go door-to-door, to the various homes of the Mongolian people and spread the name of the church. Challenging enough as it was in the States, imagine the difficulties of that in a foreign country; in a culture so utterly distinctive, and in a language so definitely different. Yet, as we were told, it would be our jobs for the next year or so.

Shortly after the sermon, we received our schedules, which looked as follows:

- 6:45 - wake up, shower, brush up, personal study
- 7:30 - depart for LDS headquarters
- 8:00 - arrive at HQ, eat breakfast
- 8:40 - briefing, prayer, scripture, daily planning
- 9:55 - depart for mission, travel, knock on doors
- 5:15 - arrive back in HQ, rest, dinner
- 6:45 - language lessons (Mongolian)
- 8:45 - reflection and prayer
- 9:30 - depart for hotel
- 10:45 - lights out, sleep

Though we were an ocean away, the constant scheduling and inflexibility made it as though we had never left. As they had strictly instructed us: outside of work, we were to only mingle among ourselves, never to leave the hotel.

The thrill that first thumped me slowly dissipated as I grew into the routine. Days had gone by as days tend to, and I became a professional at speaking words I did not believe in. As I exhausted my energy on this otherwise senseless cause, I looked at my peers, who had not once flashed hints of curiosity or questions regarding authority. It was easy to distinguish those who had come from more affluent families and those who had never left the solitude of their homes, but even in the case of the former, it was apparent that they shared the same sense of unfamiliarity. After all, the job was all that we knew; all that we understood in this distant, removed country.

Back in the hotel, the mornings were quiet. You could barely hear the rumblings of the morning call, only the unceasing sound of water as it poured from the showers. A more discerning observer would note the solemnity in the bus as the missionaries gathered, to face yet another day of outreach, preaching, and rejection. And can you blame the Mongolians for turning us away? Seeing two complete foreigners knock on your door, whose poor attempt at Mongolian seems more mockery than speech?

"Well, this is what we do," Elder Ward would tell us. "We keep trying and trying, until something sticks."

On our better days, my companion and I would be invited in for some tea, where we would share and exchange our respective cultures. If we were lucky, we would make some good contacts and invite them over to the church, where there'd be shared activities with the other Mongolian members and recent converts. Typically, this would include a feast over some Mongolian dinner. Khorkog, a lamb dish cooked inside a pot with potatoes and carrots, was a favorite of mine.

Sundays were the only day where we were given some flexibility, with no expectation for preaching or service. It would also be the day where missionaries would relax, write to their families, and as best as they could, engage in a space outside of religion. Even tolerable at times were trips to the city, though those were strictly controlled, and with an official from the church always.

Perhaps the one benefit that came from the rigorous religious itinerary was the bond that I developed with my companion, Mary, who like myself, was burnt out after a few weeks of fruitless attempts. Up to this point, I have upheld my Mormon persona with ease. To her, the other missionaries and the church, I was still a diligent, obedient Sister following the Holy Ghost and preaching the word of God. There was no reason for me to break my character, though I sometimes speculate if other missionaries were doing the same.

"We have spent the past four hours knocking on doors, only for people to aggressively gape us down. Why do we even try?" she would inject intermittently.

A notable, weird quirk about Mary was her insistence to be on the right side of me at all times; not that it bothered me, but the lack of pedestrian walkways also meant that we were accustomed to walking on the cusp of the road with the cars, which made her unusual behavior dangerous at times.

As we spent our days walking aimlessly, we came across a distinctly purple house in an otherwise regular suburb. Unlike the other homes in the area, which had clear architectural influences from the Soviets, this house was modern looking, futuristic even. On its front wall was a single, giant glass window, and a narrow, beseeching door that served as its singular entrance. Naturally, we were curious, given how striking and unique the house was, but even more peculiar was the assortment of sheep that were gathered in front of the house. Merino sheep, Suffolk sheep, Texel sheep, none of which were native to Mongolia. Yet, here they were, sitting and purring at the face of this purple house.

Odd as the assembly of sheep was, there was no caretaker around. It was impossible that they were wild; I found myself incapable of words, not that there was a conventional way of describing a random mishmash of sheep.

The congregation of creatures watched us as we made our way to the entrance. Mary looked at me as I looked at her, our eyes exhibiting the shared tokens of uncertainty.

I gave the door a knock, which was unmistakably solid and of quality, and waited. The three minutes of silence led me to knock again, only this time, harder, and in series with an additional two more knocks. It would be an unobservable amount of time before steps were audible from within the house. The footsteps grew louder, but they were also gentle. At some point, the footsteps disappeared altogether, before reappearing as slippers being dragged.

The door opened to the face of a man, dressed in his pajamas and with a flustered look. He was spectacularly bald. Not in the unflattering, derogatory manner that people of receding hairlines might be labeled as—it was more that the bareness of hair was an inescapable part of his personality.

Though it was well past noon, it was clear that he had just woken up.

"Hello, how may I help you?" said the man.

During missionary training, there would be recommended tactics on how best to appeal to people, namely that most of the previous missionary approaches would be to knock on doors, speak for a few seconds, and then have the door slammed in front of your face. Given the abysmal history of this, a pivotal strategy would be to do whatever it takes to get "through the door," because once inside, the chances would be exponentially better, or so we were told.

"Hello, sir, how are you doing today?" asked Mary as she extended her right arm for a handshake.

"I'm good, thank you," he replied as he yawned. "This is certainly quite a sight. Not one that you would often see, if ever, especially in these parts."

"Yes, well, we have traveled quite a distance to come here and speak with you. My name is Sister Mary, and accompanying me is my companion Sister Emma. If you don't mind, there are a couple of questions we'd like to ask you today."

"Is this about the sheep? I'll have them sorted out soon enough."

"No, sir, I'd just like to take a few minutes of your time to fill in this survey concerning your opinions on a few things, like, for instance, your views on religion, or family values?"

The man squinted as he studied the survey, paying considerable attention to the question on friendship as he slowly jotted down his thoughts.

"Will that be all?" said the man as he returned the sheet of paper.

"Thank you very much for answering these questions. What we

actually have is a brief message that goes hand in hand with the survey you have just answered. Mainly, on items like where we're from; why we're here on earth; and what we'll be doing after leaving this life—call it a spiritual message of sorts. If you're willing, I'd like to ask for your permission to step into your home and further discuss the mission we're on and the message we're carrying."

There was an unambiguous, ineffable moment that occurred as those very words left Mary's mouth; like we had agreed to partake in something we had no knowledge of. In the split second that I was perceptive to, I felt movement coming from the house, like an awakened soul whose heart was lit on fire.

The man was wide awake at this point, his penetrating gaze fixated on Mary. He looked ever so slightly on edge. "Are you sure this isn't about the sheep?" he asked.

"No, not at all. We would just like to come in and say a prayer for you."

The door just slightly opened, he pushed it wide for us. "Very well. Come in then, please."

We followed the man inside his home; into the sight of well-placed furniture and impeccably designed ornaments. Through its hallway, dozens of different candles were burning low by its side. In the center of the living room laid an altar; of what exactly, I wasn't sure. The whole place was like the lovechild of a Buddhist monastery and an IKEA bedroom catalog, carrying an aroma I can only describe as poignant. Streams of light filled the space from the giant glass window.

The man went into the kitchen and offered us some tea, which we had kindly accepted. "To be honest, I can't remember the last time I had visitors. I'm quite the hermit, as you can tell," said the man.

As he found a comfortable position in his armchair, I noticed the tiers of bookshelves tucked away in the walls. One held a sizable collection of books, neatly organized in paginations. Through a quick glance, I could see he held a selection of classical books. He must have been an avid scholar.

"Thank you for having us today, it means a lot to my companion and I that you would take the time to hear us out. If I may, I'd like to share a story with you?" asked Mary.

"Please, I'm all ears," he said.

Standing from her seat, Mary began our usual recital. "Long before the inception of time, long before there were humans, there existed a God. A God whose greatness is unsearchable; whose love is immeasurable. With his power, this God created the magnificent planet we call earth, and with it, the beautiful life that we are familiar with, and that we bask in. Our God came to earth, and he established a perfect church, so that we may know how to celebrate Him. But, tragically, the corruption and evil of men made remnants of His lessons, and the simple truths of His were instead replaced by the philosophies and corruptions of everyday men. I'm sad to say that the truth, once held dear by humanity, is now lost in the sullen forest, concealed in mists of thick darkness. As we lost our path to the light, we decided to follow our own; not of God's, but ourselves. And now, we wander from the purity and grace that came from God."

Mary took a pause to sip some of her tea, which I mirrored out of awkwardness. The man remained expressionless all the while, his mind seemingly occupied by something else entirely.

"We have come with good news," she continued, "for The Church of Jesus Christ of Latter-Day Saints teaches us that God is not lost, and is in fact, right here for us to follow—if we choose to be saved by grace. The church is looking for new members and would be delighted to host you in one of our upcoming events."

The man pondered, sitting stiffly still.

"It's been a very long time since I have dealt with Mormons, or heard that name: The Church of Jesus Christ of Latter-day Saints."

"You know about us then?"

"Yes, while I was in Montana, though that was a long time ago," he said. "First and foremost, I must thank you for coming all the way here and offering salvation. The entry to heaven is not cheap, as I'm sure your flight ticket wasn't. Unfortunately, I must decline. I'm currently active in a different belief, something else entirely."

"Our church members come from all sorts of backgrounds, many of them converting from different religious backgrounds. If you don't mind me asking, what religion is it that you practice?" asks Mary.

"I don't necessarily practice or belong to a religion. There are, however, some beliefs that I hold, and some things I do unswervingly, with which conventional religion is incompatible. In my view, any religion that has salvation in its core is fallible." replied the man.

"What do you believe in, then?" I asked. It was the first time I had opened my mouth.

Without a word, the man glared at me. To this day, no one had looked at me with the same degree of intensity as the man did. But, as unsettling as it was, his gaze was of a gentle kind, a vividness that could warm the coldest of places.

The whole matter lasted less than a second.

"Yesterday, as I sat in my living room, I was able to see the stars. Specifically, the seven Dipper stars that make the Great Bear. It was not something I thought possible, given the haze and pollution covering the sky, but they radiated at me, called for me. These stars— there were thousands of them if not more; some I could name, some I could not—were all present, having emerged from the emerald sky at twilight. It was during this that I realized something I had long forgotten in my solitude; that they represented everything of importance to me. In existence and out of reach, they were fixed forever in the sky that those before and after me were to experience all the same. Indestructible, like memories I could forget but not destroy."

"Everybody has something they believe in," mused the man, "But religion doesn't care for that. It's a lot like love; what is given has nothing to do with what one seeks."

I felt a wave run through my mind, a ripple that went past sorrow or sadness. A tremendous wail shook me, vibrating through my bones, and then to my heart. Deep into my soul, I felt my every fiber resonating—no one could help me, not unless I helped myself.

"You ask me for my beliefs. But that's never really the question, is it? The truth is that I believe in God, but not as an almighty deity or the face of a religion. I believe that what people call God is something within all of us; not in you or me, but in the little spaces in between. Consciousness pervades the universe in all its form—to experience itself as a cow grazing grass or a mushroom releasing spores. So the birds fly long in the sky, where we watch arrogantly in our misplaced superiority. But they are wiser than us. They experience life for what it truly is, and we mistake it to be but everything else."

The man let out a warm smile as we waited in silence. A powerful energy entranced us from every direction; constellations from above radiating through down to our skin. An undeniable light flooded us; and neither rising nor dropping, Mary sat with me in discord, her gears churning internally. Transient pieces of her mind flowed through mine—mixing with all that is me, making their way into my being.

"Right over there; through the corner of the living room. That's where the sheep go through. Let me call for them," he said, motioning towards a secluded doorway by the left side of the floor.

Mary and I sat in astonishment as the assemblage of sheep made their way into the house. The centrally placed altar, now burning, became the source of gathering for the creatures—which were now numbering among the hundreds.

I was in paralysis, my body like a fish floating in water. The man placed his hand on my palm, whispering unrecognizable vowels to me as I slowly drifted, unconscious. "Things become clearer in the dark," said the man, except not with his voice, but as visuals; in the stream of consciousness that was my mind, fluttering in and out like question marks without beginning or end.

"I see your spirit for what it is: in this decipherable state, looking at a map, having an unruly desire to go to this place. There is no reason for wanting to go to this place, except to see it, experience it. Curiosity in the truest sense; an unmistakable sense of conviction. Your soul is treading the earth somewhere, urging you to it."

But where?

13

It was dusk by now; the sunset having passed a few hours ago. I was a shoulder to lean on as Emma finished her story. "Sorry, that was a lot. I didn't mean to go on for that long."

"Please don't end there," I said. "I'd really like to hear the rest."

She rubbed her face and swayed her head, her eyes still displaying remnants of tears. "The bald man," she said, after some time. "It was no coincidence that we had knocked on his door. He knew everything that had happened and everything that was going to happen. It was all planned out. Every single thing."

"What *do* you mean by that?" I asked.

"I...I don't know," said Emma, sounding disorientated. "Things got really murky afterwards. I was practically in a vegetative state by then. And the sheep...."

"The sheep? What about the sheep?"

She didn't respond. A noticeable amount of time passed before Emma spoke again. "Sorry, I think it's best if we stop here for now. There are many things I still don't understand; many things that I cannot make you understand. There are still so many things I cannot even explain to myself."

We sat by the back of the trunk, our faces to the view of the crystalline night sky. Regardless of the perspective one chooses, the depiction of the purple house was no coincidence. I knew now without doubt that the bald man served as a considerably significant center-piece to my journey up to Montana. It was as though he was plastered as a smudge over my glasses, injecting himself in my every experience. But even then, he was just one mere thread to the overall fabric; the other weaves were equally just as confusing—the glowing box; the recurring appearances of sheep; Lorenzo's baffling disappearance. The entirety of these circumstances left me in a strange tumult. Like a haphazard mix of canned soups, no singular essence was easily decipherable.

Irrespective of my situation though, it was important that I keep Emma out of this. She had already gone through a lot, more than I could have ever imagined. Fragments of her story still drifted heavily in the air, sounding stronger. The sense of heaviness oscillating.

Orion's belt towered over us as Emma continued resting beside me. The stars showered with an intensity I had never experienced before. Was there any truth to what the bald man had shared with Emma? I couldn't immediately tell, but I sensed heavy wounds still cutting at her—taunting and jabbing at her with every thought. It was the kind of insidious darkness I was all too familiar with.

"I could use a drink," she said, abruptly ending the silence.

"Me too. Know a place?"

"Yeah."

∾

Adjusting our car seats back to normal, Emma revved the engine and gave the pedal a strong push. Her truck reverberated powerfully along the ghostly roads as she spearheaded our collective desire for alcohol. Throughout the ride down the mountains, not a single soul was visible—there was darkness, surrounded by more darkness.

Gradually, the narrowed road got wider, and we eventually arrived at a secluded freeway exit. It took about twenty minutes more of continuous driving before we arrived at a small outpost of buildings.

We scanned around for parking, but the lack of street lighting made it difficult to see. Emma managed anyway and parked her truck by the entrance of a bar; coincidentally, next to a police car, operated by a man in uniform, who seemed like he was dozing behind the wheel. I speculated he was only there to act as a deterrent for whatever past problems this place had.

We walked past the slumberous cop and made our way into the bar.

The establishment was noisy and cheap, the kind of hole-in-the-wall bar you would expect from a small town. Grunge music was audible at the back of the room; a small number of people were gathered there by the jukebox. Presumably, they were regulars, and from what I could tell, they were arguing over which song to play next.

Emma and I found a comfortable seat by the pool table. Two older men were talking by the table next to us. Though I was no expert at eavesdropping, it sounded like they were in a deep discussion with regards to woodcutting.

"It's been a while seeing you again, Emma." said the bartender as he approached us. "Is this your new friend?"

"Embarrassing me as always, Doug. Could you get us two rum and cokes? Oh, and some fries, please."

Doug ran off with our order. It was now past midnight.

"Before you say anything," Emma said, slightly flustered. "Everyone in the town knows everyone else. Rural life is kinda like that."

"I'll bet."

"Anyhow, I've told you enough about me. What's the real reason you're headed to Montana? I think I deserve some honesty now, don't you think?"

I searched my pocket for my wallet and took out the photo of Lorenzo. "I'm looking for my friend, who recently went missing."

"Missing..?" she mumbled. She looked over the photo for several minutes. "Any specific reasons why?"

"I have my hunches," I said. "But it's nothing concrete. My suspicions are that he ran away from home, but I also know it's not as straightforward as that. To tell you the truth, I'm confused. Deeply confused."

"What are you confused about? That he ran away to Montana?"

"Well, kinda. But in terms of practical matters, I have absolutely no idea what to do. Zero. Like, if he did actually flee to Montana, then how do I go about finding him? Clearly, he doesn't want to be found. So what then? It's a nightmare just to think about it."

"I see," said Emma. She seemed to be listening carefully to what I was sharing. Meanwhile, Doug arrived with our drinks and basket of fries. "What about the box? What does that have to do with all this?"

I had no readily available answer for that. I could only shrug. "They're related, somehow," I said finally. "But I'm still figuring that out too."

She picked up a handful of fries and sprinkled them with salt, then nibbled at them. "Strange man, you are."

"What's that supposed to mean?"

"It's whatever you want it to be."

I took a sip of my drink and grabbed a few fries. Reflecting on my situation, I could hardly believe the series of events that had occurred in the course of a few days. "How did you end up back here?" I asked. "After that whole trip to Mongolia?"

She cleared her throat. "Long story short, the bald man helped me escape from the church and the messy situation that ensued after. I broke all ties with my family, and have been rehabilitating in San Francisco with my brother since."

"Is there a reason you've decided to come back here then?" I asked.

"Yes. Though you might not find it a satisfactory answer."

"Which is?"

She stuffed a generous amount of fries into her mouth. "That I had no choice in the matter."

"You had no choice?"

"That's right, for now at least."

"What does that mean?" I pressed.

"That I come back here every few months to pay my dues."

Your dues? "I have no idea what that means."

"I don't expect you to," she continued. "It's not something I'd ever hope to explain. But practically speaking, it means that I have to come back once in a while."

"So, you're indefinitely tied to this place?"

"I wouldn't phrase it like that."

"Well, how would you phrase it?" I asked.

"It's slightly more complicated. As a person, I'm free to go anywhere, but my spirit is stuck here. It was part of a deal I made with the bald man."

I took more sips of my drink. "Is this one of those stories where you sold your soul to the devil?"

Emma's cheeks were beginning to flush. It was very obvious that the alcohol was getting to her. "No, no, nothing of the sort. It's more like I left my old world behind to come to this new one."

"Like, you swapped realities?"

"Not like. That's exactly what I did."

"You're kidding."

"No, I'm not. That's how I got out of that whole mess. You'll understand if you tried it," she said, giving me a completely earnest look.

"What do you mean, *you'll understand if you try*? How does one go about trying to swap realities?"

"Well, the first step is to go to Mongolia and find a bald man with lots of sheep."

I looked at her in disbelief as she started dissolving into laughter. "I'm totally screwing with you," she said. "Yes, the bald man helped me, but none of that reality or soul swapping stuff. There's still some unfinished business I have left in Idaho, but don't ask me about it. Perhaps I'll tell you when things are finished."

I nodded. I had only taken a couple of sips from my drink, but the alcohol was hitting me harder than usual.

"Do you smoke weed?" Emma asked, out of the blue.

"With my roommate in college. But not much anymore."

She gazed at me, her hand resting on the table. "If you're interested in revisiting your old habits, I have some at home..?"

It had just occurred to me that she was inviting me back to her place, but more notable was the fact that I had nothing else planned. I had quite impulsively decided that I was going to follow her, with little regard as to what was going to happen.

"Sure," I said. "It's been a while."

"Sweet! The stuff I have is decent, but it's still nothing in comparison with the buds in California," she said. "Also, I think it's better if you drive. I'll give you directions to my place."

We left our drinks unfinished as I settled the bill. The police car from outside was still there when we left, but the cop was now wide awake, fiddling on his phone.

Emma passed me her keys as we got into her truck. I revved the engine, and asked for directions.

"I kinda forgot where I lived," she said. "But! Keep driving! I'll tell you as we go." I couldn't tell if she was being serious, but it was a nightmare trying to understand her baffling directions. Instead, I took out a map on my phone and had her navigate me to it.

We drove for about fifteen minutes. It was hard to discern much, given the dark. But at some point, I arrived at a cross-street.

"You can park here," she said. "My house is right on the left."

The house was some odd juxtaposition of a new building that was nevertheless starting to fall apart. There were a few casement windows by the front of the door. It was a standard, single floor American-style house with an overly spacious yard. As ridiculous as it may sound, a place like this in San Francisco could easily sell for a million, if not more, depending on the neighborhood.

The living room was large and well furnished. The combined kitchen and dining room made for an extended design, with a sliding door separating the bedroom. But perhaps most amazing was the outside patio, which served as an opening to the exquisite view of the forest. It was unlike anything the city could offer.

Emma sat me down on a giant sofa in the living room, behind which was a giant mushroom tapestry. She went into the kitchen and came back with a glass bong, already equipped with an extended ash catcher. I noticed the remains of some old hash in the bowl piece

.

From underneath the table, she pulled out a cigarette lighter and an ashtray. "I think you'll enjoy this," she said. To start, she placed her mouth on the bong opening and ignited the bowl piece. Then, she began inhaling, incrementally increasing the pull of her breath as the water inside started its churn. Once there was enough accumulated smoke in the main chamber, she lifted the bowl piece and sucked all the vapor into her lungs. She waited a few seconds before opening her mouth and blowing out the smoke. She motioned for me to do the same.

I mimic'd her flow and achieved a similar result. But, unlike Emma, I was coughing endlessly after the first hit. "Don't worry about it," she remarked. "It happens when you haven't smoked in a while."

We repeated this cycle three more times until we had exhausted all the buds. The marijuana high was subtle. But then, slowly, came a light buzz, which eventually developed into something warmer; something fuzzier. I closed my eyes and imagined a papaya fruit, which then transformed itself into a McDonald's combo meal with chicken nuggets. I started to feel light and kind of weightless, as if my body were levitating above the ground. "Two dollar combo meal...."

Emma, all the while, was giggling nonsensically next to me. She couldn't stop pointing at my feet. Were my shoes too big? I wondered what it'd be like if humans walked on their hands. Probably not that efficient, I thought.

As I sank deeper into the couch, Emma grabbed my arm and rested her head onto my shoulder. Seeing her dilated capillaries meant one only thing: we were both immeasurably high.

"You look stoned," she stated.

"So do you."

We started embracing. Reality now seemed insignificant in comparison with time, which was getting perceptibly slower and slower. I was also beginning to get hungry. Really hungry. Soon, all that was left of me was my potato body; floating endlessly in the imaginary continuum that was my craving for the McDonald's combo meal.

"Hey, I have a question for you!" asked Emma.

"Shoot."

"Have you ever been in love?"

I took a moment to think it over.

"I think so, or at least, my understanding of love," I replied.

"Which is?"

"We all have this person that we love in our imagination, like an ideal, flawless dream lover that comes from our mind. The bitter truth is that regardless of how perfect the person I meet in reality is, I will always be comparing that person to my dream lover. Eventually, I find the differences between them, and if I can live with the difference, then I allow myself to fall in love."

"And you have met such a person?" she asked.

"I have met a few people like that, yes."

"Oh really?"

"All of them existed at different points in my life, which is a scary thought since none of them would be compatible with me now. But the intensity and affection that existed then were always true, and in a way, will always be true," I said.

Emma silently nodded, as if she was correlating my points with her own emotions. "So, you're still in love with all of them?"

"I guess you could say so."

"What's it like then, falling in love?"

The marijuana high made it impossible for me to stop talking. "It's like seeing everything you hold dear manifest into a person. And this person, you tell them everything; you share hopes for the future. When something miraculous happens, you celebrate it with them as though they were part of your livelihood, and as you get to know each other, it becomes a question of not what you could with them but what you couldn't do without them. They laugh with you, they cry with you. They magnify the beauty within you; music sounds brighter, colorful. There's a well of joy that you can now pull and draw from. And within all this, you open your heart and become vulnerable to things you were once scared of, with an understanding that nothing is unachievable or beyond overcoming."

She reached across the sofa and kissed me below the ear.

"I want to sleep with you."

14

There are several reasons why habitual marijuana smokers exist. For one, it heightens the senses: a whiff of pine in a warehouse sale could transport the sniffer to a lush, mountain forest deep in Patagonia. A slice of cake has every taste bud receptive to any level of sweetness waiting to be absorbed. No question. Smell, touch, sight, taste, sound —all become enhanced with the devil's lettuce; sex included.

When we were finished, the hands of the clock on the wall indicated that it was well past four in the morning. The lights were out, the room sparsely lit by the stars glistening through the windows. We were both fully naked, her chin resting on my chest, her arms around my neck.

I gently disengaged my arm from her waist, reaching out for the cup of water by the tableside. I took a sip and quenched my thirst — the cold breeze from outside was fluttering through the curtains.

"I died that night," she said.

I met her eyes.

"The man and his sheep. I don't know what they did, but some internal exorcism resounded within me—a kind of damning, piercing pain that would whirl in circles. But as I was enduring it, my perceptions began to alter; soon enough, the pain became nothing to the wave of euphoria that was to overtake it. I dissolved into eternal emptiness. My consciousness was releasing and experiencing simultaneously; and through the recesses of my mind, an unrestricted mode of mindfulness was unleashed. I was in a dream. I did not know when it began, or if it was even mine, only that I slept for a long time. And then, one day, I awoke to a different life."

"To a different life?"

"To a different life," Emma repeated. She adjusted her position, peering at me. At that moment, I remembered something; something very important. But I couldn't put my mind to it.

"Sometimes, I try to move on," she continued, "but as painful as the memories were, I know that deep down, I never want to let go. In a way, it's the only thing that I have to prove that I'm real. That life is real."

I cleared my throat. I didn't know how to respond.

"I'm jealous of you," she said, out of the blue.

"Jealous of me? Jealous how?"

Emma didn't answer me. She snatched the comforter from my hands and wrapped herself like a burrito. It wasn't long before she was asleep.

Mouth closed, she breathed silently through her nose, her head resting on my extended arm. I stared at her beautiful hair, trying not to gaze too much, as if I was the earth looking at the sun. Yet, all I could see were radiant lights, glistening through my closed eyes. The difference between sand and sea. Between reality and dreams.

I smiled, and joined her in deep sleep.

I woke up in an empty bed, to the distinct sizzling of avocado oil. Emma was in the kitchen busy at work; the assortment of eggs and sausage scattered across the countertop led me to believe that she was preparing breakfast for us. "Omelet or sunny-side up?" she asked.

"I'll have whatever you're having," I said.

She took out a blue carton of milk from the fridge and poured me a glass of ultra-pasteurized milk.

"Cheese? With your omelet?"

"Sure."

Emma dumped a generous omelette-meat combination, still hot

from the frying pan, on my plate. I cooled the food with my breath, before stuffing the big chunks of sausage into my mouth. I took large gulps of milk as I ate. The combination was surprisingly tasty.

"I'd toast us some bread, but I forgot to grab some on my grocery run," she said.

It only occurred to me how hungry I was after I took my first bite. "It already tastes delicious enough as it is," I said. "Thanks a bunch."

Emma responded with something, but her mouth was too full for me to make out her words. "Sorry, I didn't quite catch that."

She took a few seconds to fully swallow her food before speaking again. "Do you have any other leads on finding your friend?" she asked.

"Nothing concrete, unfortunately," I said. The more I thought about it, the more apprehensive I got. "The only thing I can do is to continue heading to Montana."

She twirled a pepper grinder over her plate. "And once you get there?"

"Honestly, I have no clue. I'm hoping things will figure themselves out over time."

Emma cleared her plate and looked down for a long time. Neither of us moved. "I'll take you to the bus station, which should lead you straight to Helena," she said. "You can decide when to leave after that." She then grabbed a napkin and scribbled some numbers on it before handing it to me.

"My phone number," she said. "In case things go south. Don't be a stranger, okay? I'd like to see you again."

I took the piece of paper and stuffed it in my wallet. "I'd like to see you again too. Besides, I have to hear the rest of your story."

I helped her rinse and pile the dishes into the dishwasher. Then, gently, she guided me back to the bedroom, where we made love again.

The house was amazingly quiet - a halo of zen surrounded the bedroom. The bright sun was making its presence known through the gaps in the curtain.

I looked into Emma's face, and then into her hair. Sunlight travelled through the voids of space to pierce through the clouds; a tiny fraction of its energy was being used to glisten the room. It struck me as miraculous that something as inconsequential as that had its place in the mechanisms of the universe; that some higher conscious body of earth did not overlook this very moment. Was this the Nirvana that the Bodhisattvas had meant?

Looking outside, the enigmatic canvas that was the forest at night was now luminous and alive.

～

We arrived at the Greyhound bus station a little after two. Emma dropped me off and gave her farewells; where she went after, I had no clue.

I sat on the first bench I could find, overlooking potato fields. My mind was drifting, but I couldn't concentrate on anything, except for that one piece from Emma's story that came to mind repeatedly: *Your soul treading the earth somewhere, urging yourself to it.*

I stood up, and snow packed its way into the soles of my shoe. It hindered my movement; I was a little out of breath. I felt lost, so utterly lost. Like an empty hollowness, within me was a fatigue that went beyond physicality—it was probably always there, hidden away in some part of my brain, waiting for its moment. There was nothing for me to do; nothing that I wanted to do. It was impossible to describe the paralysis overwhelming me.

I ripped open a pack of gummy bears. I had hoped that the sugar from the candy would energize my body. But instead, a phone call came.

"Idaho would be the last place I'd guess," came a woman's voice. "But then again, men are prone to do strange things."

It was Jess.

"Did you know that avocados are fruit?" she asked.

"No, I can't say that I do," I said.

"You can tell if they're ripe based on the weight and darkness. You can even speed up the ripening process by adding a banana," she continued. "It makes for a tastier spread on bread."

"Where's this all coming from?"

"I read about it online, thought you should know."

I could hear her chortling through the phone, her mouth directly against the microphone. "So it would seem that you have found your-self in quite a predicament," she said.

"That's one way of putting it," I said.

"Going after your friend like that."

How did she know that? "He would have done the same," I said.

"Are you sure?"

"Is this really what you're calling about?" I asked.

"One of many things, yes." Jess said. "If it makes you feel better, you're headed the right way."

"Oh, so I'm not going crazy then? He's in Montana?"

"Probably."

"What do you mean *probably*? It's a simple yes or no question."

"It's not so straightforward, unfortunately."

"Care to elaborate?" I asked.

"I have a shirt, and I'm telling you it's black. Not blue. Not white. Not any other color found in the color scheme. Just a plain old black shirt. If you had asked me what color the shirt was, it'd be a simple answer: it's black. But that's not what you're asking, is it? No, you're asking me *why* the shirt is black, which is an entirely different ques-tion; and how could I possibly know why? I just know it's black."

I grasped my phone. Was there a message hidden somewhere in there, or was that supposed to make sense?

"Listen, I'm not in the mood for these kinds of games." I said. "Can you please stop being so ambiguous?"

"Ha, but where's the fun in that? Don't forget—*this is your world*, Mister Yam. It's up to you to decide where this story goes."

Beep-beep. I looked at my phone's black screen. She had hung up on me, again.

I shook my head. *You're asking me why the shirt is black.* I left the analogy to brew in my head. What kind of useless metaphor is that? It was so absurd that it even had me laughing.

I put on some headphones and played some of the best works by Debussy. There were too many things going on, too many items to consider. I needed to clear the clutter of my mind. I took a deep breath and looked up at the sky. Clouds and blue tints came to view, alongside an unrelenting craving for pizza.

Okay, I was hungry, or so my brain had convinced itself. I pulled out my phone and searched for the nearest diner, which was just a couple blocks away.

I lugged my items around the deserted walkways and walked into a diner. I found a seat at the bar section and ordered myself a single slice of pizza. As it arrived, I took a generous first bite and felt the grease oozing out, the excess oil sloshing around in my mouth.

I felt queasy after the second bite and made my way into the bathroom. Standing in front of the sink, I gathered my hands and splashed some running water across my face. I had to be gentle so as to not further antagonize my already flaring pimples.

When I was done, I took the paper towels by the dispenser and dried my face, not before looking at the mirror. Unshaven and unkempt, I could barely recognize myself. The acne across my left cheek was reflaring, as were the blackheads all over my nose. Wonderful, I thought. Was the recent stress to blame?

I rinsed my face another three more times before making my way back to the bar. From my wallet, I took out and straightened the photo card found in Lorenzo's diary. I placed my fingers against it— on the corners and then on the center—hoping for some miraculous clue to reveal itself. From a purely physical standpoint, there was nothing unusual about it—the bald man, the purple house and the strange herd of sheep—but I knew that behind this plain piece of photo lay an answer somewhere. That lingering feeling of being whisker's away from something. What was I forgetting?

I settled the bill and lugged my baggage outside the restaurant. Then, I searched for a nearby hotel online. Searching for Lorenzo was key, but I needed proper rest to do that. Never once did I crave for a hot shower more than today.

After some unremarkable scrolling. I found a three star hotel within walking distance. I rang the front desk and was shortly received by someone.

"Hello, this is Nicholas from the Bariston hotel speaking."

"Hey, do you guys have a bedroom available for tonight?" I asked.

"Certainly. Just one night?"

"Yes, that'll be great."

"Will there be anything else?" he asked.

"I'll be there in twenty minutes. Thank you."

I hung up the phone and made my way to the hotel. It was located just five blocks west and two blocks north of where I was standing.

Though it was just a short walk there, the path was filled with rows of deserted stores. The whole area was hushed and still; I'd never seen such desolation in a town. No other person was walking the streets, no other vehicle was occupying the roads. If there was life here, it was very well masked.

Following the directions on my phone, I eventually arrived outside the hotel. Despite the snowy weather, my body was drenched in sweat, as was my hair and my pants. A puddle began to form on the side of my left ankle, which quickly froze in the snow.

I stood outside for a few seconds, waiting for my sweat to dissipate. The building itself was only four stories tall. In any other city, it would have been considered small, even imperceptible. But here, in this city, it stood shoulders taller than anything within its vicinity.

Entering through the revolving door, I found a lobby bigger than expected. To my left was a lounge area, and to my right, a...fireplace? It was hard to tell, but mirrors were scattered across the ceiling walls; a common technique employed to hoodwink depth perception. Upon closer inspection, I could see the cruddy grease of paint oozing, concentrating in the areas around the edges.

I approached the front counter and was greeted by a young man. Presumably it was the clerk I had spoken to earlier on the phone. He had some of the most interesting eyebrows I'd seen.

"Hello, I called earlier—"

"One moment, please," he interrupted. The man was busy jotting down some notes on a piece of paper, chuckling.

"Sorry about that, I had to handle something urgent," he said. That was a lie. From the tone of his voice, he sounded like he was flirting with someone else over the line. Perhaps it was a woman he had just begun dating. "What can I help you with today?"

"I called earlier about one night's stay," I said.

"Ah, yes! Certainly. Allow me to handle that for you" he said. The man took down my information and started typing indistinguishable words on a computer.

"We have a number of rooms available. Would a regular queen room be okay?"

"That'd be fine."

I took out my credit card and paid the deposit, along with payment for one night's stay. The clerk ran my card against a machine and passed two key cards to me. "To my right is an elevator. Make your way up to the third floor and your room will be on the second door to the right. Have a pleasant evening."

I gave my thanks and grabbed my stuff to the elevator, and then to my room. As I tapped the hotel room open, a lavish king bed revealed itself to me, alongside a fancy wide desk. I guess I had unintentionally been upgraded.

Parting the window curtains, I observed the entirety of Idaho Falls. The buildings were all the same cookie-cutter, one-story composition architecture abundant in suburban America. And though it was only five o'clock on a weekend, there was barely anyone out and about.

The lingering desire for fresh clothing popped into my head. I dropped my bags and made my way to the bathroom. I stripped myself and prepared for a luscious shower. I ran the provided bar soap across my body as water trickled from the showerhead. Like polishing a porcelain anew, I cleansed all the accumulated dirt from my body. Not the most momentous thing to do, but a thing to do, nevertheless.

I thought about my coworkers. What would they think about the situation I was in? Confused, maybe, but I'd argue they would remain indifferent most likely. As with all in corporate life, we remained a lone column in a vast, unending spreadsheet—imperative, but unimportant.

I exited the shower and wiped myself dry. Then, I changed into some pajamas and laid on the bed. As a point of curiosity, I switched on the television and ran through the local news channel. Flashing statically on the screen was a dog—a golden retriever had gone missing. The news report featured the pet owners, who were seeking support in their local community to galvanize efforts for a neighborhood search. Later on, they featured clips of elderly parents distributing flyers alongside their kids, with a small segment of it dedicated to a group interview with the high school students surveying the town.

An undeniable smile swept me. Small towns like these might not have the glamour of larger cities, but they had an elusive charm that was personal and special to their community. It was wholesome. It was representative of what I found important.

I turned off the television and stretched myself across the bed. Then, I stood and drew the curtains shut. No light could enter the room once I did. I was surrounded by total darkness.

In a room like this, with the blinds closed and the curtains drawn, existed a darkness equal to the soul. Staring at the ceiling, my sight and sound synced. I started mumbling to myself. Memories filled my mind. People that I'd met; family that I had. Goals that I had desired; values that I had lost. I was able to recall them with great vividness, my mind a canvas to a brush.

Feeling the alcoves of my consciousness begin to weaken, I looked around, into the shadows surrounding me. I could disappear from the face of the earth tomorrow and the world would go on without batting an eye. I understood life as complicated, with infinite layers and convoluted fabrics tugging and pulling at each other. But one thing was abundantly clear—I would not be missed.

In the absence of light, anything is possible. So I held my breath in the vacuum, counting the seconds as they went by.

1, 2, 3...

My thoughts began manifesting into images.

58, 59, 60...

I let go. There was nothing else to see.

86, 87...

I found freedom. Losing all hope was freedom.

I was back in a hallway, the candles along it still faintly glowing. Enigmatic and eerie, there was a discernible smell as I walked to the living room. The altar and furniture from before remained unmoved, except that there was no door this time. "Hello!" I shouted. "Is anybody here?"

I sniffed the air. I couldn't smell anything. I couldn't hear anything. There was no voice that greeted me. Just silence. But for the swallowing of my throat, pure utter silence.

A few minutes or more went by as I stared motionless at the altar, observing the dried-out embers. My face was sweating, but I had no desire to be cooler. I felt my hair thinning out; the pulsation of my sinuses. In the darkness, there was no way of validating these feelings. I could only resort to my intuition that everything was okay.

I decided to venture beyond the living room. It was dark, but the glow from the candles made the opacity more tinted than solid. There was nowhere to go but forward. One step at a time, I told myself. Deep breaths and big steps. My mind, usually rumbling, was being muffled unlike usual. How much clarity can one achieve by zip-locking their thoughts? Apparently quite a lot.

Now and then, I would hear the sound of my feet being dragged. I walked for a while. How long exactly, I did not know—except at some point, I arrived at a stairway. It was a long one; each step had its own weight to it. I couldn't recall the last time my feet were so heavy, but I took each exertion slowly; each step carefully.

Within the never-ending darkness, I continued climbing. The gap between my legs grew wider and wider, until finally, they were flat. An intense sense of vertigo struck me as I stopped walking. Like a breeze of chilled air, it struck powerfully. Then, it was gone. There was nothing else here, only darkness.

"You came back," said a voice. A smell from my childhood filled the air. "I didn't think you'd be here so soon."

"I came here to find you," I said.

"Oh, really?" it said. A shadow was moving in the darkness. It seemed like it was neither friend nor foe. "And why is that exactly?"

"Because I'm lost. Really lost. My mind is worried that something terrible is going to happen, but my gut tells me something worse; that something terrible has already happened. I don't know what to make of it. Do you understand? I don't know if what I'm doing even makes sense."

"What do you not understand?"

"Everything. Of course there are still missing pieces I have yet to find, but even with the pieces I have, I don't know what to make of them," I answered. "All I know is that everything started on that train ride from Berkeley. Then it was one bizarre situation after another, until finally, Lorenzo disappeared."

"Lorenzo…" the voice mumbled. "You are looking for him?"

"That's right."

"Are you sure you're remembering this correctly?"

"I must be. That is the conclusion I had reached. There's no alternative to me."

This time, there was no immediate response. It shifted in the shadow, its actions removed from sound. Then, eventually, a lone sigh. "If that's the case, then why are you here?"

"Because I know that you hold some kind of key. Is that right?"

"Key?" it asked. "What do you need a key for?"

"The box," I said. "I know the answer is in there somewhere. I need to know how to unlock it."

The voice laughed. It resounded in the darkness. "Help me understand something, Mister Yam," it said, the tone of the voice becoming heavier. "You say you are looking for your friend, but that you are also looking to open the box? You can't have it both ways. You have to pick one of them."

"What on earth does that mean?"

"I can't tell you that which you already know."

"I don't understand," I said. "You tell me that I know you, that we worked together to keep me from forgetting. But try as hard as I might, I can't recall anything. Who are you?"

"You want to know who I am? You already know who I am," the voice said. "All you have to do is to remember.."

At that moment, light started penetrating the walls. The air in the room felt warm, and then hot. Blisteringly hot. I clamped my eyes closed as an intense, sweltering wave of heat pushed against me.

Shadows, candles; the vacant aftermath of a room. I was passing through consciousness, from one reality to another. The air exploding, my heart convulsing. The strong pull of a vortex absorbed us and condensed us to a black hole. Light did not exist here.

Only darkness.

15

It was around seven or so when I woke up. Without thinking, I donned my clothes and packed my suitcase, and headed down to the hotel's cafe. I was hungry. Unusually hungry. Even after waking up, it was impossible for me to start my day without some kind of food in my stomach.

I grabbed a random seat and poured myself some fresh orange juice, also grabbing a bowl of watermelon and a plate full of scrambled eggs. I was surprised with how voracious my mouth had become; it took me just under two minutes to exceed the daily recommended breakfast intake. No wonder my affinity for buffets.

Heading to the hotel lounge, I dropped my keys and did an early check-out. I took out my laptop and booked the next available bus ride to Montana. Navigating the web pages was near impossible, but I eventually bought a ticket. The total cost of the trip was just shy of nine dollars.

"Thank you for your purchase! Please show your ticket number: #E412NT upon arrival at the station's platform."

I felt some relief, knowing that I had some sort of mission in mind, to find Lorenzo. But that serenity was immediately eclipsed by the buzzing migraine festering at the back of my head. My mind suddenly fizzled, as if a cord had been pulled. Was it lack of sleep? Potentially. I speculated that it had more to do with my caffeine withdrawal though, so I went back to the cafe and chugged a cup of coffee.

Leaving the hotel, I walked to the station and picked up my ticket. Unlike yesterday, the station wasn't a ghost town—a few other groups were hovering by the waiting area, throwing peculiar looks in my direction.

I tried my best to keep to myself. It didn't work. All I could do was throw an equally peculiar face at them. It was like boxing with my eyes; my awkwardness against their nosiness. There were no winners, but it did make the time pass faster.

When the bus finally arrived, the driver stepped outside and waved at us to form a line. There were only about twenty people for one hundred seats, or exactly one fifth of the potential travelers.

I threw my butt on the first seat available, just left of the driver. Plugging in my earphones, I had on queue a podcast about gluten-free bread. The person narrating was using a deliberately mellow voice, tapping the hidden desire I had for the carbs.

A crust with a thick crunch. A well-fed sourdough starter. Eating with just the tongue—

I fell asleep before that section was done.

Saliva was dripping from my lips when the bus driver made his way to me.

"We're here," he said, nudging on my shoulder.

It took me a while to regain my senses. I rubbed my eyes and stretched my arms, yawning no less than three times during the process. Sure enough, the bus was parked in front of a station, void of any other passengers.

I departed with my belongings. A quick glance at my watch revealed that it was slightly past noon. I thought I was early, but from a certain perspective, I made it just in time.

Helena, Montana. What did I know about this place? Nothing. Perhaps the furthest place South-East Asians had ever ventured. I thought about the Lewis and Clark expedition that first discovered the state. The Corps of Discovery, as the group was called, was political in nature; it was commissioned by the then President Thomas Jefferson, shortly after the Louisiana Purchase in 1803, to establish American sovereignty in the region. Under the command of Captain Meriwether Lewis and Second Lieutenant William Clark, one of the main objectives of the expedition was to explore and document the newly acquired territory; to map a practical route across the western half of the continent; to establish American presence in the area before other colonial European powers could put their hands on it. Yet, as important as the realization of those goals were to the epochal expedition, they also achieved incredible success in the millions of wildlife discoveries they made while traversing the unknown west. Scenery amongst sceneries; landscapes over landscapes of beauty; the true triumph of the trip was a matter of differing perspectives.

I decided to spend the rest of the afternoon wandering the city, trying to unravel where Lorenzo might have gone. I figured that any clue, however small, would be better than nothing. Of course, such a task was still no piece of cake. Helena might be tiny relative to other cities, but it was still a city.

But size wasn't what daunted me; it was the cold! Dragging my bags across the street and down three solid blocks on the snow covered pavement was all it took for me to realize that I had completely inadequate equipment. My South-East Asian blood proved vulnerable against the freezing frost.

I stopped into the first clothing store and bought myself a blue puffer jacket. I couldn't find one in my size, only those twice my size. But I didn't mind; as far as money was concerned, I was paying an unbelievably low amount for what the equivalent would have cost me in San Francisco.

Ripping off the price tag, I was floored with an aura of coziness as I put it on. The sense of relief came with a number of epiphanies. For one, the store was packed to the brim. Evidently, the cold winter here did nothing to dampen the spirits of the residents, who were out and about shopping.

Second, as I stepped out of the store, I observed how much more bustling the area was. Already, there were a dozen more stores available than in Idaho Falls. Crowded wasn't the word I'd use, but life was certainly doing its job here—couples kissing; kids running. I observed a sizable line forming in one of the coffee shops across the street, and another at a restaurant down the block.

Such a sight might not have been a surprise to others, but I was in total shock. If reality differed from person to person, why did we city people speak of life as this singular dimension? Who are we to judge the people that live here? Who'd enjoy the calm lifestyle that can be found here?

The more I thought about this, the more impassioned I became, but soon the excess energy in my brain dropped off and I began to feel dizzy. Desiring some caffeine, I waited in line at one of the coffeeshops and ordered myself an Americano, filled in with an extra third shot.

The medium-roast taste was enjoyable, and the caffeine prevented grogginess. But a hot drink wasn't enough; infiltrating my headspace was an unrelenting desire for a long, elaborate shower.

Located next to the shop was a hotel, which was also conveniently located on top of an Irish pub. I appreciated the proximity of it and checked in the lobby. It was noticeably larger than the one in Idaho Falls; unlike the previous hotel, the place was fully packed. There was even a tour group gathering at the entrance as I walked to the front desk; my guess was that it was for a national park tour.

A woman in red greeted me as I walked up to the counter. She began to furiously pound the computer keyboard as I gave my name and my details.

"Hello," I said.

"Good afternoon, Mister Yam…" she said. Her voice choked slightly upon saying my name. "How many nights are you planning to stay with us?" she asked.

"I'd like to stay for three weeks," I said.

"Three weeks..?" She stared at me blankly, as if she'd never heard those words uttered before. "You'll be staying here for three weeks?"

"Maybe. Maybe longer, actually. I haven't decided yet."

"I'm assuming this is for a business trip? I can setu—"

"Err, no, not really," I interrupted. I was about to say more, but I kept my lips shut. "I hope this won't prove to be an issue?"

"Oh, uhh, no! Absolutely not! We'll be happy to accommodate you. Though, for such an extended stay, hotel policy is to establish a weekly payment system. Would that be okay with you?"

"Yes, that's fine. You can set it on my credit card."

As with the previous clerk, she took my credit card and plunged it into the machine. She typed a few more random things onto the keyboard, before leaving for a room behind the concierge. Moments later, she returned with a printed invoice.

"Please place your initials on the points I have highlighted in blue, and sign at the bottom of the page. A weekly deduction will occur every Sunday, and you can opt out at any point before the next billing cycle. Once you have concluded your stay, your deposit will be returned to you via your payment method within three business days after."

I jotted my initials and signed the double stacked pink pieces of paper. How many people actually read these things?

"Is there anything else I can help you with today?" she asked.

"Actually, there is one more thing," I said. "Would it be possible for you to remove the bed from the room?"

The clerk looked at me with her mouth wide. "Excuse me? Did you say you wanted the bed removed?"

"Yes."

A few notes of silence.

"May I ask *why*?"

"I'd rather sleep on the floor," I said.

The clerk peered at me. The movement around her mouth indicated she was debating on whether or not to say something. *I don't get paid enough to deal with this*, her face said. Yet after a few seconds, she regained her professionalism and returned a smile. "Please give me a few minutes while I ring management about your requests."

She took a cellphone from under the desk and returned to the room in the back. I took this as an opportunity to survey the place around me. The lobby was smaller than at first glance; the mirrors around the room did an excellent job amplifying the illusion of depth. And not that it mattered, but there was a large, potted plant by the fireplace; it was most likely a synthetic fake, given the artificial texture of green. Even so, there was an element of comfort that came from its presence.

"I just got off the phone with my manager," she said, returning. "We can remove the mattress, bed frame and foundation, but it'll take us about a day or so. In the meantime, we can house you in a regular queen room. Will that be fine for you?"

"Yes, that sounds good," I said.

"Please hold on for just a moment."

She pulled out a box full of keycards and ran them through a machine. She does this while inscribing a room number on my key holder. Once she was done, she passed it to me, and similarly with the clerk in the previous hotel, she gave me basic directions to my room.

I grabbed my bags and gave my thanks. Taking the elevator upstairs, I walked into my conventional queen hotel room. Immediately, I stripped my clothes and prepared for the bathtub with the lavender shampoo provided. If there was a bachelor's guide to modern day pleasures, having your body submerged in warm water would be one of them. The process—waiting for the water to fill, adjusting the temperature, soaking in the bath, relaxing in the bath, drying from the bath—was an underrated art.

I changed into some new clothes when I was done. Throughout my journey here, I paid no attention to the deteriorating state of my shoes. Now, with some breathing room to work with, I left the hotel and walked into the nearest shoe store.

I tried to bring up Lorenzo's photo every chance I interacted with a person. In this case, it was with the sales assistant who was helping me shop for a new pair of sneakers. "Excuse me, do you happen to recognize this person?" I asked him. I took out the photo of Lorenzo, but all he did was shake his head. "Sorry. Doesn't seem familiar to me."

I left the store with my new kicks and walked the stretch of town again, revisiting the coffee shop from earlier and purchased myself a slice of cake. I brought up Lorenzo's photo, and again, the results were disappointing.

"Nope, I don't recognize him," said the cashier.

"I have worked here for six years and I have never seen anyone like him," the baker interjected behind the glass panel.

"He looks like the Spanish guy from that cooking show competition," a random bystander remarked.

That last comment made me chuckle, but I was otherwise unable to offset my overall state of dejection.

The difficulty of the search was beginning to weigh on me; I was starting to recognize just how strenuous this was going to be. Like finding a drop of vodka in a glass of water, an impossible task.

Feeling dispirited, I took out my phone and gave Emma a call. I found a great deal of solace when I heard her voice.

"I take it that you're finally in Montana?" she said.

"Yeah, it's a lot colder than I expected."

"How's the search going?"

I sighed. "Not great. I'm at a dead end here; though I can only blame myself for that. I was so fixated on coming here that I didn't consider at all what I would actually do once I got here."

"You're way too harsh on yourself. It has only been the first day, no? I'm sure you'll find something, eventually," she said.

"Thanks. I'll try to keep that in mind," I said. "But I've also been thinking: even if someone did end up recognizing him, how will they know where he went after? I'm literally begging for a lottery ticket."

"Have you thought about posting online?" suggested Emma. "On social media—in one of those local community groups? It's possible that someone may have seen him there."

I thought about it for a few seconds. "That's a pretty good idea, beats doing nothing."

I went back into the hotel, and then into my room. Once inside, I dialed room service for a basket of fish and chips and began typing up a post:

Attention: In search of a missing person!
- Male.
- Brown hair.
- Black eyes.
- Athletic build, about six ft tall.
- Some may consider him a poor man's Diego Luna.

Last seen in San Francisco approximately one month ago. Please contact (415)-300-3823 with any leads.

I reread the post twice before publishing it. "Do you really think I'll get somewhere with this?"

"Maybe. Maybe not. Though I have a feeling you will," she said.

"Why?"

"Like you like to say, it's just a hunch."

The doorbell rang. I thanked Emma and received my fish and chips from room service. Fresh and crispy, they made for a delightful meal as I licked my plate clean.

I once read that a happy gut was correlated with a happy mind. It was no wonder, then, that I slept so well that night. The heavy weight of duty freed itself, if only for a bit.

I made my way down to the egg station at the hotel's cafe for breakfast. Short of other options, I ordered scrambled eggs with toast as a middle-aged couple bickered behind me. They were Caucasian looking, but they weren't conversing in English. European tourists, I speculated. Germans, maybe? If I were still a teenager, I'd strike a conversation with them purely out of curiosity. But, alas, the anxiety of adulthood wouldn't permit such things.

Fresh cooked breakfast on a plate, I scouted the vicinity for an unoccupied table and ate my meal alone. I quickly snagged a mug of black coffee along the way, alongside a cup of apple juice—sugar, spice, and everything nice. From my seat, I watched the clerk from yesterday glancing around the cafe and the different tables. Inevitably, our eyes connected, and she gave me a courteous, professional smile.

I tried my best to match the affability; but instead, I shifted direction and stared awkwardly at the salt shaker in front of me. It wasn't that I was inherently dreadful in social settings, but there was nothing I wanted to talk about. Nothing for me to talk about; nothing that was even worth bringing up. I'd come all the way here to find my friend, but I had no strategy, no inkling of what I was even doing. What kind of conversation would that be?

I finished my breakfast and left for the lobby. Parking my legs at one of the luxurious sofas scattered across the room, I admired the synthetic plant in the lobby. Since I woke up, I hoped for a response from the online post I wrote yesterday. But there was no luck there.

With no plan in mind, I watched the hands of my watch land at nine; and then at ten; and then at eleven, before I decided to move. A solid two hours had gone by, and all I had done was glare compulsively at the fake fern potted by the fireplace.

I had to do something. Something more than nothing. Something that remained low effort.

I made my way to a nearby cafe and parked my laptop at one of the high tables by the corner. To support the shop hosting me, I ordered a cup of coffee whenever I had to take a leak, which was around every two hours or so.

Shortly after noon, I received a single phone call.

"I read your post online. Who's this man? Why are you looking for him?" came a man's voice.

"It's a friend of mine. Have you seen him?" I asked.

"No. But if you do, please let me know."

"Excuse me?"

"I like his jawline, and his black eyes. You should know that I'm in the market for a man like him. Perhaps, when the dust settles down, you can set us up?"

I hung up on him. A lonely man looking for some company? It was hard to tell if he was being serious or not.

A few minutes later, I received another call. "Our town doesn't have space for folk like you. Better pack up and leave."

I heaved a sigh as he hung up on me. So much for the United States of America.

As I sat endlessly at the cafe, I watched the weather turn sour. The sky was completely covered in clouds with no traces of sunlight. If not for the cold, everything seemed cast in gray; even the macchiato I was sipping on. A winter storm could ensue at any moment, and nothing would change about my life. Except, perhaps, another dull moment for me to remember and forget.

I ended the day with no new leads and ate a panini chicken sandwich for dinner. When I was finished, I walked back to the hotel and saw a clerk different from yesterday waving at me. He informed me that the room I had requested was now ready and handed me two new keycards.

I gave my thanks and grabbed my items from my former room. Then, I took the elevator and made my way to the new hotel room. As expected, the room was sizably more spacious without the bed. There was only a desk and chair by the corner; all the more perfect.

When I awoke the following morning, the same cloudy gray sky from last evening greeted me. I felt great sleeping on the floor. It was as though my spine was realigned, with each vertebrae comfortably adjusted. Of course, these were just figments of my imagination; it was very well possible that none of these things actually occurred within my body.

As like the day before, I cycled through the same routine— washing my face, heading down to breakfast, drinking coffee—and like yesterday, I caught the female clerk from the front desk staring at me. Except this time, she wasn't smiling. If anything, she gave me a tense glare —one that spelled trouble. Was there something about my presence today that bothered her?

I didn't think of it as much and left the hotel for the same cafe. Despite having just eaten breakfast, my tummy was still unsatisfied. So, alongside my latte, I ordered myself a prosciutto sandwich, topped with onions, arugula, olive oil and parmesan. The sandwich was delectable, and I finished the entire thing within four huge bites.

Shortly after noon, I received a phone call from a teenager. "Why find a missing friend when you can make a new one?" He spent the next twenty minutes promoting an online video game called League of Legends. It sounded like an interesting game—and a frustrating one. But again, no new leads.

Having eaten too much, I ended the day early and headed back to the hotel. I entered the lobby and walked past the front desk when I noticed the clerk from breakfast peering at me. When we locked eyes, she had an inviting look on her face. Except it didn't seem like the type for a party.

Discreetly, she gestured for me to come to her.

I slowly walked towards the concierge. Standing directly in front of her, she shot a quick glance across the lobby and surveyed the space around her. It was evidently clear that there was no one else around us. Just her, myself, and the same, impressive synthetic potted fern by the fireplace.

"We have to pretend that we're talking about something," she said. "Management is pretty uptight about interactions with guests."

"Okay" I said. "I'll talk about hair conditioners and you can tell me whatever you wanted to say."

She gave me a peculiar look. The kind that said - *was there something off putting about the bathroom amenities provided?* Whatever her initial confusion was, she shrugged it off and cleared her throat. "I read the online post you wrote yesterday."

My eyes widened.

"The man in your description. Brown hair. Black eyes. Athletic, about six feet tall? He was here about two weeks ago."

I started reading the ingredient list of the top selling condition on Amazon: "...sodium cocoyl isethionate, polyquaternium-7, glycol distearate, glycerin..."

"I didn't really catch anything else; it was a really brief exchange. What I'm sure of, though, is that he stayed here for a night," she said. "I checked him in the hotel earlier that day, as I did with a dozen other guests. Except he was also with another person. Some old man, I think? Whatever the case, the weird part came later that day, when I went into the elevator to collect my stuff—"

"Wait, did you say he was with someone?" I interrupted. "Was the other guy bald?"

She shook her head. "He could have been bald, but I wouldn't know. He was wearing a hat when I checked them both in."

"I see."

"Anyhow, there's something else I wanted to talk to you about-"

Ring-ring, came a call to the front desk. She looked nervously at the push button telephone, and then at me.

"Let's talk about this somewhere else. It's too risky here," she said, twitching slightly. "My shift ends in thirty minutes. We can meet at a bar a few blocks from here."

"Tell me where to go and I'll be there," I said.

She tore a piece of paper from the printer stand nearby and drew some directions to the place. "Let's meet here. And please, don't tell anyone about this."

I took the note from her. "Talk to you soon," I said.

She nodded awkwardly at me, and then picked up the phone.

I took the elevator back to my room. Something strange happened in this elevator, huh? I wondered what she had meant by that. The boat was still stranded in the sea, but there was at least some idea of where to go next.

16

I changed into a button-up shirt and left the hotel, following the directions from the clerk. Snow occupied the sidewalk unlike anything I'd ever seen, but eventually I made my way to a tiny, lively bar on the outskirts of town.

The place was packed to the brim with locals outfitted in football jerseys. They were drinking and dancing to American classics—Garry B.B. Coleman, Ray Charles, Frank Sinatra. As the only Asian there, I noticed a couple of stares at my direction; curious stares though, not threatening ones.

I pulled up at the countertop and ordered myself the house's shot of whiskey. The bartender poured me a generous amount, which I downed in one swoop; a surprising cherry oak aftertaste lingered in my mouth for a while after. I also let out an embarrassing burp after I wiped my mouth.

An exceptionally rowdy table from behind me was hosting a yellow contest. Drunk and loud, two tall, unshaven men were arguing heatedly about something. I could only discern three distinct words given the noise—Democrats, dumbasses and 'the deep state'. It took their respective wives in the group to calm them down.

"Sorry I'm late, I had to do some last minute work," the clerk said, patting my shoulder from behind me. She took me by surprise, and was also noticeably late. "My manager showed up right as I was about to leave."

"Don't worry about it," I told her.

We moved towards the back of the bar, to an obscure table by the corner. She unwrapped her scarf and ordered herself a fresh mojito. Social pressure compelled me to do the same.

"How's work?" I asked.

"Boring as hell," she muttered. "It pays the bills for now, but honestly, I can't wait to leave."

Her drink arrived; she took a small sip of it. Then, her eyes beamed at me as though she was analyzing the length of my eyebrows. "I can't get a read on you," she remarked.

"What do you mean?"

"The request regarding the bed in your room. Who does that? And, also, your name. Why are you named after a sweet potato?"

Talk about insulting! I confronted her about her impoliteness.

"Sorry, forgive me. I didn't mean to be rude," she said. "But back to the crux of this; the guy that you were looking for? Could you show me a picture of him again?"

I took out the polaroid photo of Lorenzo and passed it to her. Immediately, instinctively, she took another sip from her drink and said: "Yep, that's him alright. There's almost no doubt about it. Though my memory of this is foggy."

"You said you met him at the hotel?" I asked.

"I didn't think much of it, honestly. I was manning the lobby at the time; and like with every other guest in line, I went through the same questionnaires - how long was your stay? What kind of room would you like? Nothing beyond the usual, mundane stuff," she said. "But as it came to his turn in line, he spoke in a peculiar, distressed way. I couldn't tell you what it was exactly—the language he used; the body language he displayed. He said he was booked in for a job interview, for about one night's stay.

"I have been working in the service industry for quite some time now—there's a kind of intuition we develop as we deal with more and more people. You could call it a gut feeling, but most receptionists possess a magnifying glass about people. Though it wasn't very explicit, your friend, and whoever the old man was next to him, were acting really obscure."

She stopped and took a few sips of her drink. "But bar the weird chakra energy, everything else about check-in was as usual. They paid the deposit and completed registration with no problems. There was, also, a decent line forming behind the two of them, so I sent them to their rooms on the fifth floor and continued on with my job. Coincidentally, the fifth floor was also where the staff room was located. Every morning before our first shift, we'd have our coffee and breakfast there; throughout the rest of the day, it would remain a break room for us employees—as a place for us to take naps. Heading to the staff room, in other words, was a pretty robotic process for most of us working in the hotel; it's not necessarily a place we employees would consciously think of going, if that makes sense?"

"Yes it does," I said.

"Okay, that's what I thought as well! But, you see, that's where all the weird, mumbo jumbo comes in. I worked most of the midnight shifts that week, to earn some extra dough. And by midnight, I mean an hour before midnight, because this is America."

"Uh-huh…"

"Well, my shift ended later that night. So I put on some headphones and called for the elevator like I'd done a million times over by now. When I finally reached the fifth floor, I stepped out of the elevator like I'd always done; my mind, deeply fixated on some stupid family drama back home. Except this time, as soon as I stepped outside, a loud, abrupt metallic bang came from behind me."

She paused abruptly, taking more sips of her drink. "The first thing that came to my mind was —oh gosh, that can't be good. There are good sounds and bad sounds, and that sounded terrible. Like, really awful. When I turned, my suspicions were confirmed—the elevator doors had shut themselves completely!

"I was shook, but surprisingly though, I didn't panic. Instead, I was able to recall with great vividness the first lesson I learnt at training, which was to feel less and think more in situations of emergencies. So I took a few deep breaths and went straight into brainstorming mode. My initial hypothesis was that the elevator had broken down. If that was true, then that would mean there would be only one serviceable elevator operating in the hotel. That would have really sucked, and also really inconvenienced the other guests in the hotel. Mind you, we had no formal training on dealing with technical issues like these. Our training was heavily skewed towards matters of hospitality, our own emotional wellbeing, and situation handling of guests. Any other topics, as we were told, would be handled by the hotel's 'upper" management. Are you following so far?"

I nodded.

"Alright, good." She looked hard at me, as if contemplating the delivery of what she was about to say. "My gut reaction was to immediately inform hotel management of the elevator. I took out my phone and searched the directory for my manager's contact number. I think I was holding my phone with my right hand and I was standing six inches by the elevator, when I noticed that I couldn't really see anything around me. I mean, like, everything around me was unusually dark."

"It was at that moment where a thought struck me: where on earth was I? In front of me was the hallway, which had turned completely alien—the red carpeting on the floor was gone, as were the room numbers around the doors. The ceiling lights I had grown accustomed to were no longer anywhere in view. Rather, they were replaced by a series of candles, numbering in the hundreds, providing a dim light."

"I swung my head a few times and blinked my eyes repeatedly. That's ridiculous, I thought. There's no way this is real, right? I mean, I really had no way of describing the scene I was witnessing, no idea of the type of situation I had suddenly found myself in. The candles were emitting a glow that was unique to anything else I'd seen; and the air, the air was strange too. It was thick, but there was no smell. There was no sound either. It was similar to how I'd imagined the vacuum in space to feel like."

With a single, elongated gulp, she downed her entire mojito. She didn't seem fazed by it though. "As for dialing the phone, that yielded absolutely nothing; the line went dead after a few, unremarkable beeps. Out of desperation, I tried mashing the elevator buttons, but that didn't do anything. None of the button lights were responding, and there was no movement from beyond the shafts. Suddenly, the emotions I had buried earlier sprang out, causing me to freak out, like really freak out. And can you blame me? Here I was alone in the dark, just trying to get home. Life was already confusing enough as it is, but now, I had to deal with this bullshit too?"

"The more I thought about these things, the more frustrated I got. I made minimum wage at a job I didn't even care for; I couldn't even recall the last time my manager acknowledged me for a task well done. What kind of shitty life was I even living? Like, why was I working so tirelessly for an entity that didn't care one bit of my well-being; that didn't give a shit about me or my coworkers! Was our sweat and labour not enough?!"

"Gradually, the uneasiness within me was instead replaced with a variety of mild annoyance, that transformed itself into a bonfire of rage. If I possessed an internal boiling point, the temperature within me had easily exceeded it. Like a bar of smelted iron, I was burning everything around me. God was I angry!"

She stopped speaking and cleared her throat. Oh jeez, I thought. Her tone was starting to freak me out. I wasn't used to having such an aggressive conversation.

"Sorry, I can get pretty involved sometime," she said, letting out a sigh. "I could go on and on listing all the various emotions I was going through at the time, but I hope that at least demonstrates the frustration I was dealing with at the time."

Her perceptiveness took me off guard. Was my body language that telling? "So, let me get this straight," I said, attempting to ground things. "You got off the elevator on the fifth floor but the doors closed on you. Later, you noticed some eerie stuff with the hallways and got scared. But that same anxiousness later manifested itself into frustration..?"

"Right, right. That's pretty spot on. Like I said earlier, I wasn't in the right headspace to deal with a situation like this. For all I knew, this could have been a hallucination. Like, this was all nothing but the result of a power outage, and I was just overthinking it."

"I see."

"So, after grounding my senses, I focused on finding an exit. First, I went through the hallways, like one or two steps at a time, making sure to avoid the candles by my feet. If I recall the hotel's manual correctly, the fire exit should be located on the fifth door, three turns right from the elevator. However, the more steps I took, the more unnatural things became. For one, the physics surrounding my footsteps were abnormal; my toes made a weird gooey sound whenever they made contact with the floor. There was also the absence of smell, which was a stranger feeling that you'd expect. It's hard to describe the sensation exactly. It's definitely something that you'd have to experience for yourself to understand."

"No kidding…" I mumbled, after some processing. The similarities between her story and my recent dreams were frightening. It spooked me even just thinking about it. "Did anything else happen while you were there?" I asked.

"Unfortunately, yes," she answered. "As I mentioned earlier, every step I took caused the uneasiness within me to grow. But I couldn't stop walking; my desire to escape was hijacked by my curiosity for whatever mumbo jumbo business was being conducted in front of me. So, picture this—I'm hugging the wall, continuing my walk. Forgetting about time, as though I'd been sucked in a wormhole. Then, suddenly, all the candles on the floors were simultaneously put out. Like a storm unraveling in the sky, a heavy cloud of darkness started pouring over me. I could no longer see my hands or legs. Moving was no different from imagining movement."

"I was utterly confused at this point. I had no idea what was going on, but the darkness wasn't enough to deter me. I needed to see if this was some elaborate scheme someone had set up. I was being pushed by my stubborn curiosity. But then, after enough steps, it did finally occur to me what was going on—that there was this terrifying nightmare lying right in front of me. I felt a black hole of misery preparing to drown me."

Seeing that I wasn't drinking, she grabbed my mojito and took a few sips from it. "As you can imagine, I was terrified! Have you ever felt your heart try to catapult itself out of your body? Parts of me that I did not know even existed froze. Then, a huge rush of adrenaline swept me. So, I made a solid U-turn and ran. I ran as fast as I could back to the elevator. I ran so fast I felt that I could have beaten Usain Bolt. My heart was going so rapidly that I thought I was going to die at any second."

"Fortunately, I felt the darkness slowly dissipate. As I ran faster and faster, the darkness became less and less absolute, until finally, I could spot a line of light in front of me. In the distance, crevices of bright light were escaping through the elevator door!"

She stopped and killed my mojito. It was her second drink before the hour. Nevertheless, my instincts were to order another round for both of us. "I'm not kidding when I said I had never been so thankful to hear elevator music," she continued. "I sprinted inside and slammed all the buttons. I also prayed to all the major religions I knew. Jesus, Allah, Buddha; even Zeus if that was even a thing—any one of them could have been my savior for all I cared. All I wanted to do was get the hell out of there."

She slouched on the table, her head now resting on her arms. "Everything after this is where things get foggy for me. I think I passed out on the elevator. I'm not sure, I can't really remember. When I regained consciousness again, there were a bunch of hotel guests trying to calm me down in the lobby. According to them, I was sweating profusely, screaming in an indistinguishable, blabbering voice."

All I could do was nod, and continue to nod; there was no other way I could react to what she was sharing.

"The rest of that day was collect myself, dealing with my coworkers and being sent home in a taxi. I downed a shot of whiskey and went straight to bed. But the next day was equally as strange; as I went back to my desk, all the records regarding your friend's stay were gone! Registration numbers, room invoices, billing records, you name it. Just like that, they had disappeared without a trace. Of course I couldn't believe it, but when I confronted my colleagues about it, they all looked at me as though I was hallucinating."

I waited for her to continue, but she said nothing more. She plucked a cigarette from her purse. Her expression calmed after her first puff. "I still go back to the staff room for lunch breaks, though I'd be lying to you if I said I don't feel scared at times," she said finally. "Anyways, that's all I wanted to share with you."

"I see."

After her exhilarating debrief of a story, she took multiple puffs from her cigarette. Then, she flicked her hair to one side and exhaled a cloud of smoke through her lips. When the joint was towards the end of its lifespan, she mashed it on the table and looked up at me. It was as though she had briefly forgotten I was even sitting next to her. "What's the backstory behind you and your friend?" she asked.

I froze, and thought for a moment. "He was a good friend of mine from college," I said. I gave her a brief recap of my story —the phone call, the bald man on the train, the disappearance of Lorenzo, my journey up to Montana. "Unfortunately, that's all I know so far, which isn't really much."

"I'm still not following," she said. "If he was last seen in San Francisco, why do you think he's here?"

I pulled out the list of numbers I had received at the pawn shop and handed it to her. I couldn't have informed her of all the exact details of course; it would have been too difficult to describe and convey all the nuances that followed. "I don't have any easy way of explaining this, but these coordinates have something to do with my friend. One coordinate points to this city."

47°27'22.3"N	112°43'11.3"W
__°51'11.5"N	130°__'19.5"W
43°__'35.2"N	___°57'23.4"W
__°20'56.3"N	___°32'42.8"W
46°13'__._"N	109°__'71.2"W

"Huh..." she said.

"It's the only tangible clue I have at the moment," I said.

"Where are the rest of the numbers?"

"I'm not completely sure," I said. "I was hoping to find some leads here."

She looked at me in disbelief. "You came all the way here based on this one sheet of paper?"

"It was a big gamble, but you've essentially confirmed my theory. So I guessed it paid off."

"Oh really?" She pulled another cigarette from her purse. "So you believe me, then?"

"I do," I said. "The place you described—the hallway, the candles, the bizarre lack of sound...I had dreams about this place. It wasn't unlike your experience." I paused and finished my drink. "The dots are starting to connect. I don't really know what that means yet, but the pieces are all here."

She peered into my eyes, her irises slightly red. She was maybe drunk, probably tipsy, pulling a few puffs from her cigarette. "Thanks for hearing me out," she said. "I already feel better just getting this off my chest."

"No problem," I said.

"Do people really call you Mister Yam?" she asked.

"Yes," I answered, showing her my driver's license. "What about you? What should I call you? "

She laughed. "Alright, Mister Yam. You can call me Sappho."

It was an hour past midnight when we were done drinking. Sappho's alcohol tolerance had long faded by then, as had my puny one. I ordered us a few cucumbers to help with the nausea, but she found the mere suggestion ridiculous and refused to eat any. It was no exaggeration to say that we were heavily intoxicated when we finally left the bar.

"Hey, I don't think you should be driving in this condition," I said as she was searching for her car.

"This isn't San Francisco. There aren't any taxis operating at this hour," she said. "Besides, if I don't get some sleep soon, I'll be completely screwed for work tomorrow. My Toyota Prius is crimson red."

I stood firmly and hooked her arm. "Look, I get it. But this isn't about you. You have to drive responsibility."

Sappho puzzled over this fact for a few seconds. I could see the thought registering slowly. "Okay, fine. You're right, but what do you suggest I do, then?"

I suggested that she could stay the night in my room.

She looked at me in disbelief, and laughed. "Are you insane? First of all, your room doesn't even have a bed. Second of all, going out with you was already a big risk. Can you imagine what would happen if they found out I was sleeping with a guest? I'd be fired before lunch."

I shook my head. "Of course I'm not asking you to sleep with me. I'm totally happy to crash in the bathtub if that makes you feel more comfortable. You could sneak out before breakfast and no one would have even known you were there."

Finally arriving at her Prius, we stood in front of the car for a few seconds as she considered my suggestion. A sudden desire to dance came over me, but I suppressed the urge by reminding myself how embarrassingly awful my high school moonwalk was.

"Alright, fine," she said, after deliberating. "But I don't want any funny business from you, okay?"

I grabbed her pinky finger. "Yeah, obviously," I promised.

Returning back to the hotel was no easy feat in the cold weather, but the alcohol in our bodies seemed to help. Dredging through snow, we shared stories about random things: my upbringing in Malaysia; her cat's eating habits; the manner in which she likes to sneeze. She held some interesting opinions regarding life in South-East Asia, but I pointed out that there was a lot of smoke and mirrors with the way the region was treated by mainstream media. But, still, she pushed me on the details. So I described my perspective surrounding identity and growing up trilingual. "It's a secular, Muslim-majority country mixed with a number of other different races. It's hot and humid; the rain is unpredictable, but the good food more then makes up for it."

"Interesting..." she mumbled. "All I know about Malaysia is the missing plane. Did they ever figure out what happened to it?"

"Uhh...we don't talk about that."

Sappho's pupils were beginning to fluctuate as we made our way inside the hotel. To my relief, the concierge was empty, but dragging her semi-conscious body through the revolving door was a challenge in itself. Once we passed the lobby, I carried her and sneaked her onto the elevator for my floor.

I assembled a makeshift bed with the pillows and blankets scattered across the floor.

By the time I had tucked her in, she had completely dozed off.

"Good night," I whispered from the bathtub.

17

I woke up slightly after noon, to the sight of my legs hanging over the edge of the bathtub. Surprisingly, I did not ache; for the amount I drank and the manner I slept, I felt remarkably refreshed. Even still, I had the lingering bitter taste of alcohol swirling around my gums—cherry oak gone astray.

I stretched myself out of the bathtub and did my usual routine—peeing; washing my hands; scrubbing the pores manifesting on my face. I rinsed my mouth and went on gargling away my worries. This time though, I noticed a lipstick on the sink.

I picked it up and gave it a quick twirl. It had a solid quality and looked fancy. The color consisted of a highly pigmented red, which leaned towards crimson. Highly fashionable from a glance, this must have been Sappho's. But what on earth was it doing here?

Returning to the room, I noticed a stack of neatly folded blankets placed by the windows. Like a Japanese department store, they seemed organized according to the color gradient of *Wes Anderson*'s tasteful palette. This was undoubtedly Sappho's doing. She must have successfully sneaked away.

I had a sense of relief knowing this, but the sensation was short lived. Her story at the bar, as suspicious as it was, served as my only lead thus far; it was all I could think of as I went on staring at the floor. Something about the hotel—or more specifically, the fifth floor and the elevator—involved Lorenzo somehow. Was it possible that he was still in the building? And why on earth was he accompanied by the bald man? Whatever my next step, I knew for certain now that the bald man had his fingers wrapped around Lorenzo. It could have been a kidnapping, I thought. Or, maybe, a ransom? Perhaps it was something more sinister beyond my imagination. Having binge watched numerous seasons of *Criminal Minds*, my paranoia was anticipating the worst case scenario. Oh god, what if it was—

Buzzzzzz. Buzzzzzz

Buzz Lightyear?

My inklings were cut short by a constant buzzing, which I quickly identified as the dial-up phone in the room. I put on a pair of hotel slippers and picked up the telephone. I felt a strong urge to respond in a thick, Soviet voice.

"*Previet*," I opened. It was the only Russian word I knew.

"Uh...sorry. This must be the wrong room," said a woman over the line. It was definitely Sappho's voice. "Please excuse me—"

"Wait, it's me," I said, returning to my Manglish accent. "Pretty good accent, huh?"

"What the hell is wrong with you?"

"I get a little cheeky when I sleep in the bathtub."

"You mean *crazy*?" she corrected, sounding slightly annoyed. "By the way, I barely got any sleep. I could hear you snoring in the shower all night."

I told her she could thank my chronic sinusitis for that.

"Sinusitis? Is that supposed to be slang for something?" she asked.

"It's a chronic nose condition I have."

"Why are you telling me this? Too much information. Way too much information."

"You're the one who asked," I said. "Besides, aren't you also the one calling?"

"I'm calling you because I left my lipstick in your bathroom, so I'll need to drop by at some point later today," Sappho said, her voice now slightly more agreeable. "I'll come over after lunch."

"Can't I just pass it back to you in the lobby?"

"Mister Yam. How dense are you, really?" she said, before cutting the connection.

Still rubbing my nose, I put down the phone. What a peculiar woman. Wasn't she worried about keeping her job? She was being rather enigmatic about her lipstick too. Perhaps it wasn't as *crimson red* as I assumed? Whatever the case, I didn't want to overanalyze it. That wasn't important right now. I had a more pressing issue to solve —the elevator at the hotel. If what Sappho shared was true, if Lorenzo was truly here, then I needed to retrace her steps and find whatever clues I could.

I tore a piece of paper from my notebook and began to sketch a map. Tracing carefully with a pen, I diagrammed every detail she shared. The incident she brought up began with the elevator on the fifth floor; I was just two floors below it. Following the floorplan of the hotel, the hallways were just slightly adjacent to the staffroom she spoke about. But I found it difficult to picture the rest of what Sappho said. I'd figured that the only way to go about this was to see it for myself.

After a quick shower, I went into the hallway, and then to the elevator. I pressed for the fifth floor. I took a deep breath and a few steps back. What should I expect? A dim hallway with candles? With a few unremarkable beeps, the elevator began its ascend upward. The display on the top right registered the floors as they went:

| 3 | ..... | 4 | ..... | 5 |

An infinitesimal note sounded when the elevator doors slid open. I braced myself.

The fifth floor greeted me—bright, perfumed and exuberant. Crimson red carpeting occupied most of the floor; on the ceiling were an abundance of recessed lights. The smell coming from the carpet was as though it was just vacuumed and lightly scented with vanilla air freshener. There was no enigmatic darkness; no strange sensations; no puzzling candles. The hallway had the same, generic features as the one on my floor.

Terrific, I thought. Still, I couldn't give up yet. Maybe Sappho had remembered the floors wrong? I returned to the elevator and repeated this process for every other floor. As the doors opened, the results were the same—red carpeting on the floor; obscure Victorian paintings on the wall; an occasional lamp by the elevator. And like the fifth floor, there was nothing unusual overall.

Disappointed was an understatement; the initial excitement of my new clue was now replaced by a smelly, unappetizing dissatisfaction. What other lead did I have, if not this?

Nothing. The answer was nothing.

Feeling dejected, I left the hotel and scouted for some carbs. This time, I ordered myself a triple-stacked bacon cheeseburger from Burger King. The burger was exceptionally greasy when it arrived, but it was also one of the more satisfactory meals I had. Buns, bacon, cheese, onions, tomatoes, lettuce, sauce and patty—the sloppy combination of ingredients was exactly what I needed right now.

Even so, there were limitations to what the human body could handle. There was no way in hell I was going to find Lorenzo by conditioning my body with greasy fat! So, I took three big pieces and packed the rest for leftovers. Then, I returned to my hotel room and prepared for a hot bath. When the water was filled to a reasonable level, I stripped my clothes and slowly dipped myself inside the hot tub. There was an immense, physical pleasure that came with the thawing of my freezing body; but alas, the day was otherwise impossible to get a grasp on. I was confused, and tired, and inching closer to a food coma, my stomach still reeling from my unhealthy lunch. Fortunately, the cucumber I snacked on yesterday helped prevent a more serious blow.

Exiting the shower and drying myself, I gathered all the blankets in the room and layered them together. Gradually, I wrapped myself inside of them. A steady, therapeutic slumber graced my subconscious, creeping its way up to my eyes. I enjoyed my lucid semi-awareness until I heard a soft knock on my door.

"Are you there, Mister Yam?" said a voice. It was soft enough where I couldn't discern who it was.

Still slightly groggy, I put on some clothes and went to the door. As soon as I pulled it half open, Sappho barged in.

"I have about an hour before my shift tonight." she said, panting slightly. She slid off her shoes and stood by the television in the room, giving me weird looks as she examined the state of the room. "I'm not interrupting anything, am I?"

"You interrupted my nap," I said, begrudgingly.

"I'm sorry," she said. I sensed she didn't mean it. "I didn't think you'd be sleeping right now. If anything, I thought you'd be searching for your friend."

"Well, I tried earlier, but I had no luck. In fact, the most interesting thing I've accomplished today was the nap I was about to take—"

"—until I showed up?"

"...until you showed up. Why are you here again?"

She ignored my question and took a can of beer from the minifridge. "Don't worry, I'll make sure you aren't charged for this."

"You're drinking rather early today," I observed.

"I'd already violated a ton of policies by coming here. What's one more rule going to do?" she said.

Sappho took off her sweater and took a seat next to me. She had a point. Not the strongest point, but a point, nevertheless.

"Fair enough." Glancing at her face, I noticed deep eye bags. I didn't plan to comment, but she looked too exhausted not to. "Rough day?"

"Nah, I was just really busy. Had to wrap up a few things at work and also run a few personal errands?"

"Errands?"

"Yeah," she said. "It required a few trips back home. Thankfully, I don't live too far from the city."

Back home. Back home. I repeated to myself. When was the last time I went back home?

"Thank you, though," she said.

"For?"

"Last night. Making sure I was safe. As silly as it was, I also appreciated you sleeping in the bathtub."

"No problem," I said.

A click, and then the pop tab of her beer came off. She took a single sip. "I still don't get you," Sappho said.

"Which part?"

"Well, everything. Since I started my job here, I usually only deal with families and tourists. It's quite strange seeing...a lone traveller like this. Not that there's anything wrong with it. It's just new to me, that's all."

I thought for a moment. "I wouldn't say this is common for me either. Quite frankly, this is the furthest I've ever ventured from the big cities."

"Really now?"

"Yeah."

"Do you like being alone then?" she asked.

"What do you mean?"

"Like, what you're doing right now—coming all the way here, dealing with all this snow," she observed "I get that you're trying to find your friend, but all of this seems pretty extreme, don't you think?"

The question took me off guard and made me kind of embarrassed. "I don't...really know?" I said. It was an honest answer. I really didn't know. "I guess it depends on the context."

"Hmm..." she mumbled. I could sense her mind churning. "But didn't you come all the way here alone?"

"Yeah, but I don't consider this being alone."

"That makes no sense."

"Well, yeah. I see what you mean. But there's a difference between loneliness and solitude," I said. "I'm not sure if I can explain it well— it's not something I fully grasp yet."

"Oh, come on," she nudged. "You have to at least try. Or else I'll think you're officially crazy."

Try? How do I go about describing this? "What I'm trying to say is that I'm alone, but I don't feel alone. Rather, I'm making a distinction between the physical fact and the emotional headspace of being alone."

She shook her head. "Can you elaborate?"

"Loneliness is this terrible feeling of being trapped, being lost, not knowing where to go, dreading every step on the way." I continued. "Solitude is different. It's like you're alone, but it's not isolating or daunting. It's more like the opposite—being by yourself, in the midst of the world; experiencing your own voice away from distractions."

"So, solitude is like wanting to be alone?"

"Well, not exactly. It's more like being alone while also being aware that you're not actually alone—but if we're not familiar with solitude, then we start to equate loneliness and solitude as the same thing; if we can't find comfort in solitude, we'll only know the anguish of loneliness."

Taking large sips of her drink, she slouched on the floor and turned her head to face me. "You're *officially crazy*," she said. "Perhaps even delusional too."

"Thanks."

"Are you always this introspective?"

"No," I said. That was a lie; introspection has no end.

"You're lying," she said.

"Maybe. Maybe not."

"Do you ever hear yourself speak? Of course you're lying," Sappho said. "But perhaps there are things we have in common."

"Like what?" I asked.

"I don't know. Do you feel like eating?"

"Don't you have to work soon?"

"I can be late," she said.

We ordered a pepperoni pizza from Domino's as Sappho shared stories about her upbringing in Montana. After graduating from high school, she moved to Seattle and worked at a budget hotel there, before coming back. "It was an interesting city, with far more things to do. But I realized that I was happier here."

"Let me guess, you were homesick?" I said.

"No, it was something else. Even though I met more people in the city, they weren't very authentic. Like, there was an invisible wall that separated me from everyone else that belonged; no matter how hard I tried, I couldn't break it," she said.

"You didn't fit in?"

"Sure, that's definitely part of it. But that's never really the question, is it? I can have a dozen friends over, and still feel alone the minute they leave. If that makes sense?"

"Yeah, it does actually," I said. For some reason, I was craving a harsh cigarette.

When she was done eating, she placed her arms over mine. We stayed like this for about five minutes, neither of us uttering a word. Then, a single, sorrowful tear from her left eye landed on my right hand; she was burying her face in my arms, as if she wanted to be sure no one else in the world could tell she was crying.

Through the window, snow kept falling. An ethereal landscape was beginning to manifest itself in front of me, filling the town with an everlasting plane of whiteness. For the brief minutes we were holding ourselves like this, I felt a slight divergence in reality. Back home, back home, I repeated to myself again. I started to think more about my journey to this country. When did I come to the United States? Why did I leave Malaysia? All my years of studying had been to purchase myself this one opportunity, to experience the golden ticket sold to me as the American dream. To experience the world from the lens of privilege, to see more truths than I could have ever envisioned. I had fought for this chance so that I could confront the heart of my being, the construction of my self-identity. If I surrendered now, I would lose more than an opportunity—I would lose my voice. That was the cost of freedom; the price I had to pay. I understood that now—I wasn't running from society, I was running from myself.

"I should probably head to work now," she said, abruptly ending the silence.

"That weird experience you had on the elevator?" I recalled, suddenly. "What was the song you were listening to on the elevator? Do you remember?"

She pulled out her phone and started fiddling with the screen. "I should be able to find it somewhere...'Mad Rush,' by Philip Glass," she said.

"I see."

"Why?"

"I'm just curious. When do you get off work?" I asked.

"My shift ends around midnight. You're not planning to stay up, are you?"

"I'll play it by ear."

She gently planted her lips against mine. Then, she stood up and slid out the door, leaving as silently as she entered. I stayed seated on the floor all the while—a thought I was holding disappeared without notice.

I closed my eyes for a few seconds, and then opened them. Just as Sappho had said, I was alone again.

By seven that evening, I was out of things to do in the hotel. I hadn't made progress on finding Lorenzo, of course, but I'd pretty much done everything else—I shattered my previous planking record of two minutes; I watched the evening news; I took multiple walks across the hallway. I even measured the square dimensions of the floor with my palms. From a practical standpoint, I had scrutinized everything remotely interesting.

I headed out and strolled the remainder of town. A diner I hadn't noticed before caught my eye. Without thought, I went inside and found a comfortable seat by the bar. Still jaded from the pizza earlier, I skipped dinner and ordered myself a cup of coffee.

In the twelve years since I discovered the caffeinated drink, I had never once understood the bad rap bitterness gets. It's usually described as an intense, disagreeable flavor, but it is anything but—well-prepared, strong black coffee with fresh ground beans has a fantastically, mouth-watering quality to them. The millions of people who drank black, filtered, or espresso will attest to that.

The coffee arrived; I took sips. Was taste really a matter of subjective opinion? And, going further, was there such a thing like an objective opinion? Suppose you had a certain "something"—a gut feeling, an inexplicable sense of things—but aren't exactly sure what it was or how to best express it. For all intents and purposes, let's use the example of coffee. Because of its ambiguous definitions and personal uniqueness, we could consider the attractiveness of coffee a matter of subjective taste.

Then, one day, you wake up at a dinner party and find yourself chit-chatting with some other fellow whom you've just met. The conversation leads to morning routines, then leads to breakfast, then to coffee. Naturally, you start a discussion revolving around it; after further deliberations, you realize that, aha, I'm not alone in enjoying coffee. This shared epiphany develops a new basis for communicating this "something" which now results in an elevated understanding of coffee. We could consider this new perspective a matter of transcendence: from subjectivity to intersubjectivity.

I'd gotten deep into this train of thought when the store manager came over to me with the bill. As with most restaurants, this was the unofficial, least insufferable way of motioning a customer that it was time to leave. I was a bit surprised, given that most diners I knew of operated twenty-four/seven, but the waiters and waitresses were already thoroughly cleaning up.

I signed the bill and made my way back to the hotel. Where was I again? Oh, right, subjectivity in coffee. If the dinner party was a house party, and more people came along in the discussion with quantifiable ways of measuring the enjoyment of the drink, then eventually, the understanding of that "something" would deepen.

I entered the lobby and called for the elevator. If the mutual understanding of it grows deep enough, then most of its personal ambiguity would be gone. By that point, we may as well consider it an "objective" fact. We could theoretically arrive at a place where the deliciousness of coffee would become a shared truth.

The elevator door opened; I dragged my feet inside. Wouldn't that be amazing? I mean, there were already a sizable number of people around the world who already enjoyed coffee, but it'd be wonderful if there was indisputable, universal recognition for its taste.

| 1 | ..... | 2 | ..... | 3 |

According to some scientific studies, it even helps with weight loss by signaling the breakdown of fat. Of course, nothing is great in excess. But taken in moderation—like two to three cups a day—I think it's fair to say that coffee was a healthy drink for most people. Mmm.. cappuccino...

I exited the elevator. After all, it contains a plethora of antioxidants. It has manganese, potassium, and, um, magnesium I think? I'm not exactly sure why these substances are good for the body. But they sound like cool things to have in the body, and—

Wait. Hold up. This isn't my floor.

I looked around my new surroundings; there was a blanket of darkness over everything around me. I knew coffee to be dark, but even burnt coffee wasn't this *dark*. No, this was something else entirely; and there was no smell to enjoy.

I turned around and pressed for the elevator. If coffee was what manifested this place, then I was clearly drinking the wrong kind. Was this Melbourne's revenge for a mediocre latte? I mean, Starbucks had to close more than half the chains they opened there. The Aussies are a hard demographic to please.

The elevator buttons weren't registering. I stood alone, somewhere.

Somewhere?

Glancing at the walls, I noticed gleams of candles lined up around the hallways. That's when it hit me—where the hell was I? This must have been the place that Sappho had mentioned in her story. There was no other explanation to the candles; they emitted a glow that was completely unique to anything else I'd seen.

My heart started thumping. I lifted my hands and felt myself across my body; my clothes were still intact, as were my glasses. Though it wasn't bright, I could still discern the edges of the wall—the candles, the kooky air, the eeriness of things. Making a karate chop with my hands resulted in not even a speck of sound. The absence of it was in itself a kind of sound; no emotional headspace could have made it less absolute.

I shut my eyes and opened them repeatedly; there were barely any differences between light and dark. I saw the walls bend and move. Or was it me that was bending and moving? It was difficult to tell. Like in a used car commercial, there was no difference between perspective and imagination.

What on earth am I saying?

I placed my right hand against the wall and the skin of my palm merged with it. There was a growing chill that enveloped me as I took more steps forward. Then, there was the air—an ambiguous, thick strain of air not unlike pollution. But sniffing the air was just a motion; there was no discernible scent.

Hugging the wall, I continued my walk down the hallway. Careful now, one step at a time. Now was not the time to be superstitious, I told myself. Distract your anxiety with something else. If I died, what would I eat for my last meal? I revisited my thoughts about gouda cheese. The saltiness; the nuttiness. Of course I would include the Dutch cheese in my final meal. Ideally, it'd be in bed with some grapes and crackers. It was something I could imagine Caesar Augustus doing.

I made a left turn. The candles in the hallway were numbering fewer and fewer. My body started going numb. My head started aching. It was now impossible to distinguish an object from a concept. Twilight crept in through my eyes like dissipating gas; the glimmer from the candles was now no different than a spectacle I could have imagined.

I continued pushing forward. I took a deep breath, but the very thought of motion was suffocating. Stop thinking, I repeated to myself. Focus only on the movement of your calves. One step backward, two steps forward. Rinse and repeat. Rinse and repeat.

Silence. There was so much silence. My footsteps weren't audible, and neither was any other movement. How long have I been walking now? A few minutes? A few hours? I was amazed at how Sappho was able to accomplish any of this: the nerve! Talk about her fearlessness, indeed. My respect for her grew tenfold.

In the distance, I sensed an unmistakable void of light. A few more steps forward and there would be nothing left. A different kind of darkness greeted me there, one that was deathly absolute. This is where the path ends; or where the path begins, depending.

I stopped and deliberated for a long time. I was at a crossroads here—my entire journey had led me to this point, and I did so with little to no hesitation. But this was different. There would be no turning back after this. Head back to the elevator and it would be the end; I'd finish my journey and leave Lorenzo behind. But what would the point of that be? After all, wasn't this what I had been searching for? Wasn't this the whole reason I had come here?

There's no need to panic, I convinced myself.

So, I closed my eyes and took a step into the abyss.

18

It was impossible to know how long I walked in twilight. I was still in the darkness, but a very different kind of darkness. Any attempts at scanning my surroundings were futile; the candles that once occupied the hallways were long gone, and with them, any visible points of light.

I felt helpless; I had thoughts of giving up. No mental gymnastics could compensate for the anguish riveting in my head. Perhaps this was what Carl Jung had meant when he described the shadow realm - deviants lingering in the unconscious mind. Was there even a point in going any further? Yes there was—according to my legs, that didn't seem to care at all about the ongoing turmoil in my mind. They just wanted to walk, and to keep walking, to a place only they seemed to know.

You could form distinct shapes within the darkness. From a certain angle, Steve Jobs was playing *fantaisie impromptu* with only his index fingers. Billie Eillish and Henry Kissinger were making surprise cameos in what I imagined to be a controversial ukulele duet. Personally, I found the lack of *vibrato* quite disconcerting.

Dancing elves were shrouding my brain synapses. Whiplash in Italian is 'when the witch hits'.

I must be going slightly insane.

All at once came a sound. A minimal, saturated droning noise. It sounded artificial, mechanical even. And like subtle variations found in a radio system, there were static undertones everywhere. Where were these projections coming from?

A familiar place; a strange place. One from another reality; one that existed here. Far off in the distance, I spotted a faint glow. Light was seeping from a room—from the crevices of its door. It seemed like a conception of unfettered imagination; it looked too pure to be true.

I tip-toed towards it.

The door had no knob, no lock, no hinges or handles. The top and bottom were so even, so perfectly flush within the frame, that there was no possible way of deconstructing it. Yet, the light from beyond carried with it an unmistakable familiarity.

Where had I felt this before?

I gave it a gentle push, and the door opened inward. A candle was sitting on the top of a table. Just barely, I could make out certain objects by it—chairs, cups, and a kettle. It seemed as though I was walking into someone's bedroom.

Then, a scent. A lavender scent swept me from my feet. From its source also came a trickling sound; liquids were being poured onto a cup. "It took you awhile," said a recognizable voice. "Take a seat, please."

I navigated through the pitch black until I touched something resembling a chair. It felt wooden, and cold; so very cold.

I placed my butt on the freezing wooden chair. Fiddling with my hands, I was still unable to distinguish anything around me. The small amount of light was limited to the table; the radius around it was just another layer of shroud.

"You don't remember anything, do you?" it continued. "I hope you realize what that means."

I gazed at the shadow facing me. The only thing I understood for sure was that I didn't understand anything at all. "Everything started with the bald man and the train," I said. "It was one weird thing after another, but I knew they were connected."

"So, the intangibles are becoming clearer?"

"No, not at all," I answered. "I still don't know who you are, or what you want."

"Is it really that important that you know who I am?" it asked.

"Why else would I be here?" I said.

Silence. And then a chuckle. Just like in my dreams, the voice sounded like something from another reality. Except this time, I could see the shifting shadows. "That's not really what you came for though, is it? To know who I am?"

Instead of responding, I sneezed. It was a strange sensation.

"You should have some tea," the voice proposed. "I find it to be quite helpful."

I grabbed the tea cup. It was already filled generously. I brought it to my mouth and took a sip—Earl Gray tasted solemn in the dark. "Tell me," I said. "What are you doing here? How long have you been here?"

"What am I doing here? I'm here for the same reason you're here," it mused quizzically. "I'm lost. This really *is* the perfect place to be lost, isn't it?"

I shook my head. Steve Jobs was now at the cadenza of Franz Liszt's masterpiece. "None of this makes sense."

"Of course it doesn't, but only to you."

I hesitated a moment. For some reason, I couldn't get myself to respond. Each breath I took brought with it an extra sense of heaviness. A stopwatch was counting somewhere. Tick-tock. Tick-tock. "The fact that you're here means that you're closer," it said. "Oh, yes. You are so very close."

"Maybe. But since I came here, I've only gotten more questions and fewer answers. How long will this nightmare last? I just want to end this nonsense."

For a long time, the voice said nothing. The setting was odd. Uneasy. It was shooting at me through the air, like a paintball. "Mmmm," it uttered. "You came here specifically to find your friend, didn't you?"

"That's right."

"Why do you suppose he left, then?"

"I don't know. That's what I'm trying to figure out." I said.

"Oh, but that is only one small part of it," it said. "You and I both know there's more to this than finding your friend."

Again with the riddles. "I don't have time for this."

"You certainly do not," said the voice.

"Of course, he is a big part of it," I said. With my pinky finger, I kept a firm grip on my teacup. "Without a doubt, he is the **biggest** part of this."

"But there is more, isn't there?"

"No, I don't—"

"All this time, you looked back on that day, drunk on the memory of its abhorrence," interrupted the voice. "Yet, instead of facing it, you chose to run away and forget."

The temperature took a nosedive. "Mister Yam, all you have to do is remember. That is the key *you* possess. Don't you understand? The sheep is drawn to *you*. The dream is there to hold *you*. The box flows through *you*. The story is *you*."

I gazed at the shadow on the wall, and felt a deep pain. The darkness was overwhelming. "I'm tired of games. I'm tired of riddles. I need something concrete—an objective fact; an actionable, tangible item to work with."

The voice sighed. "Mister Yam, if it were up to me, I would have already told you. But, unfortunately, I can't tell you something you already know. The process of discovery lies within you."

I could feel a gentle presence reach out to my pocket. An envelope? It was handing me an envelope. "What is this?" I asked.

"Something you've forgotten," it said.

"Something I'd forgotten?"

"As with most things with the mind, it was always there. Buried deep inside of you. I can only hope you see it through."

Immediately, instinctively, I fell onto the floor. My chair had collapsed on itself.

"You better hurry, Mister Yam. While you still have time."

Darkness came to fill the space after those words. The little furniture I recognized shaded itself into the shadows. I had given thought to every word shared with me - they stung me as I repeated them. I recognized them, somehow; in some dark universe parallel to my own.

My awareness sucked into a deep wide whirlpool, I closed my eyes and took a deep breath. Dread entered me slowly. I began to realize what this was all about.

You better hurry echoed in my mind.

19

I filled up the bathtub. The immediate desire for a hot, long bath was all that preoccupied my mind. My teeth were grinding; the shivering rippling through my body was uncomfortable and uncontrollable. Watching the water trickle required some unfathomable level of discipline.

Drip-drop. Drip-drop.

I couldn't restrain myself; the urge was too strong. I sank in the bathtub before it was even half filled.

Lukewarm water greeted me at first. But slowly, the temperature began to pick up. Like thawing a chicken breast, the water became warmer and warmer, until I could feel the fibers in my muscles begin their defrosting. Soon, warm steam filled the room. A makeshift sauna ensued.

I cut off the tap and submerged myself in the water. I opened my eyes expecting blue, but all I saw was gray; a kind of unremarkable, dull gray. If life was a dessert, it would be a moldy cheesecake. An expired chocolate tart from an economy class airplane meal.

I pressed my forehead against the walls of the bathroom. The elevator was crazy; the voice from my dream was there. Yet, I couldn't recall anything specifically. What was I forgetting? Lorenzo, the bald man, the box—heaven forbid Emma was in that mix too. They were like little dots joined by an invisible line; a confusing, immeasurable line.

"Ughhhhh…" I grumbled. I did not know what I was hoping to say, but I was thankful that I could hear myself.

I climbed out of the bathtub and wiped myself dry. The carpeting was cold as rocks, so of course I took a seat on the floor butt naked. "Ughhhhhhhhhhhh….." I grumbled even louder, "I knew it was the goddamn sheep!"

The sheep? What on earth was I saying? I buried my face onto the ground. God, was I feeling confused. I always hated that cursed mammal. Perhaps I should go to the nearest gun range and acquaint myself with a rifle. Maybe they could give me marksmanship pointers on hunting for sheep.

I thought about calming myself. I needed to center myself again, somehow. How about yoga? I recalled Pallavi Sharma and the yoginis having their own methods of returning to Zen. They'd probably start with a few stretches, and later, an asana pose, like downward dog.

The notion resonated in my head. So, putting on some fresh clothing, I sat with my knees touching the ground. Such a position was already a struggle, but I went further and stretched my arms as far as possible.

My spine at an apex, I took a deep breath and let out a sound.

Ommmmmmmmmmm.

Though my body was uncomfortable, chanting seemed to have helped. Quite a pleasant sound too, I thought. Mmm. Meditation.

Ommmmmmm. Ommmmmm.

I touched my hair. I enjoyed having hair. I'd be terribly upset if my scalp turned hairless.

Ommmmmmm. Ommmmmmm.

I imagined a woolless sheep. It was rather unassuming, and looked like the type that wore a beret. We were seated in an outdoor cafe somewhere in Milan. It was a perfect morning, and we were enjoying some pizza bianca.

"Could you be a good lad and buy me a cappuccino?" it asked. It had a ton of wool. "Frothed milk with cacao nibs if they're available."

"You don't have the money?" I said.

Ommmmmmm. Ommmmmmm.

"I'm a sheep. We don't believe in a monetary system," it remarked. "Besides, I don't have my wallet on me."

"Fair point," I said. "But coffee's not cheap, and I already spent all my money on the air ticket here!"

"Ha!!" laughed the sheep. "You're already making excuses for yourself. But fine. I'll make a deal with you. Buy me two caramel macchiatos and I'll tell you how I got this limited edition *Maison Margiela* beret."

Knock-knock, came from a door.

"Why should I trust you? You're a talking sheep," I said.

"Have some faith in me. I'm here, aren't I?"

An audible knock-knock sound kept repeating itself on my door, followed by a woman's voice. "Hey, are you still awake?"

I halted my chanting. I heard the sound of a bag being dropped, followed by the reverberation of approaching footsteps. I changed into some light clothes and went to the door. Without asking who it was, I opened the door.

Sappho slipped inside and shut the door. The congestion in my head was still there, but the sight of her made me feel slightly more at ease. "I just got off work," she said. "Did you just wake up? You don't look so good."

"I'm fine, thank you" I said.

"Are you sure? Your face looks kinda pale."

"Don't worry about it. My face always looks pale at night."

She gave me a skeptical look. She knew I was lying, but didn't press further. "Whatever you say, then."

I glanced at the can of beer by the refrigerator, but decided against it. "I just came back from the elevator," I said. "You weren't exaggerating one bit. It's definitely real. All of it."

The enthusiasm on her face was replaced with distress. "What happened?"

I opened my mouth, but no words came out. My mind was more fragile than I cared to admit. "Sorry," I said. "Words are hard right now. I need to put my thoughts in order."

She drew close and felt my forehead. "You're shivering," she commented. "I'll boil you some hot water."

I sat and watched her prepare the coffee pot. As it came to a boil, she poured it into a cup and ripped open a packet of green tea. She handed it to me as the tea bag was still swirling.

"Thank you." I took a gentle sip. The colors in the cup were dissipating and re-emerging as the leaves mixed in with the crystalline water.

"You know, you can be honest with me," she said, taking a seat next to me. "You don't have to keep this to yourself."

"Thank you. You have been very kind to me," I said. "Just as you described, I went to the fifth floor. No light. No sound. An indescribable strangeness, as though I was in a world different from ours. And yet, there was no mistaking it. It was the place from my dreams."

"Dreams? You have had dreams about this place?"

"Yeah. The hallways. The books. The tables. The palpable sense of familiarity. Old senses. Old voices," I said. "Though it's not much, things are starting to link up. I'm beginning to connect some of the dots."

But where to start? I couldn't look at it as a whole; I needed to unravel each fiber individually. If I spent too much time looking at the big picture, everything would be out of focus.

"I see," she said. Sappho pulled a cigarette from her bag and lit it in her mouth. "It seems like you've been thinking about this for a while now."

"Trust me when I say I'm not doing a good job," I said, sitting upright. "I don't know that much more than you do at this point."

Her head facing the ceiling, she snickered at me. Then, she took a few, generous puffs. "Would you like to have some?" she asked. "Don't worry, the smoke detectors here don't even work. We haven't renewed them since last year."

I nodded and took the fat joint from her. "Thanks. Can't say I'm the biggest fan."

Sappho opened the mini-fridge and grabbed a bottle of Budweiser for herself. "That's what growing up will do to you. It'll make you smoke things you don't even want to smoke."

"Uh-huh," I said. I took a few more puffs before setting it aside. Then, I pulled out an envelope from my pocket. "I found this on my trip to the fifth floor."

She reached out and felt it. "Interesting," she said. Sappho bent it slightly with her fingers while taking small sips from her beer. "Looks like a note. Have you read what's inside?"

"No, not yet. Let's find out."

Grabbing keys from my bag, I ran the tip of over the envelope and tore open the seal. Emerging from the hole was a single sheet of paper, folded multiple times over. A large, messily written title was on the top of the paper.

The Life of Boris?

An array of numbers was underneath it.

47°27'22.3"N	112°43'11.3"W
46°51'11.5"N	130°75'19.5"W
43°34'35.2"N	102°57'23.4"W
44°20'56.3"N	103°32'42.8"W
46°13'31.9"N	109°84'71.2"W

The paper was up to Sappho's face. Her eyes swiftly operated as she scanned from left to right. "What the hell am I reading?" she remarked.

"The rest of the coordinates," I said. "They are unmistakable for anything else."

"Coordinates?" she muttered. "Coordinates to where..?"

"Remember what I showed you at the bar?"

She shook her head. "Nope."

"Okay, well. You wouldn't by chance have a map on you, would you?"

"Let me check." She dug through her handbag and pulled out a booklet. "We hand these out at the lobby for free, mainly to tourists. There should be an outline of a map somewhere in there."

I took the pamphlet from her and flipped through it. There was a detailed map on the bottom left, which I then stretched open. Pulling up my phone, I went down the list of coordinates and marked their location points on the map with a pen. Exhausting all of them resulted in an area that resembled a minor arc of a circle.

"Looks like a treasure map," she said.

"It kinda does, doesn't it? My guess is that the purple house was located somewhere within here."

"Purple house? What purple house?"

I pulled out the polaroid photo of the bald man and placed it on the floor. Sappho realigned her eyes to focus on it. "That's him!" she observed. "That was the guy I was talking about."

"I know."

"Why didn't you tell me this earlier?"

"Because I didn't want you to think I was crazy," I said. "But that's beside the point. I think my missing friend is here."

"You think the bald man kidnapped him and brought him to that purple house? With all those sheep?"

"I'm positive about it," I said. I plopped down onto the floor and killed the remainder of the joint. "By process of elimination, that's the only place left to check. Though I don't suppose there's a simple way of going about it."

Sappho shook her head. "Nope, not at all. Based on the map, it'd be around fifty miles of land to cover we'd have to search. And we'd be doing it out in the snow too."

"We?" I looked up at her, slightly confused. "What about your job at the hotel? Don't you have to stay here and work?"

"So what if I miss one week of work?" she said, with merriment. "This whole sheep scenario makes for an interesting puzzle. I'd rather spend some time helping you."

Her proposal made me nervous. I didn't really want to involve someone in this, but I needed some help. Trekking through the Montana wilderness was a tall order, especially in the dead of winter. "Are you sure?"

"Yep, you bet. Besides, what would you do if you didn't have me?

Fifty miles of snow is a lot, especially considering the elevation and terrain that would need to be covered. For you to go alone and find a house like that? In the middle of all this snow? You'd be hopeless without a partner."

I'd be stupid not to consider her point. "That's the question I had as well. Is this even a good idea?"

"No," she said in a deadpan voice. "I would not recommend this trip to any sane person."

"But...?"

"Ships are safe in harbor, but that's not what ships are for," she remarked. "Did you really come all the way here to find your friend, just to quit? Seems pretty silly, even for me."

I heaved a sigh. "Yeah, you're right. I can't just give up now. But I also can't help but feel that we'd be walking into a trap."

"What do you mean?"

"I don't know. I can't put my finger on it," I continued, "the whole situation just seems a bit strange. Finding a house like that, in the middle of all the snow? We'd be crazy to try it."

She popped open a new can of beer. "Which is why we'll need to plan it out. First, we'll need to make sure we get the right equipment; and I don't mean 'California Summer' camping gear. I mean proper winter camping stuff—midweight base layers, zero-degree sleeping bags, closed-cell sleeping pads. The essentials, essentially. Synthetic fleece will become your best friend."

"How do you know so much about camping?" I asked.

"I'm from Montana," she said. "You gotta know stuff like this to survive up here."

"I guess you're right..."

"I know I'm right," she said. "Relax, Mister Yam! We got this. Besides, having complete faith in another person is one of the best attributes a person can have."

"Is that a quote from somewhere?"

Sappho allowed the tiniest possible movement to shape her mouth —a smile so unlike any smile I've seen that it could be interpreted as anything else. "Does it matter? Once we have the right preparations, everything will fall into place."

～

After spending all night discussing our potential strategy, we laid down a list of action items we had to get done. Namely, due diligence, logistics and equipment. Sappho was quick to bring up Ed Viesturs, who had a notable approach to mountaineering—*"Getting to the top is optional, getting down is mandatory."*

"We gotta optimize for survival," she said. "Even if it means packing five days' worth of food for a two day trip."

"Speaking of which, what even is *food* here?" I asked.

"Freeze-dried food. It's durable, easy to carry, and pretty tasty too. Though I suppose there's no harm in bringing protein bars as well."

We divided our respective tasks and went to work the following morning. After submitting her leave of absence, Sappho left for home to gather trekking gear for our trip. Meanwhile, I visited a REI store and spent the next few hours trying to map out logistics.

"You're not planning to go backpacking in this weather, are you?" asked the sales assistant as he approached me. "We're in the middle of a pretty rough winter season."

I nodded. "I know it sounds like a suicide mission, but, unfortunately, I'm going to have to."

Are you serious? said his eyes. "As an enthusiast and fellow professional, I hope you're well informed of the risk surrounding such a trip."

I continued to nod my head. I already knew what I was doing was incredibly reckless and stupid. "Assuming you had a gun to your head, what would you do?"

Standing unusually still, the man stifled and pondered in front of me. Then, he brought me to a room filled with maps and highlighted the different types of mapping options.

"Overview maps usually have a scale of somewhere between 1:50,000 and 1:100,000," he said. "Personally for me, I think commercial recreation maps are the best, since they're updated more regularly. They also include other details outside of topographic data. I don't recommend shaded relief maps."

I didn't really understand at all what he was sharing, but I bought all the maps in question with the hopes of Sappho dissecting them for me. It's quite possible that I was being scammed, but the guy seemed knowledgeable and genuinely sympathetic.

"Good luck, buddy. You're going to need it," he said. Not the most encouraging words you'd want to hear from an expert.

I also bought myself a number of essential gear, including but not limited to: a 55 liter backpacking pack, a zero-degree sleeping bag, a winter tent, thermal clothing, and freeze dried food for the snow. Though insulated underwear was not a formal necessity, Sappho strongly recommended it, and I complied. After all, it was better to be safe than sorry; there was no telling what could happen in the cold, especially in the winter forest by ourselves.

Returning to the hotel, I hauled my purchases to my room and began organizing them. I made an arrangement with the hotel to stash my valuable items whilst I was gone. They agreed, and even did so for free.

Feeling good about the preparations I've done, I was disappointed with Sappho, who had brought with her a sizable number of fancy toiletries alongside our equipment.

"Why are you bringing a hair dryer?" I asked.

"I like to always have one with me," she answered. "Who knows when my hair will get wet? Or when I'll need to dry it. I like the flexibility it brings."

"I don't see how—"

"My point still stands," she interrupted. "You'd understand if you had long hair."

"Okay fine, whatever." I wasn't in a position to argue with her; she knew way more about camping and the Montana landscape than I ever could.

Facing the bed, we poured through our items and began organizing them. Sappho had written an itinerary earlier, and so we used that to categorize our stuff into various compartments. "Don't put the tuna can next to your underwear," she pointed out.

Pulling out the maps I had collected, she was surprised at my selection. "Not bad. How'd you know which maps to get?"

"Uhh…I didn't. The guy at the store chose them for me. He also wished us good luck."

"Sounds like a nice guy," she remarked. If only she knew.

With her ruler, she drew a few lines and connected the points.

"Looks interesting," she said. The points seem to have a kind of shape."

"I know right?"

After having finished packing, we equipped our gigantic backpacks and dragged ourselves down to the lobby. No one seemed to recognize Sappho in her winter gear, even as she accompanied me checking out. Eventually, we made our way down to her car in the parking garage.

"Ready?" she asked.

"Not at all."

PART III

20

When Lewis and Clark set off on their great expedition west to Newfoundland, no place claimed more of it than Montana. The Corps of Discovery covered some thousand miles within Montana. More than in any other state at the time, it was the land where they saw more wildlife than humans; where they gorged themselves on mutton and buffalo meat; where they simultaneously sweltered in blazing heat and beheld their first snow in midsummer.

Yet, despite the difficulties, they were unrelenting in their mission. As history would tell us, it was not only a great exploration into America's vastness, but an insight into its scientific nature. The Lewis and Clark team observed and collected plant and animal specifics, absorbed the Native American cultures they passed through—and by mapping the landscape, put form to the unknown.

The expeditionary team contributed considerably to the biological knowledge in North America. They pioneered a set of world-class standards in the field and introduced new ecological methods of study to the Americas. A vast collection of wildlife were documented, measured, and described because of them. No doubt, a significant part of our observable nature is better served as a result of their efforts.

But what did they know about sheep?

~

As Sappho pulled up to a gas station to refuel, I went up to the porta potty by the side and released a few litres worth. Despite its unappealing optics, I found few things in life as enjoyable as a leak during a road trip. This was especially true on the off chance one finds themselves cooped up in the car for too long.

My bladder emptied, I zipped my pants and returned back to the car. Sappho was in her seat, gazing distractedly out of the window. Since we departed the hotel, she had not uttered a single word. It was as though she was in her own universe, her eyes transfixed on something I couldn't see. I read somewhere that shared dreams were a thing—was it possible that she was imagining the same anti-capitalist sheep I spoke to at the cafe? And its unreasonable requests for a free cappuccino? I thought about this, and wondered if Sappho would have been more altruistic with it.

She revved the engine back onto the freeway. For the couple of hours we had been on the road, fields of snowfall stretched wide and endlessly. Periodically, there'd be windmills, or bridges. But not at any given moment would they triumph over the remarkable backdrop that was the snow-capped mountains. This scene went over for hours and hours—a singular road, followed by a singular road from the other way, stretching endlessly without bounds, leading towards destination and origin.

It was four o'clock when we pulled up to the motel. Except for a blue sedan, we were the only other car in the parking lot. To say that the place was *typical* would have been deceptive; there was an cold, unnatural vibe to everything in sight.

"This is our motel?" she said—her first words since the morning.

"We already went through this," I answered. "It was the only available hotel within ten miles."

The place was deserted. Completely deserted. No generic lobby music greeted us; not even a soul was manning the desk.

How would we get our keys then? Turns out, our keys were already prepared for us, as denoted on the pick-up tray by the counter. "Dear Mister Yam, thank you for choosing Adoga reservations. The keys to your room can be found here. We have also extended complimentary late checkout for your stay with us today. Have a pleasant evening!"

"I don't like this place," she remarked. "Has a strange smell."

It did have a strong smell. Almost as strong as the unrefrigerated *Cubetti Di Pancetta* from Trader Joe's I left at work once.

"It feels like we're trespassing into a kitchen," I said.

"A kitchen?" Sappho turned around and looked at me. "Why a kitchen?"

"Let's try not to think too much about it. We're just here to sleep."

~

Grabbing our belongings from the car, we made our way into our room. It was a surprisingly large room, but the amenities were dated —it felt like a time capsule. Instead of a cable television, there was an old transistor radio. And there were no lamps or nightstand, just a single fluorescent light bulb hovering over us. If I were a poker regular, I'd make a three-bet raise that most of these were products from the Sixties.

We settled our bags and unwound in the bed. Despite not having done much, I felt exhausted. Sappho was also visibly tired, though the extent of her fatigue wasn't quite as obvious.

"Sorry," she said. "I'm feeling off today. I'm not usually this reserved."

"Don't worry about it," I said with a smile. "It happens."

Through the curtained windows, the sun was beginning to set as the winter clouds came out. From the snow white came a shade of black, strikingly similar to the color of a grape, before turning darker; and then obsidian.

We sat on our beds, running through our itinerary again. I chugged a gallon of water as Sappho narrated the plan—the beginning portion of tomorrow's trip would be connected by roads, but the rest of it we'd need to cover by foot. In theory, we should be able to cover the key areas within three days, but there was no telling what the reality on the ground would be. Sappho insisted that we pack a week's worth of supplies to be safe; she even went the extra mile of bringing a portable filtration system.

"No active snow this week..." she said, scrolling through her phone. "You have no idea how lucky we are."

"Should I be glad that I don't?"

She shook her head. "It is unfathomable to me how you've survived for this long, Mister Yam."

"Let's hope for the best then," I said. "I'm already on thin ice."

Later that night, we shared a bottle of wine and watched an Adam Sandler movie on my phone. Then, we sneaked into the shower and took turns massaging our backs. It didn't take long for the hot water to run out, by which we had already dried ourselves and gotten into bed.

"I'll set my alarm for six tomorrow," I said.

She didn't respond. She was already deep in sleep, her delicate breathing audible around the room. I tucked her in and set the alarm for the morning tomorrow. Shortly after, I put on my puffer jacket and took a walk outside.

First came the wind. Then, the freezing dark. A mix of cold and snow greeted me, alongside a bunch of emptiness. There was emptiness surrounding me; emptiness all over me. The hush of wind came and then diffused itself around me, into my being. What was I, outside of flesh? This person, this self. This version of me was nothing more than a cumulation of experience. Everything had come from somewhere, and would eventually evolve into something else. I was nothing but another iteration of myself. If there was no meaning in this world, we would have never known. Just as if there was no smell in the universe, and therefore no scent to discover, we would have never realized its absence. Having a nose would be without meaning.

A wet cough shoots out from my lungs and catches me off guard. Clearly, the universe did not enjoy my nihilist views.

With no avenue for my feelings, I snuck back into the room.

The morning was wet and unforgiving.

I woke up thirsty, and reached for my canteen, only to find the water inside already half-frozen. Instinctively, I searched my backpack for my propane burner and began to boil it. As it began to warm up, there was nothing I craved more than a hot cup of coffee.

"Could you make me some coffee too?" asked Sappho, who had just risen as well.

I took out a packet of instant coffee from Kroger and split it between the two of us. The taste was unremarkably bland, but the warmth and caffeine more than made up for it.

"Tired?" she asked.

"More cold than tired," I said.

She let out a gentle laugh. "Show a little spirit. It's just the morning."

After our little coffee session, we wrapped up our stuff and packed for the car. The parking lot smelled of strong gasoline. "Ugh, I hate the cold," she remarked out loud. It took Sappho a few attempts at the engine before it finally started.

Little rays of sunshine escaped through the thick clouds as we drove out of the motel. The road we were on had surely seen better days, but the nature around it said otherwise; giant and dynamic, the trees here had liveliness unlike any I'd seen. They'd stare back as I stared at them, but they had no opinions about me. And the sky; the most miraculous orange tint filled the sky. The parts of it that glistened on the salted snow road made for an unforgettable synthesis of white and light.

We stopped at the first McDonalds in sight, just a few miles away from our first stop. Standing by the kiosk, we ordered two hash browns, two egg McMuffins, and two cups of coffee. I ate my share and still felt unsatiated, so I ordered two more hash browns, two more egg McMuffins, and two more cups of coffee. "You eat a stupid amount," she commented.

"You know, there's a nicer way of saying that."

"How are you not fatter?" she continued.

"Must be good metabolism, I guess."

Once we were done, we drove to our first stop. According to the map, it was on an obscure corner on the edge of a discontinued, abandoned highway. This was where we'd start our search; at the cusp of a deserted road, in the middle of nowhere.

She parked her car on the side of the road. A gust of freezing air blasted me as I opened the car door. Even with my vest, down jacket, and triple-layers of clothes, the cold was still unrelenting. The intensity of the wind here was something else, like it belonged to a different ecosystem.

From my backpack, I put on a pair of thicker gloves and made a kind of clapping sound. The sound dissipated as fast as it had begun. We were alone. There was no one else here but the two of us. "The rest of the coordinates lie deep in the forest," Sappho said. "We've got around six hours of sunlight before it gets too dark."

I contributed in the only way I knew how. "Mhmm," I said.

"Let's be mindful of pushing ourselves, though," she continued. "The last thing we'd want is for someone to get hurt."

We loaded our backpacks and huddled together. I took out my map and set our bearings. We'd have to cover at least ten miles today to keep to our five-day timeline. "We'd just have to walk a few miles up north for today," she said, nagging at me. "Shouldn't be anything too difficult."

I nodded. With the car behind us, we began our trek inward. Thankfully, the entrance to the trail was conveniently located in front of us. It only took us a couple of minutes of walking before we were officially inside the national forest.

Sappho navigated us through pitfalls of logs while we squeezed through snow-covered juniper trees. Day old snow would gently rub against my hair as I pushed away thick branches. Silky and cold, there was a decent amount of snow accumulated around my body. But it wasn't anything unmanageable. If the weather reports stayed accurate, we should expect sunny days for the majority of the trip.

We walked like this for a while before we left the main trail, transitioning into a secluded path parallel to a now frozen river. The estuary eventually led us to the opening of a hill, which was followed by a sign that read "Welcome to Lolo National Forest!"

Sappho scouted for a fallen log and to take a short break. It took me a while before I found a comfortable position that didn't poke my butt. Outside of our own breaths, everything was silent. Layers and layers of solitude sheltered the forest, buttery and rich like folds of a croissant. The little sounds of life that managed to break through were like rare specters of energy.

"Youve got to be kidding," she blurted out

"Something wrong?" I asked.

"I packed the wrong pad thai."

"The wrong pad thai? There's such a thing as 'wrong' pad thai?"

"Of course," she clarified. "Spices are completely different."

I had no strong urge to contribute, so I nodded my head to everything else she ranted about. When she was done, we re-equipped our bags and began our trek inward. There was a steep, noticeable incline, but the path eventually flattened out. "I forgot how out of shape I was," she remarked, panting heavily. "This used to be so much easier."

I gestured in agreement. Stretching my hands, I relaxed my palms and felt the air. There was a stark difference to how it felt. "I can't believe how much difference elevation makes."

We had a short break after spotting a frozen stream. As we crouched by the rocks, snow-capped mountains continued to fill the backdrop, except they were larger and more animated. If you looked carefully, you could observe them observing you.

"Let's get moving," she said, nudging my shoulder. "We can sightsee later."

We walked by the stream for the next hour or so, stumbling upon pods of broken ice along the way. The water was something I was too curious not to try. I scooped a generous amount in my hand. As I thought, it was simply miraculous. The taste couldn't be captured in words alone; it was an experience that required all five senses.

I offered Sappho a sip. "Incredible," she remarked.

∼

By the time we arrived at our first coordinate, I was drenched in sweat. Evidently, the thermal clothing I had bought from REI was doing a good job. Too good of a job.

In the dozen miles we had walked, the climate had reinvented itself multiple times. It was simply impossible to tell where we were, except on Earth; but even that was hard to believe at times. The only color outside of white was our clothes.

"I don't think there's anything here," said Sappho. It was clear from her face that she was disappointed, but it only took her a few seconds to get over it. "We should take a break."

I nodded enthusiastically. My body had never ached so badly; having made it this far, I doubted we would have problems with the rest of the trip.

From my backpack, I took out my propane burner and camping cookset. Then, I tore open a packet of instant chocolate and prepared us two cups of hot cocoa. It took a long time for the water to boil, but the satisfaction of a hot drink in this weather was immeasurable. "This is really good," Sappho remarked.

"From where I'm from, it's called *Milo*," I said.

"*Milo?*"

"Yeah, it's a brand that sells chocolate instant powder."

"I'll keep that in mind."

After we finished our drink, we began trekking again.

"Would you ever raise a sheep?" asked Sappho.

"A sheep? Like, as a pet?"

"Yeah."

I hadn't thought about it before. The only pet I'd ever considered before was the sausage dog. "No, I don't think so," I said finally. "They seem like a lot of work. Just imaging the amount of food they'd need to be fed, plus all the housekeeping requirements like shearing..."

"Makes sense," she said. "They do sound like a lot of trouble."

"What about you? Would you?" I asked.

"I think I'd consider it. Life has a nicer ring with sheep in it."

I recalled my conversation with the woolless Italian sheep. With all the trekking today, I've had a change of heart. I should have bought the sheep its cup of cappuccino. It was the right thing to do.

Maybe on a different occasion, we'd even have steak and lobster at a resort in Maui. Unless it was vegetarian. Then I'd suggest some butternut risotto instead.

"What do you think sheep do in their free time?" she asked.

"In their 'free time'..?"

"Yeah," she continued, with a completely serious face.

"Ummm...probably graze on grass?" I answered. "It's a hard question. I mean, what do humans do in their free time?"

"Eat. Sleep. Shower? Shop? Errands? I don't know. There are so many things."

"Exactly. It's probably the same with sheep."

She booed at me. "Cheap answer."

"What do you want me to tell you?"

"I want you to think about it!" she exclaimed, passionately. "Unlike humans, sheep don't do much. All they *do* is eat grass. All they *want to do* is shag one another."

"Please explain to me how humans are any different."

Sappho didn't respond. Instead, she stopped for a few seconds to reclaim her breath.

Then, a breeze, a strong one, blew directly at her face. Her left cheek covered in snow, I could hear Sappho chuckle uncontrollably. "Looks like nature didn't agree with me," she said.

The evening sun hovered above us as we called to an end our day. We were now deep in the forest, having successfully covered one coordinate, and within arm's reach of the next. Though we had exceeded our walking expectations, there were still no signs of a house. No signs of Lorenzo. No signs of anything but the tundra we had infringed upon. Life here was stiffly still; the snow could have been suspended in motion, and neither of us would have noticed.

There was a thick, frozen stream by the camping spot. Sappho gave me instructions on starting a bonfire—first, you take a rope and stretch it as wide as possible. Then, you pluck a few loose strings from it and plant them at the bottom of the wood. Ideally, they would be small, dry pieces of twigs. The thinner they are, the easier the fire catches. Once the setup is done, you'd create a small wind opening within the wood as an area you'd blow into.

"Alright, look here, Mister Yam," she said. Sappho took a little zinc bar from her pocket and repeatedly struck an even tinier metal rod against it. Sparks flew. "Once the rope catches fire, blow gently into the hole so that the branches get it too. When there's a small fire, that's the signal for incorporating the larger wood pieces. Got it?"

I absorbed her directions as faithfully as I could and made multiple attempts at the fire. It took a few dozen tries before there was some semblance of a spark. Unfortunately, it did nothing for me; none of the wood caught fire.

"Alright, give me that," said Sappho. She clearly found humor in my ineptitude. "You have to be more gentle. You're being too harsh."

It took her only three strikes of the zinc to achieve a small fire. "Now, quick! Grab some wood" she said.

I grabbed a hatchet and searched for wood; spotting a nearby tree, I chopped its branches down, and then broke those pieces down further. Within twenty minutes, I had accumulated enough wood to last us the next hour—not that we were planning to stay up for that long.

"Hungry?" asked Sappho. She enunciated that question rather cheekily.

"I'm game. What are you thinking?"

"Dehydrated pad thai from Mountain House," she answered, with a smirk. "The backpacking classic."

"How do you prepare it?" I asked.

"Boil some water, mix it in with the bag for a few minutes, and...I think that's it? I'm pretty sure that's it."

"No kidding..."

Sappho was not exaggerating one bit. For freeze-dried powder to make such a wonderful dinner was nothing short of remarkable. I couldn't stop gushing over the fact that 'cooking' like this was something that even existed. Not only was the meal hearty and delicious, it also provided a kind of warmth that I would, ideally, never ever take for granted again.

"Let's pack up," suggested Sappho. "The earlier tomorrow, the better."

I agreed. Our bonfire, though impressive, was being dwarfed considerably by the cold winds howling around us. I began rinsing our cooking gear and stashing our trash away. Meanwhile, Sappho decided that she'd assemble our two-person tent all by herself. Since our trip began, I have been nothing short of amazed by her knowledge and prowess in everything. While I had failed miserably at my one task of starting a fire, she had succeeded in all she had set out to do.

When the hands on my watch pointed exactly at eight, I entered the tent and buried myself in my sleeping bag. Sappho soon followed, and hugged me from behind.

I didn't respond. I pretended I was asleep—and silently enjoyed the affection. "Everything's going to be fine," she whispered in my ear. "I believe in you."

Her words made me heavy. A deep emotion from my childhood resurfaced and ate at me. It was something my mom would always say to me throughout my difficulties. It made the loneliness more bearable.

I shut my eyes and let out a few tears. Then, I cried myself to sleep.

21

The clock struck eight and I woke up in an instant. The sun was out, tiny rays of it seeping through the trees and the mesh tent screen. I stretched my hands, and then my legs. Everything below my torso suffered from a degree of soreness, the slightest movement requiring additional effort. No question, the strenuous hiking had taken a toll on me.

I zipped out of my sleeping bag and added a jumper to my already sizable layers of clothing. Small chunks of snow tacked around my hair as I put on a snow beanie. I took a piece of tissue and cleared my foggy glasses. My fingers were cold; my hands were cold. I put on my gloves to conserve whatever remaining heat I could.

An array of packaged food and wood greeted me as I exited the tent. I stood there, hands over the dried embers of our bonfire, trying to gather my thoughts. With great difficulty, I processed what had transpired.

Sappho was gone. She was no longer here. None of her stuff was here. The camp had been vacated. It was similar to a feeling I had recognized at the end of both of my previous relationships; the aftermath and consequential act of being lonely again.

Searching through my bags and equipment, I had deep-rooted hope that she would have left a message. But there was nothing. Trekking through the dark, she was probably already back by her car.

Why had she left me? Why did she wait until now? I closed my eyes and felt a great wail ripple around my chest. My heart said pain. Piercing pain. I could feel it all so clearly. But I needed to stop thinking. There were already enough questions as it is, and I wasn't in the right state to digest her sudden disappearance. Everything that was happening to me was far beyond any domain of apprehension.

I returned back inside the tent. From the front-zipper of my bag, I took out the map. The surrounding forest was so incredibly vast. How did Sacagawea do it? Or any modern traveler for that matter? Was there even a difference between intuition and chance?

I notice my mind starting to wander in the realm of despair. I'm pulling it back with a tight lease though. I wanted to push on. I needed to push on. My morale had been crushed, yes; the lingering pockets of hope I held, squashed; the sheets I once slept on, swept from under me. But none of it was a mortal blow. I was not dealt a mortal blow.

Regardless of the circumstances, brooding was fruitless. I had to see things through.

~

I rekindled the bonfire with the leftover wood and prepared a hearty breakfast: a pack of dehydrated beef stew with two loaves of bread. Sappho had left some equipment with me, but I had no idea what to make of it. Scavenging through her items, I set aside the stuff that was light and buried the rest. Leaving no trace behind seemed like the responsible thing to do.

Waiting for the water to boil, I packed the tent and prepared my bags. I would eat, drink some coffee, and then leave. When my stew was ready, I did exactly that - putting on my knapsack and continuing my trek.

The remaining stretch consisted of some miles to cover; at least two more days of hiking if I pushed myself. I try not to think about it, but there was no denying the challenges of covering the distance alone. I needed to make sure I did things carefully, and slowly. Right and wrong are sometimes a question of timing.

Already, more unmelted snow greeted my shins as I pushed deeper into the forest. The noise of my footsteps, swallowed by the density of the vegetation; my optimism, puckered by the endless trees in view.

On ahead was a series of never-ending branches and snow, a perspective further gleaned by the thick clouds forming. My frame of mind, already fragile, was not helped one bit by the deteriorating state of my knees; the aching was noticeable. Hard enough as it was to balance my gear, I now had to worry about increased elevation and resistance as well.

Despite this, I keep on trudging. I had lost my mind, but not my soul.

The trail came to an abrupt end after about a few hours' worth of walking. There was barely any light that seeped through the dense vegetation ahead, yet according to my map, that was where I needed to go.

Hands above my shoulders, I pushed through the icy aspen trees as early symptoms of frostbite began to develop around my ears. The hills started getting steeper, the trees towering taller and taller. I cautiously climbed up a makeshift path as the air grew thinner. Physically, there was pain all around my body, from the tendons of my shoulders to my hamstrings.

More trees; more rocks. There was snow; there was so much snow. Up above the branches, the frozen vapor blotted out the sky. I confused a right turn for a step I already took. I couldn't discern an entrance from an exit. Like a recursion back to square one, all paths lead to nowhere.

A wide range of emotions tugged at me. Had I gone astray? I pulled the map out again and read it left to right. If my intuition had a mouth, it'd sigh at me. I couldn't validate the facts completely, but the feeling was certain—I had wandered off the trail. Deep in the forest, I was lost and alone.

I stood and contemplated my situation. The bridge above me had collapsed; the weight of things falling over me. I was a tiny Martian, on a new planet, trying to make sense of the environment around me. Was I suffocating on the unfamiliar air? Or had I taken oxygen for granted?

Cold wind swept under me, dancing in circumference from toe to nose. I gazed up at the sky. A chunk of snow fell on my face. As tiny portions of it crept into my nose. Instead of swallowing mucus, a gut instinct swallowed my thoughts - the chapter was not over. Lingering energy hovered around me, urging me to look closer. The vibrating intuitions of my bones did not lie, could not lie. A faint power was calling for its discovery and it would not subside.

Knowingly, but very slowly, I reached a simple conclusion—I was approaching this wrong. All wrong. Conventional wisdom had gotten me nowhere; I needed to listen to the body. What were the words whispering underneath my breath?

I stopped in my tracks and dropped my knapsack, scavenging meticulously through all my items. No, I couldn't give up! I couldn't surrender to death! Even if no one would miss me, even if my existence proved a mere stain on someone's chapter, I couldn't just walk out on life.

I shook my body from top to bottom, magnifying the essence buried within me. Come on, I nudged myself. There must have been a variable I was missing; some key I was missing.

Key?

With my two hands, I clasped the box from my bag. Immediately, I felt an energy pulsating through me from top to toe. I could see a gentle glow of light ooze through its frame; reticent gleams leaking through its crevices. It traced its way from my fingers to its fibers.

I stood in awe as I watched the tiny iotas drift and circle the box. Lights orbited around me with a glowing dot carried by its own distinct solar system, enveloping my hands in a field of white halo. I shepherded the delicate veins of luminous energy over my body. Listen to the light, my dad once told me - *use your heart, search for what you already know is true.*

I closed my eyes. There's a ringing in my head that's picturing the brightness as a sound. It was loud, but it seemed familiar, and of recognizable taste. Deep breath after deep breath, I lay on the ground and spread my arms. From above me, I was being replenished fully; the light reminding me - being alive, in the midst of the world, with every experience flicking through my bones. Remember the world you were in. Remember the world you needed to leave behind. Remember the world you needed to rediscover.

Open your eyes.

Open my eyes? My eyes were already open. And just as before, the view was nothing but snow.

Then, within the snow-capped forest came the most miraculous sight. Illuminating light from the stars shot down through the clouds and shimmered onto everything in view, like some blast of angelic revelation. I shook my head in disbelief as the halos of light transformed the landscape into a vast sea of whiteness. At that moment, I felt the rotation of the earth along its axis.

I stood motionless to the reverberating light pouring through the clouds, realizing now how narrow minded my previous expectations of nature were. The landscape transformed into a vast sea of whiteness. It was beautiful, it was miraculous. It was a scene from Oscar Wilde's dream.

I opened my heart to the gentle indifference of the world and recognized the profound miracle of my being. Touching the bark of the first tree within reach, I felt my hands merge with it. Connecting to its soul, I felt its beating heart enveloping me.

I saw the air, and then I saw the atoms, and then I saw the atoms that make up the air. Everything was frozen, figuratively and literally. I could see the snowflakes hanging in the air; the discomfort around my body becoming imperceptible. I could move again, but time and its indomitable press were gone.

My legs start walking on their own, to a place only they seemed to know. Like entering a different universe paralleling my own, it gradually layered over my consciousness like a transparent robe.

So I walked, and walked, and walked.

Snow packed into the gaps in my boots, but trivialities didn't slow me.

As long as there was light, there was a path forward.

Clear of thoughts, I followed my legs.

My mind running adrift, I surrendered myself to fate.

22

Bright sunlight from the windows scintillated down onto my face as I roused myself awake. Fireplace near me, thick quilts over me, I found myself loosely tucked in on a chesterfield couch, its arm panels acting to support both my head and heels.

I untucked the blanket and sat up. Circulating around the room was a golden morning aureole; its light enveloped me like French butter. My memory remained hazy—there wasn't much I could recall after passing out in the snow. But if I had to make an educated guess, I slept at least a day. The temperate condition of my body convinced me of that; the fatigue from hiking, a lot less palpable.

Dozens of different candles were laying low by the floor as I scanned my vicinity. A pot of tea, now boiling, was whistling nearby. Without question, I was in someone's house. But the interior design of the place was some strange blend of traditional and abstract; an experimental mixtape between Mozart and Kanye West.

"Hello," I shouted. "Is anybody here?"

Silence. Absolutely nothing.

I stood up, the whistling effects of the teapot now reaching an apex. I rushed into the kitchen and removed the pot from the burner.

"Your tea's done boiling," I shouted again, to deaf ears.

Hands on the cooktop, I tried to iron out my thoughts. Where in the world was I? I knew I was in a house. I knew I was in *someone's house*. But any further speculation was pointless; I was too hungry to function. Any attempts at thinking were dislodged by a strong yearning for Belgian waffles. "I'm hungry, so I'm going to raid your fridge, okay?!" I said out loud, somewhat hoping for no response.

I opened the fridge. A fully stocked pantry greeted me: an abundance of fresh produce layered next to cured meat from the deli. Like columns in an spreadsheet, everything was labeled and organized.

I mulled over my options for a moment, but a sudden desire for an Italian sub sandwich came to mind. Salami and provolone stacked between two sourdough loaves; I drenched the sloppy creation with olive oil. Once I had assembled it on the counter top, I ate the entire thing in five bites. But I was still hungry, so I assembled another similar sandwich with tomatoes and ate it, albeit slower. I chugged a gallon of milk.

My hunger now satisfied, I turned my attention to the house itself. Towards the corner of the room was a fireplace. There was some fresh wood by it, chopped symmetrically in length and in great detail. In its center, an altar stood planted, dried of any recent use. Approaching the mysterious shine led to the discovery of some unlikely objects: two vinyl turntables, a subwoofer, and a mixer, all of which were spread randomly across the ground. An extensive collection of techno records were also present, stacked alphabetically just a few feet away.

Who was this, a monk that disc jockeys? I ran my fingers over the audio equipment; a sizable amount of dust was accumulating around my nails. I came to recognize some of the artists from the records - Marcel Dettmann; Ellen Frattz; Richard David James. The person in question had fine taste in techno, that I knew for sure. Yet, it had been a while since any of this was used. Maybe a year since it was last touched?

Careful to not disturb the items, I tip-toed around the remaining furniture and took a closer look at the back of the room. A wooden bookshelf was tapered to the wall, and left of it was an entrance to a stairway, which I climbed.

Arriving on the second floor, I found a loft with two rooms. Both were roughly of the same size, but where one room had a table, the other had only a bed. Without much thought, I went into the bedroom first. It consisted of only three things: a bed frame, a mattress and a dresser. The sheets were neatly made, but there wasn't a pillow in sight. And the dresser held nothing remarkable: just a collection of men's underwear, sweaters, shirts, and pants. I ran my hands against the walls in the room, hoping to find some inconspicuous secret tunnel, but my attempts were in vain—it was an exceptionally ordinary room.

Moving onto the office space, I inspected the desk. On the top of it was a polaroid photo and a few letters. The picture itself was dark and ethereal. It was my guess that the picture was not fully developed; any inference from it would be speculation at best. Opening the desk drawer revealed a stack of papers. Again, nothing remarkable—you could replace the room with a cubicle from an accounting firm and no differences.

I ran my fingers over the table just as I had done downstairs. This time, there was barely any dust on my index finger. Evidently, there was some fresh activity here. Possibly within the last three days? Whoever this person was, he or she had only disappeared recently.

I lifted the sole window in the room and swept aside its curtains. Thick clouds greeted me, as did giant pine trees and blankets of snow. From my position in the room, the sky seemed nothing more than a scenery to be enjoyed. The same was with the weather.

I turned my face to the ground. I expected snow, but in the midst of the estate lay a pasture full of green...and sheep. Immediately, instinctively, I recognized it. Just like in the photo, there was an assemblage of sheep, matching that photo.

I looked at the spectacle in silence. A rocket ship full of turbulence hit my chest, rippling through my body like a sine wave without bounds. Unless my eyes were failing me, the wooly mammals were ignoring the snow as if it was some kind of mere inconvenience! They were, quite impossibly, grazing on grass that should not have existed.

I closed my eyes. I took a deep breath. A sizable cloud hovered over the house, only to shift north and dissipate. After having searched for so long, here I was at the cusp of it all: I had finally found the sheep I had been looking for. Except that I had no answers.

I climbed the stairs back down to the living room. I rested on the sofa bed and closed my eyes. The last thing I wanted to do was think. The time for understanding was long gone; there was nothing I could do but sit and wait. Like swimming during a hurricane, I prayed, and hoped that my God was the right one.

~

The sky was sullen when I awoke, but outside of the darkness, nothing else had changed.

I went into the kitchen and turned on the lights. I opened the refrigerator and did a more extensive inspection through the pantry. Not only were the ingredients of impeccable quality, but the range was extensive enough to be its own grocery store. There was even a compartment in the fridge dedicated to dry-aging meat.

Underneath one of the kitchen cabinets was a tiny cellar, where I found a random bottle of wine and poured myself a glass.

I boiled some salt water for pasta, and then later, prepared a cast iron pan with bacon, cheese and eggs. When the noodles were cooked *al dente*, I sauteed the concoction together and made myself spaghetti alla carbonara.

I brought my dinner to the couch and ate by myself. I took two sips of my wine. Earthy and mineral, it must have been French. Red burgundy, perhaps? As before, I ate my meal within five bites and cleared the wine glass with two gulps. Afterwards, I went upstairs and took a quick bath.

With the large showerhead and sizable water pressure, I meticulously scrubbed my face and body with the shampoo provided, the scent of which a pleasant papaya extract. Feet on the marble tiles, I started to imagine a parallel version of me somewhere else. Had that one girl I met at the park not rejected me, how different would life be? What priorities would shift, or even emerge from such a relationship? New love discovered, old love forgotten; the circumstances of my life would considerably change. How terrifying, to imagine the power of a single outcome.

I exited the shower and dried myself with a towel. I changed into some new clothes and made my way back to the living room. Picking up the gas starter, I made my way towards the dried wood nearby and began preparations for a fire.

Warm and cozy, I read Hesse by the fireplace.

23

I was in the mezzo of a markedly smooth poop when I heard a soft thud from downstairs. I couldn't discern its source until a second thud was audible from the front door. With my pants caught between my ankles, there were about five more consecutive knocks on the door before I collected myself and made my way down the stairs.

I opened the heavy wooden door, and standing there a few steps away was an old man. He wore a cowl scarf on his neck, and looked fashionably distinct because of the bucket hat he was wearing, but there was no mistaking his face—the birthmarks around his forehead, the button nose, craggy jaw, and high cheekbones. Facing me was the bald man from the train; the bald man from San Francisco. It was surreal, seeing with my very own eyes the person I had by now imagined a dozen times over.

"You're finally awake," he said. He wore a pair of floppy slippers, a loose robe, and a pair of merino gloves. "For a moment there, I didn't think you were ever going to wake up."

"Neither did I," I responded. He didn't seem one bit concerned with the snow enveloping us. "I also didn't imagine I would meet you here, in this way."

"The world is full of surprises, isn't it?" he said, after some laughter. His voice was calm. "I hope you don't mind me coming in?"

"No, of course not."

He dragged his feet towards the door. Once inside, he took a seat on an armchair by the fireplace. "Did you find the fridge well stocked? I made sure there was enough bacon in there."

"Yeah, it was. I appreciated it a lot."

The man took off his hat, and the shining refractions from his bald scalp blinded me. It was a powerful sight to behold. Everything seemed insignificant in comparison. "You are tired," he said.

The man observed correctly. My body was in an indolent state. I could barely stretch my legs. It wasn't just a physical fatigue, though; my mind was also exhausted. No matter what I turned my thoughts to, there was nothing but excruciating ache. "How'd you guess?"

"Intuition," he laughed. "When you grow old, you become more perceptive of certain things."

I nodded. "So, you knew about this whole situation from the start?"

He ignored my question. He dragged his feet into the kitchen, then began to prepare some tea. "Pu-Erh leaves from Menghai," he said, as he sprinkled them into a boiling pot. "You won't get any better than this."

"Menghai, China?" He nodded and prepared me a cup.

Accepting it, I angled myself forward and gulped a sizable amount. I could tell that the tea was of a high quality, but I wasn't well versed enough in black tea to fully appreciate its complexities. "Where are we?" I asked.

"Physically?"

"Physically," I said.

"Hmm. Physically, we're in the sheep farm. This is where all the sheep come from," the bald man said, amused.

"The sheep farm?"

"Correct."

"That doesn't make too much sense to me."

"Of course it doesn't," he continued, "in fact, there's a lot you still don't understand. But to be frank with you, there's not much else to know about this place. *It's the sheep farm! It's the sheep farm!*—don't I sound like a maniac for saying that? The location really isn't that important."

I shook my head. "I'm not following."

The bald man shook his head too. "My dear boy, don't you get it? We needed to create a destination in your mind!" he said. "Everything that transpired was nothing more than an elaborate blueprint we created. Now, ostensibly, things didn't have to occur this specific way; we tried other, more conventional methods to catch your attention. But the sheep were the only thing that stuck. Nothing else was quite as effective."

He stood up and made his way to the bookshelf. He fiddled with his fingers for a while, and eventually pulled out a book from the second row. "You needed a story. A convincing, believable story. It was the only way."

Walking towards me, he handed me a book. The title read *The Life of Boris*. "And quite a story it was, wasn't it?"

"This story was your doing?"

"You are certainly a sharp one. Again, it was merely written as a means to communicate with you."

"So that I'd come here?"

"So that you'd move on," he said. "So that you'd understand."

"Understand? Understand what?"

The bald man heaved a sigh. He stood up and hovered next to me. "Mister Yam, you really are so stubborn! But since you insist, allow me to explain—since that dreadful day, you decided that it'd be better to create two distinct realities in your headspace than to face the pain of what happened. Every time the truth popped up, you'd run further. Further from the world around you and deeper into the world that is you. The lie you had created was so extensive you even manifested me into existence! Though, speaking freely for a moment, I'm not in a position to complain..."

I shook my head.

"But these worlds, these truths, could only stray away from each other for so long. A conversion was necessary at some point. A return to normalcy—as Warren G. Harding put it. Too bad he was such a terrible president!"

I shook my head again.

"C'mon! Think about it!' The bald man laughed, and proceeded to refill my cup of tea. "Let's start with the beginning. You came here to find Lorenzo, didn't you?"

"Yes," I responded. "All the clues pointed here."

"But you already knew where he was," he said. "As a matter of fact, you spent this entire journey *knowing* where he was. Yet, you decided to come here anyway."

I took more sips of my tea. It wasn't as calming as I'd hoped. "Is that why you confronted me on the train?"

"You knew how important the box was to him. I couldn't allow you to throw it away like that."

"Really now?"

"Yes," he said unequivocally. "Discarding it won't change anything. The truth remained the truth; and you knew this. You knew it from day one until today. You knew long after the career fair. But what have you done since? Going to Berkeley for tea? It was an elaborate plan no doubt, but you knew there was a timer within all of this. All of this had to end some way or the other."

I went silent. More silent than I had ever been. Refuting and disbelieving would have done nothing for me; if anything, it would have added to the agony.

"I'm upset," I said. "Very upset."

"I know. And you have every right to be."

"Tell me about Sappho then," I asked. "Was it really necessary for her to have abandoned me like that?"

The bald man narrowed his eyes. "She...was someone we didn't account for. Her involvement here was a mistake."

"You chased her away, didn't you?"

"No," he answered. "It was her own choice, and her own doing. She knew what lay ahead. She could have sensed it herself. But she was never meant to come here."

"Wasn't it her choice to follow me?"

"Yes, but you confused her just as much as you confused yourself. How could she follow you? It was inevitable for her to leave."

"Even after all this?"

"You didn't leave her a choice. She was the only one that could see past your lies. Just as you had lost your mind, any step further and she would have lost herself as well."

My chest hardened upon hearing this. I took a few deep breaths before I could even open my mouth. "I...."

"This was as far as her mind could have gone. Her absence here was the best thing that could have happened to you—for both your sakes."

I closed my eyes. I didn't want to believe it.

"Ever since that day, you'd done nothing but hide. Hide against the backdrop of a lie. Hide against the very facts that you'd continuously ignored. But the only thing that matters is the truth. That's why you're here now, got it?"

"The truth...?" I shook my head. "The truth...?"

"I can't tell you what you already know."

I shook my head. I shook my head a few more times.

"There was nothing else you could have done. But enough from me. I've been talking too much. I'm sure your friend will answer the rest."

I covered my face. I couldn't smell anything. I couldn't see anything.

"When will I see him?" I asked, finally.

Looking directly at me, the bald man stood up and collected himself. "That's up to you, isn't it?"

I had a lingering feeling things would end up this way. Since that fateful day, darkness was introduced to me. I had thought that with more time, I could have done something. Changed something. But the truth was that I had never felt so worthless. Even my own shadow was laughing at me.

I knew that it was implausible for things to return to normal after, but I suffocated on the shock. It was always something I held in the back of my mind, but I had to find my own way of making sense of what happened.

I drank my last glass of wine and set a timer for myself. Midnight tonight at the cusp of twilight. The bald man was right; there was no point running away anymore. These demons needed to be gone. I needed to rediscover happiness for myself.

Dragging myself to the living room sofa, I wrapped myself in a blanket and took a nap on my back. When I woke up, I went into the bathroom and took a long shower. I changed into a warm jumper and prepared the fireplace.

Sitting by the flames, I watched the fire wood crackle. It was only a few minutes past midnight when I last checked my watch.

"I hope I'm not late," Lorenzo said.

"Better late than never," I answered.

24

The wood creaked. "I took my own sweet time to arrive here," he said. "I hope you're not upset at me."

"Tell me the difference between anger and stupidity and I'd have Marco Pierre White sear me a steak," I said. "That was one of the very first things you pointed out to me when we met."

"Ha! I didn't think you'd remember. To be honest, I didn't really understand where I was going with that."

"Me neither, though that's how I knew I'd be great friends with you."

Masquerading in the dark, Lorenzo stepped out from the shadows and took a seat by the fireplace. Next to me. "I've been watching you, you know. I didn't think you'd come all the way here just to find me."

"I was always wondering what that feeling was; that little oddness that lingered at the back of my mind. I should have known it was you."

"I'm cheeky like that, aren't I?" he laughed. "But I knew that you'd eventually figure it out."

"It definitely made things trickier," I said.

"It could have been simpler. Yet, the point of it all would have been lost if it were."

"Really now?"

"Yeah, of course," he said, "the longer route's always more difficult, but that's also what makes all the difference-"

"Given that you don't find yourself lost."

"Well, you're here aren't you?"

I couldn't respond. Lorenzo continued to speak. "By the way, I didn't take any part of your journey here for granted. There were a number of events that had me worried. The part where you almost died in the snow? Even for me, that was a real scare."

"Mhmm," I nodded. "How did you manage to save me from that?"

"Me? Don't thank me for that. That was all you."

"Nonsense."

"Indeed it was. As a matter of fact, this entire thing was all of you. If you didn't already know."

"What about now then? Is this all me as well?"

Lorenzo let out a cough in the shadow, as if contemplating. He seemed hardstuck on what to say. "You know I can't answer that. Remember what I said to you?"

"What?"

"I have a shirt, and I'm telling you it's black. Not blue. Not white. Not any other color found in the color scheme. Just a plain old black shirt. If you had asked me what color the shirt was, it'd be a simple answer - it's black. But that's not what you're asking, is it? No, you're asking me why the shirt is black, which is an entirely different question; and how could I possibly know why? I just know-"

"Okay, okay. Fine," I said. "I get it."

"The phone call was fun," he laughed. "I'd never thought I'd find your reaction so funny."

I nodded. "It seemed stupid in hindsight, but what else could I had done? I wasn't counting on doing it alone; there had to be some other forces pushing me. Guiding me. There was no way else I could have gotten here."

"I know."

We both went silent. Lorenzo seemed to be glancing at the ceiling, fiddling with his fingers. "We had so many good memories together. It seemed like it was just yesterday. But those experiences...those memories.... they feel so distant now," he said. "It never occurred to me that those things would just end. Like, I don't even recognize them anymore..."

"Life's like that, right?"

"Yeah, I guess so."

We fell silent again. I sensed great anguish in my friend. "You were so good to me. You treated me so well. Yet, I made you go through all this madness for no reason."

"None of that is true."

"Only according to you. The fact is, I had been nothing but pain to you," he said, his voice cracking ever so slightly. "Quite frankly, I have been a terrible friend to you. No one should be subjected to what I made you go through, just to get here and—"

I cut him short. "Let's not talk about that yet. I'd like to figure out a few things first."

He paused, and then nodded. "Right, of course..."

"Why the bald man? Why not anyone else?"

Lorenzo kept his eyes on me. He said nothing at first. "I figured he was the best way to catch your attention. I don't think anything else would have had the same effect. Don't you recall the countless times you'd freak out over the prospect of going bald? I knew it'd had a lasting impact."

I shook my head. "He was surely effective. But, if you would have just told me in person, none of this would have happened."

"Yeah, but it would have made things harder, and worse." he said, elongating his words slightly. "I'm not here to defend myself. If there is any blame, it is mine alone. You have every right to be angry."

He was right; I was angry. But what could I have done about it? "I don't want to argue," I said. "I've been arguing with myself enough as it is."

"I know. I heard it all." Lorenzo stood up and walked into the kitchen. He came back with two glasses of water, one of which he handed to me. "Like I said, I've been watching you from the very beginning."

Taking a sip, I thanked him and set it aside on the floor. "Explain the sheep to me, then. What's that animal all about?"

"It wasn't anything particular," he said. "It could have been anything else, but I decided a sheep would be funny; and cute. You could call it a matter of personal taste - my way of cementing my memory within you."

"I don't follow."

He laughed. "It falls in line with Tarkovsky's idea that one should always attune themselves with nature. That sort of symbolism... the reflection of yourself; of your perception and being. By associative process and with a vivid enough image, we can ascribe meaning to anything."

I thought about his words. "The meaning of things..."

"That's right," said Lonrezo. "Hopefully, the next time you see a sheep, you'll think of me as well. Existence can't be limited to just the body, right?"

I snickered at him. "That's unnecessary symbolic, don't you think?"

"I know, and I'm sorry for that too. But it couldn't be helped," he said. "The whole thing would have been meaningless without the sheep."

I closed my eyes. I felt a thought come and go; a trail of dread followed. "I...don't really know what else to say."

"That's fine. Not talking is fine."

Silence. It was a long one.

"Not too long ago, you'd promise me a new porcelain bowl after you broke mine," I said. "Though it's too late for that, I'd need you to answer this question out of compensation."

"Go ahead."

"Why'd you do it?" I asked.

Finishing his glass of water, Lorenzo didn't respond. At least not immediately. "I don't know," he answered. "Even to this day, I can pretend and say that I understood my actions. But humans hardly understand the things they say they do."

"You're beating around the bush. You know I need a better answer than that," I said.

"I wrote you a letter...."

"The letter isn't good enough. I need to hear it directly from you."

Lorenzo sighed. Embers from the fire continued flickering at us. "Alright, go ahead.."

"You're dead, aren't you?"

I don't know how long we sat in silence, but face down onto the floor, Lorenzo didn't react. He sat motionless like that for a long time. Whether or not it was a minute or an hour, it was impossible to tell.

"Yeah. That's right," Lorenzo answered finally.

25

"When did it happen?"

"Four a.m., before dawn," he said. "I'd figure that the bridge would be tall enough. All I had to do was jump, and...I'll spare you the details."

"I spent that whole morning looking for you, but I couldn't figure out where you were," I said.

"I'd figured that much," he said, sounding apologetic. "I didn't mean at all for you to come find me. The box was only supposed to reach you a few days later, but someone at the post office must have screwed up the delivery date."

I shook my head. "A few days later?"

"You weren't supposed to know until later. Much later. The whole thing at Berkeley was done at dusk for a reason; mainly because I didn't want you to be involved with the...initial mess of it."

I didn't respond. My stomach churned so audibly it could have invented its own note.

"It was ultimately all my fault," he continued, "I knew I couldn't keep it a secret forever, but I wished I had given myself more time. To digest everything right. To make sure this was the decision for me. But...the suffering was too much."

"I don't understand," I said.

Lorenzo stretched his hands and hovered them lightly above the fire. "To be honest with you, it didn't start off as intentional. It was gradual. The disassociation began with just one person, and then two, and then three. Soon, fewer and fewer people kept in touch with me. And..." he paused. "I think you get the idea."

I turned away from him. A tear graced my cheek.

"There's a lot more I could share about that," he said. "But I'd rather keep the details to myself. If that's okay?"

"Were you scared at all?" I asked.

"Of course I was scared," he stated, immediately. "But I was also really exhausted. And tired. Instead of dreading a nightmare, I would wake up into one. So..." He paused again. "I would crave sleep often."

We fell silent again. It was the worst one yet. "Speaking genuinely for a moment," Lorenzo continued, "there wasn't much I regretted. I felt this pain since I was a kid - happiness wasn't something I recognized naturally. I understand how awful that must sound, or feel, but imagine what it must have been like for me. I felt like a wilting flower with a drooping soft stem; and instead of waiting to decompose, I decided there was a quicker way."

"I think you acted incredibly stupid," I said.

He heaved a sigh. "I can understand why you think that way. I'm really sorry."

"But things are better now, right?"

"Yeah, I think so," he answered in the darkness. "Are you angry at me?"

"Of course I am. But what good does anger do? I don't think either of us would benefit if we kept on brooding about it."

"So, you forgive me then?"

"No, not yet. It'll take me a while to get there," I said. "But who knows? Maybe I'll find a fluffy sheep and forget about it."

Lorenzo laughed. "Ha! I hope so."

Shrouded by the darkness, we sat silently like this for a long time. I thought about the ridiculous bald man and the story of boris and the theater with the man and the kid in the pawn shop with his sister Emma and her history with the mormons and my time in the hotel and Sappho with her elevator story before my trip to find you in

Montana in this house and found you I did. Yet, I knew. I knew that the interactions here were nothing but stories I had imagined for myself.

"The reality was always there, buried somewhere within me. But I never realized how deep the hole would be," I said. "It's not too late for me, is it?"

"It's never too late, Mister Yam."

"Right..."

A few rays of light seeped through the walls as Lorenzo pushed himself upward. "I should leave now then. I've already taken too much of your time."

"Okay..."

"I'm glad you found me."

"Me too," I said.

"Goodbye."

"I love you."

With one swoop of his hand, he put out the fire. Then, as if blending in with the shadow, he dipped his feet into the wall and stepped inside of it, disappearing as quickly as he had arrived.

Eyes focused on the wooden floor, I lay on my side and cried. A gentle trail of moonlight filled the floor from one of the crescent windows on top. There was no omen; no guidance from any higher power. My head was empty of everything but the memories I had retroactively censored. Why did it take so long for me to come to terms with it? Why couldn't I have just accepted and moved on? I knew the answers, but I couldn't accept them. I needed a belief; I needed something better than the truth.

I dragged myself to the living and pulled the box from underneath the sofa. Had I done the right thing by choosing to suppress it all? Maybe not. But I had to believe in a world outside of my mind. I had to believe that he was still alive. Even if my actions were fruitless, even if my narratives were lies. I had to believe that there was something worth chasing. How else could I endure the world?

I closed my eyes and felt the slow thumping of my breath. I tried to recognize the heartbreak that I had so fortuitously suppressed. I was a hovering speck of dust in the sea of void that was space. No smell; no sound. Just myself and I—floating endlessly and senselessly.

With my arms around the box, I blew the dust from its surface.

I took out the letter and read it for the second time.

2 6

LORENZO'S LETTER

I had meant to write to you sooner and do a proper job of explaining everything. There are many different things I wished to tell you, but to elaborate on them piece by piece would require a level of conviction that I did not have. Part of it was that the faith that I still harbored; that these feelings—these "realities"—would naturally dissipate over time. But the turmoil within me only grew as a result. And little by little, the choice became clearer.

Which is that I have decided to end my life.

I have this strong urge to justify my actions, but it's not something I could ever hope to explain. And since I've never spoken to anyone else about this, there would probably be a lot of different speculations as to the circumstances surrounding my death. This is why I have specifically written this letter to you. It was important that you know before anyone else.

I apologize in advance for imposing such a burden on you.

God. If it hadn't been for you, things would have been so much worse. I would have surrendered myself to overwhelming despair and not once attempted escape. Motionless on the beach, I would have drowned solemnly in the tides of misery that came in strong waves.

Such depression was never unique to me, but as you knew, my mental health was increasingly deteriorating when we met.

Within me, of course, was an enduring belief that this was not all there was to be. I still had faith in my perceptions, in my perspective, that things would turn around for the better. Hope, as they say, is one very strong drug. And I did find hope—or more specifically, I found company. I found people that cared for me.

You wanting me was the beginning of me wanting myself. It made me realize that I was not alone. In my conversations with you, I would always exaggerate my social dilemmas, but none of those things were true. It was all an excuse for me to feel like I belonged. You have no idea how badly I "wanted" it—to understand what it meant to not feel lonely. It was the only way I could cope with myself.

Three or four times a day, I would lock myself in my room and stare at the mirror. It was always a puzzle to me why I hated myself so much, but all I saw was darkness in my reflection. I was in a deep cell, bound in chains I myself had created. Every time I sank deeper into my despair, a petal would wither away. I wish I could express how lonely I was. How cold and miserable it was down there. But sometimes in these moments, I would hear your voice. "It's a trap!" you would shout. "You can escape from this!"

Perhaps if you had extended a hand, I would have had the strength to pull the remainder of myself out from my jail. But I was never able to produce the strength. And try as you might, I went back straight to darkness. It was always like that for me, but at least with you, there was lingering hope for me to find my own way out. I had always hoped that such courage would propel me out of my hole someday, but it never occurred. There was no easy ladder for me to escape with.

The height of the Bay Bridge is about one hundred and eight feet, or roughly fifty-seven meters. Right next to Berkeley, the final step for me will be quick and easy. And for the most part, it will be painless as well. Jumping from the top will mean that I left the world much faster than I entered it. But it'll be okay. Humanity will do fine without me.

Maybe if we had reconnected earlier, we would have met under heartier circumstances. But nothing would have changed. Everything would have been the same. I'd understand if you'd think I'm selfish, but what else could I have done? When I was struggling to make sense of the future? When I was struggling to imagine any kind of future? When I was struggling to picture myself in my future?

～

The box I've enclosed with this letter is a special one. It was passed down from my grandmother to my mother, and then from my mother down to me. I am passing it down to you because I'd like to think that someday, you'll pass it down to someone special as well. Consider it a token of sorts.

With regards to my family, they will be receiving a similar note like this in the future. But for my sake, please keep this a secret until then.

～

I can't write anymore. I'll be leaving now.

I love you, but I guess that's not the point now, is it?

～

Thank you.

***

ACKNOWLEDGMENTS

Lauren Humphries-Brooks - for her wonderful editorial work.

Faris Waiteasa, Michelle Teplitski, Jordan Wu - for their diligence in reviewing the manuscript.

Chelsea Tan, Jacqueline Chao - for their thoughtfulness in designing the book cover and logo.

Mei Khien, See Kin, Hweii Chiee - for their teeming love and support.

Other family and friends.

PRINCIPAL SUPPLIERS

Wild Sheep Chase; The Wind-Up Bird Chronicle; Dance Dance Dance
Haruki Murakami

Steppenwolf; Siddhartha
Hermann Hesse

Reclaiming Conversation
Sherry Turkle

The Imaginary
Jean-Paul Sartre

Description of a Struggle and Other Stories
Franz Kafka

The Flock
Mary Hunter Austin

ABOUT THE AUTHOR

Yeng K Tan was born in Kuala Lumpur, Malaysia. He now lives in San Francisco, where he spends his time daydreaming.

www.yengtan.com

Made in the USA
Las Vegas, NV
02 January 2024

83838642R00142